PRAISE FOR *A DISCERNING EYE*

"Art and theft. It's always an intoxicating combination, and Carol Orange captures the high stakes in her beguiling, beautifully written debut novel, *A Discerning Eye*."
— Marcy Dermansky, author of *Very Nice*

"Through its loving and lovable protagonist, Portia Malatesta, *A Discerning Eye* takes the reader on a journey that's both tense and wonderfully escapist. Carol Orange's rich knowledge of art history and powers of visual description demonstrated throughout elevate the adventure into the realm of John le Carré sophistication."
— Evgenia Peretz, *Vanity Fair* contributing editor and screenwriter

"Braving Colombian drug lords and the mean streets of Medellín, the intrepid art investigator in *A Discerning Eye* takes readers on a wild ride in search of the historic art heist of thirteen masterpieces from Boston's Isabella Stewart Gardner Museum. Carol Orange spins the brazen theft into a fascinating, well-researched thriller in the growing art-crime genre."
— Anne-Marie O'Connor, author of *The Lady in Gold: The Extraordinary Tale of Gustav Klimt's Masterpiece, Portrait of Adele Bloch-Bauer*

"Carol Orange's *A Discerning Eye* is an intricate tale of art theft, bolstering a sensational plot with finely crafted characters and evocative settings—an enthralling novel not only for suspense seekers and art connoisseurs but everyone who enjoys a fabulous romp."
— Alev Lytle Croutier, author of *Seven Houses* and *Harem: The World Behind the Veil*

"A beautiful read. An outstanding plot. An amazing female sleuth. I loved this eventful and absorbing journey through the gilded streets of Boston's Back Bay to the dangerous Colombian byways of the Medellín drug cartel. The reader follows the art historian and gallery owner Portia Malatesta as she decodes trails left after a tragic art heist leaves a prominent museum denuded of more than a dozen masterworks. Carol Orange tells us that the choice of a Vermeer means more than the cash value of a painting—the human heart is compromised as well."

—Miriam Brody, author of *Mary Wollstonecraft: Mother of Women's Rights*

"Take a museum heist of thirteen classic works of art, throw in an outraged and clever art dealer who takes it upon herself to create a profile of the thieves, and mix in an FBI sting, and you get an intelligent, fascinating mystery that leads the reader on a high-stakes, international chase to solve the questions of whodunnit and why. Carol Orange, with her vast knowledge of the art world, has created a story that will keep you on the edge of wherever you happen to be reading *A Discerning Eye*."

—Charles Salzberg, two-time Shamus-nominated author
of *Swann's Last Song* and *Second Story Man*

"Carol Orange's debut is a whirlwind of a read. An art heist from a Boston museum motivates a clever art dealer to help the FBI recover the stolen masterpieces. With marital tensions, a tempting flirtation, and dangerous encounters with a Colombian drug lord, *A Discerning Eye* keeps the reader guessing. You'll be swept up in this fast-paced adventure, while learning about great art along the way."

—Nicole Bokat, author of *What Matters Most* and *The Happiness Thief*

A
DISCERNING
EYE

A
DISCERNING
EYE

CAROL ORANGE

Copyright © 2020 Carol Orange

Published by Cavan Bridge Press, New York City

Edited and designed by Girl Friday Productions
www.girlfridayproductions.com

Cover design: David Drummond
Project management: Devon Fredericksen
Image credits: MJTH/Shutterstock, llllaiiii/Shutterstock, cdrin/Shutterstock, Lukasz Szwaj/Shutterstock

ISBN (paperback): 978-0-9987493-6-5
ISBN (e-book): 978-0-9987493-7-2

Library of Congress Control Number: 2020910541

First edition

Stolen art is often lost for good.
Anthony Farmer, *Poughkeepsie Journal*, January 10, 2005

I don't know of any good work of art that doesn't have a mystery.
Henry Spencer Moore (1898–1986), English sculptor

Everywhere the human soul stands between a hemisphere of light and another of darkness . . .
Thomas Carlyle (1795–1881), *Sartor Resartus*

Empty frames haunt the Gardner. Shadows linger where paintings once hung. What monsters grabbed our beloved bounty? Defiling such a treasury! The Dutch Room, forlorn without its prized Vermeer, shudders in silence. Rembrandts, formerly adorning a wall, beg to reappear. Even Flinck's Landscape with an Obelisk *has vanished. Mournful, despondent, the refrain reverberates in the Blue Room where Manet's mustachioed man no longer resides. In the Short Gallery, Degas's drawings are missing. Grief persists unabated. "Find us and bring us back to the light," the thirteen shout in unison.*

—Portia Malatesta

CHAPTER ONE

April 10, 1989

The Concert

If Portia Malatesta had realized the depth of her brother's despair, she might have acted differently. She might have recognized the clues. She might have pieced them together. She might have called the police.

On this overcast spring morning, she was on her way to meet Antonio at their favorite place, the Isabella Stewart Gardner Museum. She replayed last Friday evening's conversation in her head as she drove her VW Rabbit along Huntington Avenue. She had asked him why he seemed distracted. He made light of it, saying he hadn't gotten enough sleep. She sensed something was wrong. He hadn't teased her in his usual loud, affectionate way, calling her by her middle name, Francesca, as he stomped around her country kitchen. Why the hell did she accept his lame excuse?

At thirty-seven, Portia was two years older than her brother. Ever since they were children, she had protected Antonio and encouraged his artistic talent. Now she shouldered big responsibilities as a mother, wife, and gallery owner while Antonio, a painter of domestic scenes, taught drawing at the Boston Museum School. Portia cherished her relationship with Antonio. He made her laugh. His devotion took many forms, from dedicating paintings to her to playing games with Alexa, his nine-year-old niece. Antonio was there for her.

Before she turned the corner to the Gardner, she passed the inviting greenery of the Fens. This wild garden in the center of Boston was part of Frederick Law Olmstead's Emerald Necklace Conservancy. With its high reeds, grassy bank, and Muddy River, the place had become a city treasure. As she parked her car in a tight spot on Palace Road, she wondered why Antonio insisted she meet him on the bench to the left of *The Concert*. His need for ritual felt a bit obsessive. She would ask her friend Margot, a psychologist, what it meant.

Inside the museum, Portia inhaled the earthy smells from the plantings around the courtyard's marble floors. Light poured into the space from the triangular skylight, illuminating the orange nasturtiums cascading down the pink fresco walls and three floors of Venetian windows and balustrades dating to the twelfth century.

She climbed the marble staircase, arrived at the first landing, where she turned right, and entered the Dutch Room. Not all the paintings were Dutch. *So like Isabella,* Portia thought, as she glanced at Zurbarán's *A Doctor at Law* and a portrait by the Flemish Rubens. She sat down on the bench near *The Concert* and waited for Antonio. She pulled a loose strand of chestnut hair behind her ear and noted, once again, how the green damask walls made the framed masterpieces appear even more refined.

She looked at her watch. It was not like Antonio to be more than ten minutes late. She told herself to relax and recalled how often she'd admitted to Stansky, her husband, that the Gardner's Renaissance collection enticed her more than the Dutch masters.

"It's my Italian heritage," she said. "Fra Angelico, Tintoretto, Giotto, Masaccio make my pulse race." She had just applied to be a docent, offering to give museum talks on Monday and Sunday afternoons when her own gallery was closed. She hoped the administration would find her worthy.

She was startled from her reverie when Antonio burst into the room, oily solvent stains on his hands, long hair tousled, eyes wide open. He kissed her cheek. "You smell good," he said before sitting next to her.

"Wish I could say the same," she whispered.

"Hey, I'm an artist," Antonio said. "Turpentine's our perfume."

Portia laughed. She felt relieved that her brother appeared more cheerful today. Or was she fooling herself?

"If only I could paint figures like Vermeer," Antonio said.

"Don't be intimidated," she replied in her big-sister voice.

"You're sweet."

Portia got up from the bench to take a closer look. She marveled at the painter's seventeenth-century invention of light, as it spilled onto the black-and-white floor from an unseen window. As she pointed to the light's trajectory with her right hand, her left grazed the soft damask covering of an Italian chair. It was the very chair Isabella sat on whenever she viewed her precious Vermeer. Up close in its gilt frame, against a custom-built stand, the painting stood on top of a small wood table near a window.

"Never fails to mesmerize." Antonio patted her shoulder as he stood next to her. She squeezed his hand.

He pointed to the male musician. "I've finally got it," Antonio almost shouted, but then he lowered his voice. "I've solved the mystery of why Vermeer chose to portray the lute player from his back."

"Go on," Portia encouraged her brother.

"He's invited us inside. He's made us focus on the two women. He's inspired us to wonder if the lute player with his silk costume and burnished hair is the lead musician or is it the woman keeping time?"

"Marvelous." Portia clapped her hands.

"If Vermeer had painted the lute player facing us, the composition would feel flat, instead of three-dimensional. Don't you agree?"

Portia had also considered this. Yet she chose to be supportive of her brother, especially now that she suspected he was depressed. "You've made *The Concert* more alive for me."

"You think?" Antonio asked.

"Yep."

They studied *The Concert* for several more minutes, savoring its ambiguities, until she nudged him. "Let's stroll around the room before we leave."

They were alone, and Antonio took her arm before pointing to Zurbarán's lawyer. "That painting reminds me of Madrid," he said. "I miss Dad like crazy."

"Me too." Portia wiped her cheek with the back of her hand.

It had been two years since Joe Malatesta died from a heart attack, leaving his family bereft. Eighteen years ago, when Portia was home from college on break, her lawyer father had taken the family to Madrid, where the Prado Museum held them all enthralled.

"Remember when I asked why El Greco's *San Sebastian* was riddled with arrows?" she said.

"He told us Spanish painters excel at drama."

"Dad was so perceptive." Portia turned away from the Zurbarán to face her brother. She stood on her toes to give him a hug, honoring their father's memory, enjoying the gentle way Antonio held her shoulders until he dropped his arms.

"Damn," he said. "I'm late for an appointment."

Portia understood. She knew how much Antonio's students valued his critiques. They began with encouragement and ended with suggestions for improvement. *Outdo yourself,* he urged. She liked the way her brother motivated others. New York art dealers considered Antonio Malatesta a promising artist. They said he painted figures as naturally as Mozart composed symphonies. Perhaps he should have been a full-time artist, but Portia agreed that his teaching skills also deserved recognition.

As they walked down the stairs, she touched the brass handrail for good luck.

Together, they crossed the fragrant courtyard and made their way to the front entrance.

Antonio held the car door open for her. His face, pale in the afternoon light, disturbed her. She didn't let on. "See you Friday."

"I'm glad we're in the same town." Antonio kissed her cheek before she got behind the wheel.

As Portia drove away, she thought about her brother. She suspected that their father's death had hit him hard. Why hadn't she comforted him when he said that he missed Dad? Was she too enveloped in her own grief to assuage his? They'd been best friends and confidants since they were kids. She didn't understand why he had become so closemouthed over the past few weeks. She promised herself that before Friday's dinner she would find out what was troubling him.

On Thursday evening, when she called Antonio to remind him of their early meeting the following night, he sounded exhausted. She contemplated rushing over to his apartment but decided her sudden appearance might upset him even more. Instead, she told him Stansky wanted his advice about which graffiti photographs to show in New York. She liked that her two men consulted one another about their art and that her husband, the well-known photographer Stanislav Winchester, had asked Antonio to illustrate his brochures.

Early Friday evening, Portia paced the kitchen floor while she waited for her brother's arrival. As soon as Antonio entered the hall, she gave him a hug and then led him upstairs to the library. She carried their glasses of Sancerre, placing them on a table next to the Victorian sofa. She hoped the wine would relax them.

"That hissing radiator's too hot," he said.

She turned the cap off and opened the middle window in the bay.

When he removed his sweater, she was rattled by the dirty, torn T-shirt he wore underneath.

"I'm worried," Portia said. "Please tell me what's up."

"O . . . kay." Antonio sighed. He knitted his fingers together and stretched his arms before they fell to his sides. "Gemma broke up with me three weeks ago," he blurted out. "I can't sleep—I cancelled my classes today."

Portia didn't know what to say. She had first met Gemma when Antonio was a junior at RISD and lived in Providence. She and Gemma had never been friends. "I know how much you love her." She moved closer to touch her brother's arm. He sat on the sofa without saying a word. "But you'll meet other women."

He took a gulp of wine. "Don't try comforting me."

"I get it. Just remember I'm here for you."

During dinner Portia winced as Antonio strained to make conversation, especially with Alexa, who wore a blue pinafore dress in his honor.

"How's school?" he asked.

When Alexa complained about the math teacher assigning too much homework, he didn't react. Usually he'd ask for details, offer sympathy, and chuck her under the chin. Portia noticed that Antonio barely touched the lasagna she cooked especially for him. He mumbled goodbye at the door as she leaned in to kiss his cheek.

Later that evening, as Portia and Stansky talked about Antonio, she couldn't stop crying. "I'm worried about him."

Stansky put his arms around her. He wiped her tears with a handkerchief. "There, there," he said. "I hate to see you so sad. Antonio seems depressed, but he'll snap out of it."

"What if he doesn't?"

"He should see a shrink."

"He definitely should, but will he go?"

"All you can do is make the suggestion."

The following morning Portia drove to Antonio's studio with homemade strawberry shortcake. The curtains were drawn. Normally so neat, the place looked messy, with papers scattered everywhere. She put her arms around him, held him tight for a moment before she patted his shoulder. At first Antonio refused, but then he took a few bites of the cake. His glassy eyes, his listless body frightened her. His heartbreak made her helpless. "What can I do for you?" she asked.

He didn't answer.

Before she left, she handed him a slip of paper with the name and number of Dr. Bender, a Cambridge psychiatrist who specialized in treating artists. "He might be able to help you find some relief," she said. "Promise me you'll try." She put her hands on both sides of her brother's head and looked into his eyes.

"Sure . . . sure," he said. "First I need to get some sleep."

It was around 8:00 a.m. on May 28, Memorial Day, when her mother called. She told Portia, in between sobs, about finding Antonio inside their garaged Buick. He had died from carbon monoxide poisoning. Portia thought she must be having a nightmare, but when she saw her hand clutching the phone cord and heard her own disembodied voice, she knew the tragedy was real. She remembered the strawberry short-cake she had baked for him and how he had hardly touched it. She remembered feeling his heartbreak but never thought he would kill himself. Stansky had warned her that Antonio seemed off after their father died—he'd given away some of his best paintings to his favorite students.

"Artists never do anything like that," Stansky had said. Portia didn't agree that it was a troubling sign. She had thought her brother was just being generous.

After Antonio's death, the church, with its Latin chants and pungent incense, so familiar to her Catholic upbringing, could not anesthetize her pain or seduce her with promises of healing. It was only at the Gardner, with its soaring Venetian courtyard and priceless art, on their bench in the Dutch Room, marveling at Vermeer's painting, that Portia felt closest to Antonio. There she could contemplate *The Concert* and find solace. It was as if Antonio's soul had seeped into the canvas.

CHAPTER TWO

January 12, 1990

The Burden of an Italian American Identity

Seven painful months had passed when Portia walked with Nick Moretti, her best collector, along quiet, snow-packed paths in Boston's Public Garden. The garden, another Frederick Law Olmstead masterpiece with its weeping willows dotting the shore of the lagoon, was close to Portia's Newbury Street gallery. It was a cold Friday morning, shortly before 9:00 a.m. Small snowflakes fluttered down like white confetti. The weather must have kept other Bostonians away, for she and Nick were the only pedestrians. While she needed to be at her gallery in an hour to meet with Aaron Stockwell, an artist she represented, Portia thought she'd have enough time. Besides, the walk would do her good. She needed Nick. He offered comfort. A man of seventy-two, he'd become a sort of father figure, giving her business advice and also making sure she took the right vitamins.

Portia thought he looked younger than his age. Recently retired from his dental practice, he stayed trim by playing golf at the Belmont

Country Club twice a week. His bespoke suits and thick silver mustache gave him movie-star appeal. Nick enjoyed playing this up by taking Portia's hand and kissing it, as if he were Vito Corleone in *The Godfather.*

"How could you?" she asked. "How could you work with such people?"

Nick had just confided that the rumors he'd heard about two of his former patients owning stolen art had turned out to be true. "They're a lesser Rubens, a faded Rembrandt, a torn Goya. No one else would touch those pieces."

"That doesn't make it right." Portia began walking faster, moving past him.

"At least it wasn't Dino Felice," he said, catching up to her. She knew how fond Nick was of his former patient, despite his ties to the nefarious Patriarca clan. She shivered whenever she read *Boston Globe* stories about the Patriarcas reportedly murdering someone who had interfered with their racketeering business.

"So what!" Portia crossed her arms in front of her chest as she stomped ahead of Nick near the lagoon.

When he caught up with her again, Nick patted her shoulder. She turned around to look at him.

"Hey . . . let me explain about my similar background with the Mafia guys," he said. "I was the lucky one. My parents were able to send me to Boston College and then Tufts Dental School. Life's like that. Similar upbringings. Different paths."

"That's a bit too facile."

"Besides, I like doing business with them because they pay me in cash. And they don't talk while I drill their teeth. They respect me," he said.

"Who wants respect from killers?" she asked.

Although Portia empathized with Nick's devotion to his Italian heritage, she drew the line at the Mafia. Her paternal family came from a Calabrian village, not the Florentine city-state she revered. Her father's ancestry harkened to a hardscrabble, often violent world. A world where giving protection money sometimes meant having bread and water for dinner instead of pasta with meat sauce. Fear and hatred of the Mafia resided inside Portia's DNA.

She continued her fast pace along the roundabout of the George Washington statue, and as Nick reached her, he grabbed her shoulders and made her stand still. "Now, my darling, don't be so hard on an old man."

"You're a rogue. A lovable one, but still a rogue."

He chastised her for being judgmental. "Be proud of your Italian heritage, even with its flaws."

By this time they had reached Portia's gallery. As they stood in front of the door, they kissed one another on the cheek. Portia said, "I'm a proud Italian, but I still hate the Mafia."

As she walked inside, she thought about her animosity toward La Cosa Nostra and hoped it didn't interfere with their friendship.

Stansky had told Portia he understood her attachment to the older man. Yet he didn't like everything about him.

"Nick takes advantage of your generous spirit," he had warned her at dinner the previous night while they ate *spaghetti alle vongole* at home. Stroking his blond beard, he said, "I don't like his barging into your office unannounced. You could be having a personal conversation. Your privacy's at risk."

"I see your point," she said. "I'll have a word with him."

For the most part, Portia accepted Nick's idiosyncrasies. At her openings—he'd never missed one since she launched the gallery three years ago—he'd get a little tipsy from the wine and flirt with Brenda, her pretty assistant. Brenda would give Portia a *please-save-me* look and Portia would glide over to tap Nick's arm, moving him toward Chris Hayes, her neighbor with the perfect set of teeth Nick couldn't resist admiring.

Later that day, Portia called Nick from her office. "Can you stop by around six tonight?" she asked.

"What's up, princess?"

"I need to keep this quiet. I'll tell you when we meet."

"Sounds mysterious. I'll be there."

For the next few hours Portia read her mail and made phone calls to her artists.

Nick walked in at six on the dot.

"You called," he said, taking her hand for the usual kiss.

Portia smelled the familiar mix of eucalyptus and lavender in Nick's hair. She admired his charcoal-gray three-piece suit. "My, you look elegant."

"As do you. You should always wear black."

Portia thought it was just like a man not to notice she usually wore black. She was wearing a simple A-line dress and her mother's double strand of pearls. Boston, with its large student population, was more casual than New York, but the art world demanded she dress well.

She motioned for Nick to sit down in the orange leather chair near her desk.

"I'm worried Stockwell is going to leave."

Portia had cultivated a friendship with Aaron Stockwell before she opened Serafina, her contemporary art gallery. On many visits to his unheated loft scattered with canvases and art books, they shared stories about Aaron's idols, Anselm Kiefer and Robert Rauschenberg. She'd bring a bottle of Sancerre, and they'd sit on his uncomfortable wood chairs while they talked and drank together. Once they had a signed contract, she advanced Stockwell $1,000 whenever he needed to pay big bills.

"I found a note from Jake Higgins at the Marlborough Gallery."

"Did Aaron show it to you?" Nick asked. "Did he talk about it?"

"Nope . . . I opened the notebook he left on my desk while he was chatting with Brenda in the gallery."

"Ah . . . so you're not above snooping."

She reminded him that Stockwell's paintings represented more than half of her sales. "I count on his loyalty."

"Aren't you the one who always takes the high road?"

Portia's cheeks turned red. She shuffled some papers on her desk. Only Nick could get away with being so direct. She knew he meant well and offered him a glass of Dewar's, which he accepted. She kept his favorite scotch inside a lacquered cabinet in her office.

"I didn't intend to make you feel guilty." Nick leaned forward in his chair. "Give Stockwell more money and more publicity. Create a picture of his future that only you can provide."

Portia had considered a similar solution, but hearing it from Nick reassured her. They discussed the details together, and she decided to offer Stockwell 60 percent of the sales price, instead of the usual 50. She'd make sure he understood this was unheard of in the art world. Besides, her genuine enthusiasm surpassed representation from a more established gallery that would give him less attention than their celebrities.

Portia appreciated Nick's help. She acknowledged the difference between her father, the safe and solid Joe Malatesta, and smart, slick Nick Moretti. When he called her in the afternoons and asked, "What's cooking?" she sensed his devotion. At the same time Portia told herself she should be more careful around him. Nick had his parking tickets fixed. Mobsters were his patients.

CHAPTER THREE

March 19, 1990

The Day After

It had been almost nine months since Antonio had died. On many nights after Alexa was asleep, Portia tiptoed into the library and replayed his saved phone messages. "Hi, Portia . . . it's me calling to check in with you." Hearing his voice lent credence to her fantasy that Antonio was still alive. When she awoke the next morning, the bleak reality made her weep until Stansky comforted her in his arms. She was grateful to him and also to Alexa, who made her laugh with imitations of Mr. Snow, her hapless math teacher. Encouraging her artists' creativity filled her workdays, yet that pleasure was offset by graphic nightmares of her house burning down.

On this chilly March afternoon, Portia closeted herself in her gallery. Her office space offered warmth and comfort. She was doing what she did best: moving photographs of artists' work around her desk as she designed the new show. The gallery was officially closed, with the phones switched off—a good time to organize Stockwell's April opening. He had promised to finish his large, evocative landscapes, even if it meant staying up late for the next few nights.

While the misty tinge of his abstractions might remind collectors of Mark Rothko, they acknowledged Stockwell's gestural brushstrokes could only be his. Portia's exhibition space served as a home for ten emerging artists' paintings, lithographs, drawings, and sculpture. She employed three twentysomething art history graduates, who impressed potential buyers with their knowledge. And she felt proud when her artists' shows were well reviewed in the *Boston Globe* and *ARTnews*. After two years of struggle, the gallery had finally hit an upward swing, though so far none of her artists had become famous.

Toward the end of the day, Portia reached for a pile of bills that lay on her desk. Underneath the top envelope was Monday's *Boston Globe*. The lead headline jumped out:

$200M Gardner Museum Art Theft

2 Men Posing as Police Tie Up Night Guards

With shaky hands, Portia continued reading the story, running one finger down the list of stolen art. A mention of Vermeer's masterpiece, *The Concert*, stopped her. Placing her elbows on the desk, she covered her forehead with her hands.

"No, no, no!" she shouted at the empty room.

After a few moments she lifted her head. Her forehead felt heavy, throbbing with tension. The framed poster of the Gardner Museum's flowering courtyard on her office wall caught her eye. *Their* special place. The Gardner. She couldn't stop crying until she looked at her watch and realized her family would be waiting for her. She somehow managed to gather a few papers from her desk and jammed them, along with the newspaper, into her leather bag. She hoped that dinner with Stansky and Alexa would help restore her spirits. Instead of walking home, she took a taxi the short distance from her Newbury Street gallery to their South End townhouse with its yellow door. Monticello Chrome Yellow had the effect she'd intended when she chose it, much to Stansky's chagrin. He feared the glow would attract too much attention. She convinced him yellow symbolized warmth and honesty.

Portia fumbled in her purse for the keys and shivered as she turned the lock. She strode down the narrow hall, overheard Stansky and Alexa in the kitchen, and threw open the half-closed door. The bright lights reflected against the three floor-to-ceiling windows, the mustard-yellow drapes reached the black-and-white tile floor, the Welsh dresser was festooned with blue-and-white English crockery, the clunky divan with its flowered cushions sat in a corner, and Normanno Soscia's aquatints of mythological heroines hung along the wall.

"What's wrong?" Stansky asked. "You look awful."

"Thirteen pieces were stolen from the Gardner."

"Oh no." Alexa, in her striped overalls, rushed over to give her mother a hug.

Stansky, who had been at the stove sautéing pasta sauce, dropped his mixing spoon. "I didn't hear about it," he said. "I was in the dark-room all day."

Portia felt the kitchen's sanctity—redolent with pasta Bolognese, oil-drenched chicken, and carrots braised with mushrooms—was violated by the robbery.

Alexa sat next to her. Stansky poured her a glass of Pinot Grigio. She was grateful to be home.

"I've lost the last link to my brother."

"They took *The Concert*?" Stansky's bushy eyebrows rose as he gulped his wine.

She nodded. "Next Monday I'm supposed to lead the Gardner tour. How can I face those empty frames? If the police don't catch whoever did this, I'll never see that painting again." Alarmed at hearing the tone in her voice—its register must have dropped an octave—she felt an accumulated sorrow in its depth. All three deaths in her family had occurred too soon, one after the other. Serafina, her darling mother, had a fatal heart attack two months after Antonio killed himself. The only real family she had left sat there at the table with her.

Stansky strode over to pat her shoulder. "I'm sure they'll be caught."

"Many stolen paintings are never found." Portia looked at Stansky. "I appreciate you comforting me . . . but I have to be realistic." She choked on her words. She grabbed the newspaper from her briefcase and took a deep breath before quoting the journalist: "The police only found shreds of canvas, some paint chips from a large Rembrandt that had been taken, and glass fragments from the frames that once held the now-missing Degas drawings."

"Sloppy work," Stansky said, before he returned to the stove. He shook basil leaves into the pasta sauce and continued stirring.

"No fingerprints. How can detectives not find incriminating clues?" she asked.

"I understand why you're upset. At least no one was hurt."

"It's a huge loss." Portia put a hand over her heart.

"Of course." Stansky moved to embrace her. He nuzzled her ear.

She stayed in his arms for a few moments, relishing the warmth.

"How did it happen?" Stansky murmured into her hair.

"Two men impersonating policemen got into the museum by telling the two night guards they were investigating a neighborhood disturbance."

Stansky returned to the pasta sauce. "Only an idiot would believe that."

"The guards should have known better—being part-time college students is no excuse." Portia reached for the *Globe* again. She read aloud the journalist's description of how the thieves handcuffed the guards, wound masking tape around their mouths and eyes, and tied them to chairs in the basement. "They also disabled the security cameras," she said. "In total they spent eighty-one minutes inside before taking off with the art."

Stansky turned away from the stove, his eyebrows raised. "That long?"

"The robbers must have known they had time to remove everything they wanted. They took pieces from three rooms on two different floors." She put the newspaper down on the table and retied the bow on her white blouse as a way of pulling herself together. Then she turned to face Stansky. "The robbery took place after midnight."

"Those bastards! They chose Saint Patrick's eve, when the real police were busy breaking up drunken brawls."

"Do you think they knew the night guards were Berklee music students?" she asked.

"They were probably smoking dope."

"That's not the point." Tears ran down Portia's cheeks. "*The Concert* wasn't protected."

"It's okay to cry," Alexa said, and in her sweetest ten-year-old manner, reached over to caress her mother's hand. "Uncle Antonio loved that painting."

"It's precious, darling—just like you." Portia raised her daughter's bangs and kissed her on the forehead, breathing in her Ivory soap scent. "Do you remember it?" she asked her.

Alexa shook her head no.

Portia pointed to the grainy picture in the newspaper.

"I can't really see it well," Alexa said.

"I'll be right back." Portia ran upstairs. She grabbed a book on the Dutch masters from their library shelves as she calmed herself for Alexa. When she returned to the kitchen table, she motioned for her daughter to move her chair closer.

She opened the book to a crisp image of *The Concert*. "See the space below. It's shadowy. Vermeer's interiors shimmer and threaten."

"Wow," Alexa said.

"Can you imagine the harpsichord's sound?" Portia asked.

"Sort of." Alexa pointed to the figure on the right. "Why isn't she singing?"

"She's keeping time for the other two musicians."

Stansky sat down to join them. In his black turtleneck sweater, he looked every inch the bohemian art photographer. He stroked his beard. "If you could read a crime scene the way you read paintings, you could be a sleuth instead of an art dealer."

Pleased by the compliment, Portia ran her fingers through her hair. "You know I love mysteries, especially Donna Leon's."

"Me too," Alexa chimed in. "I want to be Nancy Drew."

"Nancy Drew has great instincts. They're almost as good as yours."

"You mean I could become a detective when I'm older?"

"You can be whatever you want." Stansky beamed at his protégé. Although Alexa was not his biological daughter, Portia knew he loved her with a parental passion. He made sure to be there for her when she came home from school. He helped her with homework. He'd bought her a bicycle for her tenth birthday and taught her how to ride it.

Portia leaned over to kiss Alexa on the cheek, and her gaze fell on the large black-and-white floor tiles. "Do you remember, *The Concert*'s floor was my inspiration for our kitchen?"

"Yes, Mom."

"It's dinnertime. Let's stop discussing the robbery," her husband urged.

And though Portia agreed with Stansky, the loss of *The Concert* festered inside her.

CHAPTER FOUR

March 21, 1990

Who's the Mastermind?

After Portia returned from work Wednesday evening, dressed in a black wool tunic and pants, the somber outfit softened by her lily-of-the-valley fragrance, she showed the *Globe* to Stansky as they shared wine at the kitchen table. Alexa was upstairs finishing her homework.

"Still no serious clues. The police know nothing," she said. "A few art thieves are the obvious suspects, but none of them have the paintings. And the most likely one, Myles J. Connor Jr., is imprisoned in Lompoc."

"Damn good alibi." Stansky put his wineglass down on the table and walked over to the stove. Portia nursed her drink. As her husband seasoned hamburgers for dinner, Portia reminded him that Connor, an eccentric con man with a Mayflower pedigree, had stolen a Rembrandt in 1975 from Boston's Museum of Fine Arts, then promised its safe return as a bargaining chip to avoid jail time for another heist.

"Recently Connor was sentenced to twenty years for art theft and drug trafficking," she said. "Have you heard he might have engineered the Gardner theft from prison?"

"Too difficult."

"We'll see." Portia thought this scenario sounded plausible. She chose not to argue with Stansky. At this point the evidence was too scant.

They had been married for five years and rarely disagreed, whereas Portia and her first husband, Henry, had often been at odds. Portia had met Stansky on West Canton Street when he gave a neighborhood party at his townhouse. Portia owned her townhouse, acquiring it in her divorce. She had wanted to be sure that Alexa had some stability in her life.

Portia fell in love with Stansky on their second date at a Hungarian restaurant in Copley Square, where she tasted iced tart cherry soup for the first time.

Stansky told her that he had grown up in a Cleveland suburb called Pepper Pike. He went to Dartmouth, like his father. He said that his life had been predictable until he went to the University of Ghana, where he received a master's degree in African history. "I was the only white guy in my class. And from the first day, I was welcomed as a friend."

"Were you comfortable being a minority?"

"Ghana felt more like home than home," he told her.

Portia wanted to know more about why he felt that way.

He told her that the people he had met in Ghana, not just at the university, but shopkeepers, farmers, fruit sellers, even waitresses, were open and friendly. "I captured their incandescent grins and trusting faces in my photographs. Ghanaians don't hesitate to go out of their way for one another."

"It was brave of you to live in a different culture."

"We have a lot to learn from them."

Portia thought Stansky's Ghanaian photographs were remarkable. But it was his humanitarian values that endeared him to her.

Later that evening, after Alexa went to sleep, Portia and Stansky sat on swivel chairs in their top-floor guest room and watched a panel of experts on WGBH float the theory that a ring of art thieves had stolen the paintings. "Makes perfect sense." Stansky turned his chair to face Portia. "Don't you agree?"

She considered the ring theory for a moment. "Not to me. I wonder if a mastermind was behind the robbery. Someone clever enough, who loves art, yet also someone sinister and greedy who conceived it and hired the intruders to steal those specific paintings."

"Why a mastermind?" Stansky turned the TV off before he sat down again.

"Because most art thefts are random. Thieves rush in. They take what's closest to the door." Portia had read enough about art thefts to sound convincing.

"These weren't even near the entrance," Stansky agreed.

"The thieves knew which paintings they wanted. As you know they stole three Rembrandts, the precious Vermeer, and a Flinck from the second-floor Dutch Room."

"An enormous heist; must be worth several hundred million."

"Yes. At the same time, in that very room, they left behind a Rubens, a Zurbarán, and a Van Dyck," she said. Stansky seemed to follow her logic. "In the ground floor's Blue Room they chose Manet's *Chez Tortoni* from a hodgepodge of valuable art. I'm wondering if there was a shopping list. Perhaps the clues lie in what was stolen."

"That's a clever idea." Stansky reached over to pat Portia's hand.

"I'd like to develop a profile of the thief."

"How?" His eyebrows rose as he looked at her.

"By analyzing each painting and looking for a common theme."

"Won't that take a lot of time?" Stansky swiveled in his chair before he faced her again.

"Yes. Of course."

"So you intend to become an *art psychologist*," he said.

The sarcasm in his voice surprised her. She didn't understand how her dear Stansky—he had always liked the nickname she had given him for *Stanislav*—could be so comforting when she'd lost her brother and parents, but then be critical of her wish to help solve this crime. She wondered what had happened to the Stansky she married, the man who had wooed her with flowers and theater tickets. He had encouraged her to invest in the gallery. He doted on Alexa, framing her drawings to hang on her bedroom wall.

Of course, he's annoyed that I'm paying more attention to the robbery than him.

Instead of challenging him or defending her plan, Portia went downstairs to their library, kicked off her shoes, and took out a legal pad and a black pen from her father's kidney-shaped desk. Reclining on the Victorian sofa, she inventoried what works of art had been taken, making rough sketches of each painting and art object next to its description. When she came to *The Concert*, her memory of sitting with Antonio at the Gardner haunted her.

Two hours later, she rubbed the back of her neck and looked at her oversized watch with its stubby black squares serving as numbers. The watch had been Antonio's, and she wore it daily. She brushed the tears away from her cheeks.

Every night that week, Portia and Stansky listened to NPR and WGBH for more information. No paintings or even leads turned up. On the third night, while they watched the news, Portia squirmed in her swivel chair. "Nothing's been found," she said. "It's depressing."

The police had questioned Myles Connor, but his lawyer assured them his client would not have butchered the art by cutting large Rembrandt canvases from their frames.

"Sounds believable," Portia said.

Stansky remained silent.

Walking to her gallery on Thursday morning, she overheard a young woman dressed in a pea coat and a striped scarf talking about the Gardner robbery in intimate terms. "Why haven't they found our paintings?" she asked her female companion, who shrugged.

Between the street talk, the evening news, her museum colleagues' sadness about the loss, and questions from her employees, Portia realized she was not alone.

Boston swirled with gossip about the robbery.

At breakfast on Friday morning, as Portia brought Alexa a steaming bowl of oatmeal, she mentioned she had begun taking detailed notes on each stolen artwork. She hoped her research might reveal a profile of the person who would choose those particular paintings to steal.

"So you've decided to become a sleuth." Stansky didn't wait for her answer. He told her he understood her desire to help find the paintings, but he didn't want the pursuit to be at his expense. "What about my photographs?"

"I gave you the first show," Portia said. "I'll sell your photographs again." She felt defensive and annoyed that Stansky was still being difficult, especially in front of Alexa. This time she decided to defend herself. "If they get away with this, no museum is safe."

"Isn't that a huge exaggeration?"

"Can't you be more sympathetic?"

"Forgive me. I'm being a jerk." Stansky walked over, and Portia glimpsed the remorse in his eyes before he gave her a hug. She hugged him back. Alexa beamed as they held each other for a few moments.

"If you find anything, how will you convince the authorities?" Stansky asked.

"I'm an art dealer and a docent. They'll listen to me. Didn't you notice that none of the important Italian masterpieces were touched?"

Stansky's eyes lit up. "Hey . . . you may be onto something. Remember Lord Duveen's appraisal of the Giotto as the Gardner's most valuable painting?"

"That's right." She was happy that Stansky had come around.

"So why didn't they take the Giotto?" Alexa asked.

"That's what I wonder." Portia brought Alexa's bowl to the sink. "It would have been simple. His *Presentation of the Christ Child in the Temple* sits on a small table in the Gothic Room."

"Like our Japanese print on the library table," Alexa said.

"Exactly."

"Only our print's a reproduction, while the Gardner paintings are real."

Portia, pleased by her daughter's comment, gave her a kiss on the head. Stansky beckoned with his hand that it was time to leave for school.

"Gotta go, Mom. I'll be home after soccer practice."

While Stansky left to drive Alexa to Buckingham Browne & Nichols, Portia, alone in her Vermeer kitchen, fixed a fresh pot of coffee and returned to the piece from Monday's paper. She studied a photograph of the empty frames on the silk walls of the Dutch Room. It looked forlorn. She was glad Isabella Gardner, who had died sixty-six years ago, was not around to witness the crime. Although she had been a strong woman, this brazen act would have caused her intolerable grief.

Portia had always considered Isabella Gardner exceptional. At the same time, she recognized her eccentricities. She didn't approve of the casual way the collector displayed some valuable art on tables or fireplace mantels instead of on walls. It drove her crazy to think that someone could bump into one of the small paintings as they toured the museum. Although Portia was a firm believer in art being integrated into daily life, and not always needing to be hung, she drew the line at masterpieces.

She leaned back in her chair. As she listened to the street cleaner whirring outside her kitchen windows, she mused about Isabella Gardner and realized that what had set the collector apart from her peers was, indeed, that very thing: how she placed a painting or object among the furnishings and flowers of her living space. She had turned her mansion into a museum with the help of dealers and distinguished art historians such as Bernard Berenson, architects, and Italian craftsmen, yet it had essentially sprung from her own sensibilities. Portia admired how Isabella had acquired art objects as mementos on her journeys, only to discover they qualified as works by great masters. One of her brilliant finds, a sixteenth-century Japanese screen featuring scenes from *The Tale of Genji*, hung on a wall of her Chinese Room. The screen was priceless, and at the same time, its dragons and musicians added warmth and texture to the room's stone carvings. Berenson helped develop Isabella's aesthetics, especially an appreciation for Italian Renaissance paintings. With later acquisitions, she was on her own.

Portia poured herself another cup of coffee and returned to the seminal question: Why did the robbers choose to take the Vermeer and not the Giotto? Both small paintings were displayed on tables and could be easily stolen. Although the Giotto was painted on wood and not on canvas, it was light to carry, though not quite as portable as a rolled-up canvas. And even though the Gothic Room was on the third floor of the museum, and the Dutch Room—where the Vermeer and three Rembrandts had been—was on the second floor, it would have taken just seconds to dash up the hallway stairs. The fourteenth-century Giotto masterpiece was more valuable than the seventeenth-century Vermeer and also more important than the stolen Degas watercolors or Manet's *Chez Tortoni*, painted in the nineteenth century.

As she walked upstairs to get dressed, Portia became more convinced than ever that this robbery was not about selling paintings on the black market. Someone had stolen them for personal pleasure.

CHAPTER FIVE

March 23, 1990

What Do Docents Know?

The Isabella Stewart Gardner Museum, now a crime scene cordoned off with yellow tape, was temporarily closed to the public. On Wednesday, Portia, along with three other docents, received a phone call to meet with two police detectives late Friday morning.

She waited for her colleagues on a marble bench inside the museum's ground floor Spanish Cloister. The room's mosaics, sarcophagi, and Sargent's flamenco dancing masterpiece, *El Jaleo*, always captivated her. Charlotte Mosley, a distant descendant of Isabella's, arrived with a tearstained face. Gloria Halpern had dark circles under her eyes. Tall, elegant Sarah Tisdale, a Chanel bag slung over her Burberry raincoat, rushed to greet them. "I'm heartbroken," she said. They all hugged one another in a warm welcome.

As docents, they enjoyed giving tours, focusing on the lives and painting styles of the major artists. Although it was a volunteer job, the Gardner docents were well versed in art history.

A detective with a choirboy face walked into the Spanish Cloister. He summoned the four docents to follow him into the museum café, where he asked them to sit at the table closest to the door. When Portia was inside the familiar wallpapered room, she smelled the freshly brewed coffee and her mind flooded with memories of sharing art-world tidbits with her colleagues. She was startled when the older detective's gruff voice interrupted. "Come here," he ordered, as he motioned Sarah to sit down across from them at another lunch table in the middle of the room.

Portia tasted bile. It wasn't a lineup, yet it seemed like an interrogation, as each docent was called one by one to sit across from the two detectives who questioned them. As she watched her colleagues being cross-examined, Portia held her hands down by her sides as still as a soldier's and took shallow breaths to keep her nausea at bay. She sat too far away to overhear the exact words, but she felt tension permeate the room.

To help steady her mind, she removed a manila folder from her oversized bag. It contained xeroxed copies of the thirteen stolen pieces of art. Last night, before she fell asleep, she had been puzzling over Manet's *Chez Tortoni*. She removed the copy of that image from the folder. While Manet's painting was ostensibly the portrait of a dapper gentleman, Portia sensed *Chez Tortoni* had a deeper meaning. Once again she studied the mustachioed man in a black top hat and morning coat seated at a table with a pen in his hand and a half-drunk glass of wine placed on a far corner of the surface. While he may have been all dressed up for a night on the town, the light on the left illuminating his face revealed the man's beady eyes and one raised eyebrow. He looked like a man who had something to confess. *Perhaps the thief identifies with him. Perhaps he is also troubled.*

She pulled out another xeroxed image, this one of the stolen Rembrandt self-portrait called *Portrait of the Artist as a Young Man*, and placed it on the table next to *Chez Tortoni*. This black-and-white etching of Rembrandt showed the left side of his face in semi-shadow. Portia wondered if the great artist, by choosing to draw himself in this unflattering light, hinted at his darker self. The juxtaposition of the two stolen images made her wonder why the thief had chosen this postage stamp–sized self-portrait when there was a much finer oil painting of Rembrandt as a young man in the same room. As she studied the apparent similarities between the Manet and Rembrandt portraits, Portia was so engrossed that she jumped when the young detective called her name.

"What's that?" he asked.

"Photocopies of the stolen art." She pointed to the two drawings.

"We're ready to interview you," he said.

"Would you like to hear my findings?"

"It's a distraction." The detective looked at her with a stern expression on his face.

Portia hid her disappointment about their lack of interest in the underlying similarities of the two stolen paintings. She shuffled the pages together and shoved the folder back into her bag before moving to the interrogation table. She patted the back of her head to prepare herself. Then she squeezed her hands together in front of her. She had gotten a paper cut on her right thumb, but it wasn't bleeding. The young detective cleared his throat before asking Portia if she could prove where she was that night.

"I was in bed with my husband."

He shifted in his chair. "Ahem." He cleared his throat and frowned. She could smell the perspiration under his arms.

His older partner intervened, asking Portia if she had any thoughts about whom the suspects might be.

"I would love to know the answer as much as you."

"Do you know Myles Connor?" He looked her in the eye.

"I don't. Though I understand he's stolen art before."

"Do you know the night guards?"

"Yes. They wouldn't steal anything," she said. "Don't you think it's odd the thieves didn't take the more valuable Italian paintings?"

"No." The older detective pursed his lips as he dismissed her. She was the last docent to leave. As she drove away from the museum to her South End home, the light rain escalated into a downpour. The sky had turned dark and ominous, matching her mood. She didn't understand why the detectives had treated them as potential suspects. And why they weren't the least bit interested in her analysis. Their brusque attitude made her angry. What's more, she didn't have much confidence in how they were investigating the robbery. She worried that if the detectives didn't take a more strategic approach, the paintings would not be found. Portia wanted them back where they belonged.

CHAPTER SIX

March 25, 1990

A Chance Encounter

Portia left her house at 9:00 a.m. for a ballet class. She hoped that by moving her body to Tchaikovsky's familiar scores she'd forget her sadness. Dancing had always worked its power for her before. She entered the ground floor studio in a Beacon Street brownstone. After greeting Shelley, her dance teacher, she waved to the thirty other students. She hung up her coat in the small vestibule and heard the pianist play a few refrains from *Swan Lake* on the small baby grand. As she took her place at the barre for warm-up *pliés*, she ruminated about her artists. Her thoughts flew to the Cuban crocodile, the latest silkscreen in a series by local painters celebrating endangered animals. The red crocodile with super-sized teeth and eight black legs painted against a bright yellow background evoked Latin rhythms in her head. Their syncopated beats clashed with the melodic ballet routines.

"Your legs are like jelly," Shelley scolded, as she caught Portia performing a sloppy arabesque. An ebullient dancer in her early sixties,

Shelley had high standards, especially for her long-standing students. She had told Portia often enough that she was "one of her best."

"I'm not paying attention," Portia admitted as she played with her leotard's neckline. She'd been dancing since she was seven, and Shelley's class, held in the low-lit, mirrored studio, was a sanctuary from her hectic life.

Five minutes later, as she pirouetted around the room, Portia missed a turn and fell on the floor. Her hands splayed in front of her while she lay on her stomach for a few moments.

Shelley rushed over to pick her up. "What's going on, my dear?"

"The robbery," Portia whispered. She reminded her dance teacher and friend that *The Concert* had been Antonio's favorite.

"You feel things too much . . . Though your compassion's endearing." Shelley gave her student a big hug and resumed teaching the class.

This was not the first time Portia had been told that. After Antonio died, grief had tunneled inside her, holding her in its grip for months. She'd wake up well after her alarm clock rang and then rush off to the gallery without brushing her hair. Later, as she walked home by herself, tears would slide down her cheeks. Her funk diminished when she played with Alexa or when she threw herself into a dramatic painting and tried to unravel its mystery. Ironically, it was her artist brother who had taught her this skill during their family vacation in Madrid.

Velázquez's masterpiece, *Las Meninas*, captivated them, at first because the painting was housed in a room all by itself with a large cheval mirror facing it from the opposite side. They'd never seen a work of art displayed in this way, and the sensation of looking at it both straight ahead and from behind made them feel agreeably dizzy. And then the composition itself, featuring the Infanta Maria Teresa in a voluminous dress, surrounded by her royal court, drew them in.

Portia had moved as close as possible to the oversized painting without setting off the Prado's alarm. Encouraged by Antonio, she entered the Infanta's world. She imagined her daily life from the painting's details. She noted that one young lady-in-waiting bent down to hold the young Spanish princess's hand, while another curtsied. She giggled at the naughty boy in the foreground and felt sure he was flouting royal protocol by placing his foot on the mastiff's back. She and Antonio appreciated the way Velázquez chose to reveal the Spanish court's peculiarities with the unruly boy, the tense ladies-in-waiting, and the grim-faced female dwarf.

"She looks composed, but do you think the Infanta's happy?" Antonio asked his sister.

"How could she be content when she's always surrounded by people?" Portia then asked her brother why he thought the artist had painted himself into the background.

"Haven't you been inside and outside a scene at the same time?"

"You're so smart, Antonio . . . Why didn't I think of that?" she asked as she playfully punched her brother's arm.

After the ballet class she walked to her gallery. As Portia raised her coat collar against the March wind, she rehearsed the difficult phone call to the SoHo art dealer who had sent her a bad check. He'd been so enthusiastic about Stockwell's moody landscapes, promising to frame one and put it in his window, that she had neglected to check his references. How she hated the business part of her work.

She'd first fantasized about owning a gallery twenty years ago when she studied the Greek statues in the basement at Cornell's Goldwin Smith Hall. As an undergraduate she romanticized art, believing that it was somehow sacrosanct. Now that she was a dealer, she found money drove the business. She also discovered there were more rogues and shady characters in the art world than she could have imagined. Only a year ago, a salesman with James Bond's charisma and, alas, Uriah Heep's ethics, had sold her a fake Picasso print. He gave her a certificate of provenance, which turned out to be forged. At the time she felt the salesman had come on too strong. He made the hairs on her arms bristle. Yet she bought it anyway. How could she resist the chance to buy an original Picasso at such a good price? Later, she chastised herself that she should have checked with art authorities. She should have known better.

Now she had to cajole a potential deadbeat into paying his bill. Before she called, she needed to cool her anger. If the phone call didn't succeed, she needed to drive to his gallery and demand he give the paintings back. Art was like any other retail business.

As she made her way to Newbury Street, Portia took a detour through the Public Garden. Its quaint bridge and seasonal plantings never failed to please her. The pansies and crocuses dominating the flower beds lifted her spirits. They'd been dampened before she left home by a disagreement with Stansky.

Near George Washington's statue she noticed a white English bulldog wearing a sky-blue sweater. "I love this breed." The breath came out of her mouth in steamy *ooohs* as she knelt to tickle the dog's chin.

"So do I," said the dog's owner, an attractive middle-aged man in a navy ski parka. "Haven't I seen you before?" His wry smile showed he was teasing her.

Tucking a strand of hair behind her ear, Portia considered him. He was tall and had dark hair, a high forehead, and an endearing gap-toothed grin.

"I don't think we've met." She held out her right hand and gave him her full dimpled smile. "I'm Portia."

"I'm Paul, and he's Cyrus," he said, pointing to the dog.

Stansky's allergy to animal dander had prevented her from giving Alexa a dog. She had grown up with Utzi, an Airedale terrier she adored, so she couldn't resist petting Cyrus again. This time he rewarded her with bulldog snorts and a wagging tail.

"Do you live nearby?" she asked Paul.

"My apartment is on the corner of Marlborough and Berkeley."

A good friend of Antonio's lived in the same building, so Portia asked Paul if he happened to know Richard Engles.

"He's my neighbor," Paul said in a melodious bass.

"Richard was my brother's good friend." Portia breathed deeply after making any reference to Antonio, and now she hoped the noise was imperceptible.

Paul laughed at the small-world connection, and Portia returned his smile.

As much as she enjoyed chatting with this attractive man, she needed to get a few things done at the gallery before taking Alexa to the library reading of *Charlie and the Chocolate Factory*. At the sound of the church bells ringing the hour, she knew she had to leave. "My gallery's administrative stuff is calling," she explained, making a face.

"Paperwork sucks," he agreed. "Where's your gallery?"

"Newbury and Berkeley."

"Close by," he said. "I'll walk you there."

"Sure," she said. Then she thought about Stansky and wondered if it was proper to accept this invitation.

As they walked along the path, they were so engrossed in conversation they almost bumped into a solemn family of four dressed in their Sunday best.

"What kind of work do you do?" Portia asked, as a teenager on a skateboard breezed past them.

"I'm a litigator."

"For corporations?"

"Yes . . . also small companies."

"What about defending people who've been wrongfully sentenced?" she asked. She had always been moved by her father's pro bono work with prisoners and couldn't help wondering if Paul shared his values.

"Funny you should ask," Paul answered. "In fact, I do."

"Well, we're here," she said. "It's been great to meet you."

"You have such riveting work in your windows." After they shook hands, Paul reached into his jacket pocket and removed a card. "Invite me to your next opening."

"I'd be delighted."

He walked away with Cyrus, dog and owner side by side, clearly in tune with one another. She watched them stroll to the corner, where Paul bent down to ruffle Cyrus's coat. *He's affectionate.*

She opened the gallery door and stepped inside, then looked at his name on the card. "Paul Tra–vi–gne," she read. As she pronounced his last name, she thought it sounded like the beginning of a Puccini aria, or maybe Verdi. It was Italian, like hers. He was a lawyer, although he seemed friendlier than most lawyers she knew. Yes, she would invite him to her next opening and learn a little more about him.

A faint scent from the card—she thought it was Old Spice—sparked a childhood memory of sitting on her grandfather's lap as he told stories about his Calabrian youth. When the aroma from her grand-mother sautéing onions in the kitchen wafted into the living room, it mingled with his tangy aftershave, and those familial smells brought back the comfort of home.

Stop romanticizing this encounter, Portia said to herself.

She turned on the overhead track lights in the exhibition space. The wide-planked floor with its recent coat of polish smelled like pine trees. Its gleam contrasted with the flat-white space. Six oversized Color Field paintings by Ann Thornycroft hung against the walls, oozing their provocative warmth into the cool room. She wondered what Isabella Gardner would have thought of Thornycroft's abstract canvases. Would the juxtaposition of primary colors entice her? Or would the simplicity bore her?

Portia took off her down coat and hung it on the hall rack with the inside facing out, just as she had done at her family's unpretentious house in Fleetwood, New York. She walked behind the reception area to check her messages. She froze when she saw the framed photograph of her mother dancing the Charleston at a family gathering. Someone must have moved it from her office shelf. She picked up the photograph and kissed her mother's smiling face. "Mom," she called. She missed her kind, generous mother. She would never forget that terrible day when she had found her on her kitchen floor—only two months after Antonio died. Portia recalled her shock that morning. Her mouth was parched. Her throat hurt. Later that night, she cried herself to sleep. It was days before she could go outside and talk with people in a normal way. She felt much older than her thirty-eight years.

Perhaps her mother's greatest gift, in addition to her unconditional love, had been naming her Portia. When she was a child, its foreign sound embarrassed her until she reached high school. After reading *The Merchant of Venice,* she'd adopted her feisty namesake as a role model, seeking to absorb the Shakespearean heroine's intelligence, risk-taking, and generosity of spirit. Now it was her beloved mother's warmth and Isabella Gardner's fierce determination that she wished to emulate.

Portia sat down at her office desk and faced the paper piled high in front of her. *Where do I begin?* she asked herself. Instead, she looked at the familiar, now tragic, poster of the Gardner Museum on her wall.

The beautiful courtyard triggered her recollection of Isabella's strong will and how her discipline had served her well in the creation

of her extraordinary palace. As the Renaissance building's construc-
tion had taken shape, Isabella had been involved in every detail, even
climbing a ladder with buckets of paint to show the local painters the
effect she sought.

Portia loved that Isabella Gardner had scandalized the Boston
society women of her day—not with her taste in art, which was mostly
traditional, but with her seductive gowns, her outrageous behavior. She
recalled how Isabella had worn a white headband emblazoned with
"Oh, you Red Sox" to a Boston Symphony concert. She had no trouble
imagining the devastated faces of that staid crowd. Yet their response
must have paled in comparison to the time when Isabella, dressed in
her black Worth gown, had let drop: "I like men best when they are
passion's slaves." *I bet they were apoplectic.*

How Portia longed to possess her idol's fearlessness. She wished
she didn't need to nurse a drink when she first walked into a room
of strangers. She wished she could be more spontaneous about life.
Her parents had taught her to consider other people's feelings before
expressing her own. They weren't wrong, but it hampered her.

At least she was able to follow Isabella's commitment to sharing fine
art with the public in a small way. She donated three paintings a year
to the Children's Fund. She also fancied she possessed similar instincts
for art, although at significantly lower price points. Musing about the
intrepid Isabella helped strengthen Portia's resolve. She picked up the
phone and dialed the SoHo art dealer's number. After a few niceties,
she got to the point. "Mr. August, your check bounced. You need to
wire the money right away or I'll have my lawyer contact you."

"Sorry . . . it's a difficult time. I promise to send a money order
tomorrow."

Although the dealer's assurance smelled like victory, she remained
suspicious. She decided to wait until the money was deposited in her
bank account before celebrating. After she hung up, she leaned back
in her chair and was alarmed by a dull weight in her chest. Was it the
gray sky? The robbery? Her late brother's upcoming birthday? Or was
it because, after five years of marriage, Stansky had become grumpy,
especially in contrast to the nice man she had just met that morning?
Since her husband worked from home, many of their conversations
revolved around household logistics. While they used to debate the

plotlines of movies and books, or daydream about places to visit, his main focus had become to-do lists. His most frequently asked questions were "Where did you park the car?" and "Did you pick up the dry cleaning?"

That very morning at breakfast, as she sipped her coffee, he had talked about the need to call window washers. "How can you live with this grime?" he asked.

"I keep forgetting. Why don't you call?"

"I'm sure your gallery windows are pristine."

"That's unfair." Portia felt hurt as she walked out of the room, running upstairs to dress for ballet class. She had an angry conversation with Stansky inside her head. She realized he didn't seem to notice or mind when she came home late from the gallery or went out to dinner with a friend. Sure, she would have been annoyed if he'd tried to stop her. She wondered if his laissez-faire attitude meant he was no longer attracted to her. Her marriage had lost its sensuality, and that made her vulnerable, even more vulnerable than the loss of *The Concert.*

CHAPTER SEVEN

March 27, 1990

The Mafia Had to Be Involved

As the days went by, the talk in the media about the art theft dwelt on false leads and dead ends. Although the museum had reopened, the staff was still in shock. Visitors stood without talking in front of the Dutch Room's empty frames. Shortly after the robbery, the museum decided to keep the plundered walls as they had been left. The empty frames served as a constant reminder to the public of their loss. And by keeping the stolen masterpieces alive, so to speak, the staff hoped for their imminent return.

To Portia's dismay, no one had been caught with the paintings hidden in a truck or a van. The collective voice of the newscasters was still focused on the theory that a network of art thieves had committed the crime. Yet Portia remained convinced one person had masterminded the robbery. If only to honor her brother's memory, she was determined to continue analyzing the paintings until she could draw a profile of the thief. Also, her museum—the museum where she worked as a docent, the museum of Isabella—deserved her full attention.

Portia was even willing to enlist Nick Moretti's help. She now realized she must overcome her revulsion about the Mafia because, in this case, they could be useful. Her gut instinct told her the Mafia was somehow involved in the heist. Possibly the faux policemen were trained henchmen. Who else but the Mafia would do this dirty work? Nick had told her the underworld had a network of its own, and gossip about who did what to whom traveled along its wires. She'd ask Nick to put her in touch with some of those very men. Maybe one of them knew where the paintings were hidden.

Late Tuesday afternoon, Portia sat at her gallery desk. She flexed her hands before she called Nick. She had never requested such a big favor from him before. But if her research was going to produce results, she needed to leave her comfort zone.

"Nick, can you stop by today? I have another problem."

"What's happening with Stockwell?"

"He's excited about his new show."

"Great," Nick said. "I'll be there in an hour."

Nick seemed out of breath when he arrived at Portia's gallery.

He sat down on the orange chair and wiped his forehead with a handkerchief.

"I'll get right to the point. Aren't you friends with Dino Felice?"

"Not a friend, but I've filled his cavities. You don't want drugs, do you?" Nick raised his eyebrows in disbelief.

"No, but I want your help." She looked straight into his cool gray eyes. She told him she'd been wondering if the Mafia art collectors he knew had heard anything about where the stolen paintings were hidden.

"I haven't heard a thing."

"All the same, I'd like you to invite Dino to lunch and ask him if he knows who's trying to sell a *hot* Vermeer."

"That's much too direct."

Portia realized Nick was right. Asking a pointed question wouldn't produce results. "Well, what's the best way to get inside information?

What do you think about inviting your Mafia guys here, one by one, for a private showing?"

"Portia, darling . . . What do you hope to gain? You don't want to get involved with the underworld. They're dangerous."

"Believe me, I know." She told him that when she was an adolescent she'd learned her best friend's parents slept with loaded pistols under their pillows. "Of course I stopped hanging out with Nancy. Her house became too scary," she said. "Now I have you here to protect me."

"True enough. But why do you care?" Nick looked confused. Then he gazed at the Gardner poster above her desk. "Oh—for Isabella, right? And, of course, Antonio."

"Hmm . . . What if I pretend to be selling a valuable *hot* painting myself?"

"Interesting idea, Portia. But . . . think it over first," Nick said.

"Perhaps, as we discuss the art, one of them might hint about the person we're looking for."

"Not going to happen."

"Can't we even try?"

"You're determined."

"Yep . . . Is inviting them here wise? Or should we meet them somewhere else?"

"It wouldn't be good for your business if word got out that you're selling art to the Mafia."

"You're right," she said. "I hadn't considered that."

She moved her fingers through the Rolodex as she searched for a quiet place that would impress them, while not putting herself at risk. "How about a private room at the St. Botolph Club?"

"That's the kind of snobby, high-ceilinged place those guys will like."

Portia was an active and respected club member. What's more, she had recently helped raise money for their emerging artist foundation. She hoped she could count on the St. Botolph staff to be discreet if by chance one of them recognized any of the Mafia figures she planned to woo. Although photos of some of Nick's gangster contacts had appeared in the *Globe* along with stories about their drug deals, from what Nick had told her, his former patients tended to dress and behave as if they belonged to Boston's Best—instead of its underworld. They frequented the symphony, shopped for designer suits at Louis's, and dined at the Ritz.

She told him she knew someone who would help her get hold of a well-executed Cézanne copy that she could present as *hot*. "Would that entice them?"

"You'll have to invent a good story about why you can't sell the Cézanne, in case they actually want to buy it. They wouldn't like being fooled or used. If they were to find out it was a fake, they'd kill you, honey, no matter how much you might charm them. To say nothing of what they'd do to me."

"You were brave enough to treat them. I can be brave enough to ask them subtle questions."

"I'm in," Nick said. "Just as long as we make sure you'll be safe."

Portia gave him a hug. They agreed that if one of the guys actually wanted to buy the painting, she could tell him the following day the "owner" had changed his mind about selling.

After they put the finishing touches on their plan, she asked Nick for a list of his Mafia patients so they could strategize the best way to invite each one. She imagined she might recognize one or two names from the recent newspaper articles on local mobster activities, but she had never committed them to memory. Nick agreed to assemble the list. He suggested they begin at the top with Dino Felice. Dino was sort of a friend, even if he was considered the king of Boston's underworld. While he sometimes spoke like a thug, he didn't look the part. He wore custom suits, tailored shirts, and striped ties. And, unlike many of his underlings, he never wore gold jewelry.

Portia and Nick were now a team.

The following day, Nick told her that he and Dino would meet at the Ritz on Thursday evening, March 29. While they ate dinner, he'd see if the mobster had any desire to buy a *hot* Cézanne and make him promise to keep it confidential. If Dino showed interest, Nick would arrange for him to meet them at the St. Botolph Club as soon as possible.

Three days later, on April 1, as the spring light poured through the windows with a luminescence worthy of Madonna's halo, Nick, Portia, and Dino sat down at the mahogany dining table in the blue President's Room. Portia offered Dino a glass of whiskey.

"Water will do." Dino placed both hands on the table. She sensed he wanted to get down to business.

She stood and poured a glass of water from a crystal pitcher sitting on the breakfront against the wall. As she handed the glass to him, her palms felt sweaty. She picked up a linen napkin, wiped her hands, and dabbed the beads of perspiration on her forehead. Then she poured water for Nick and herself, drinking hers in small gulps. Water helped her cool down. Yet nothing could alleviate her angst. Although he had died when Portia was twelve, she felt her grandfather's disapproval of this meeting with Dino Felice as if he were still alive.

Back then, as she lay under the blankets in her wallpapered bedroom, she had overheard beloved Nonno downstairs, railing against New York's Italian underworld in a loud conversation with her dad.

"They're scum. They make us look bad," he said.

She remembered how one Sunday lunch at Angelo's on Mulberry Street they had run into "Uncle" Giovanni, a distant relative. He was known to be a Lucchese capo, so her parents ignored him. Portia had been mystified by their behavior at the time, but as she grew up, she, too, avoided any contact with the Mafia. Until now. To assuage her guilt, she mouthed Machiavelli's famous words to herself: *The ends justify the means.*

"What a beautiful place," Dino said.

Portia watched as the empty brown eyes in his florid face moved around the room. He was short and balding, and he wore a tailored dark-gray suit. "Let's see what you've got."

She reached into her black carryall bag and pulled out a bulky package wrapped in brown paper. As she put it on the table, she gazed out the window onto Commonwealth Avenue and observed tiny green buds peeking out from bare branches. The magnolia trees looked innocent, exactly as she used to think of herself. Now here she was, speaking with a known Mafia boss. Yes, she was doing this for a higher purpose, but she was doing it just the same. While her stomach churned, her hands didn't waver as she removed the sticky tape from the package— it made a screechy noise. She took out the small, framed painting, a Paul Cézanne still life called *Pot of Flowers and Pears.*

The original hung in London's Courtauld Institute of Art; this was a copy of an earlier version of the Cézanne masterpiece belonging to a private dealer. Evelyn Beatty, a patronizing consultant, had once bragged to Portia that she knew a talented painter from Raleigh, North Carolina, who painted Cézanne copies. When she spoke with Evelyn, Portia had used the ruse of a client wanting to hire a muralist who could create Cézannish landscapes for her dining room, and then learned about the existing copy. Making that phone call to Evelyn and then picking up the faux Cézanne on consignment had made Portia uncomfortable.

At dinner the night before, Stansky kept asking her if she was ill. She hardly ate anything and couldn't sit still.

"Don't you like my steak tonight?" he asked. "What's wrong?"

"My stomach's a little upset. Nothing serious."

After Alexa went to sleep and she was alone with him, she complained about feeling "bleary-eyed from dealing with Stockwell's demands." He didn't question her further. She decided not to tell Stansky what she was doing with Nick and the Mafia. He'd be furious and think she was nuts. It wasn't like her to hide what she was doing. The deception made her cranky.

Dino, Nick, and Portia stared at the Cézanne still life on the table.

"That's gorgeous," Dino said.

She gave the painting to him so he could hold it. "Cézanne put a lot of thought into each brushstroke." She pointed to the pot of flowers in the painting. "He rarely painted flowers because he was afraid they'd wilt before he finished."

"Interesting." Dino studied the painting without talking at first. "Too bad he only painted one flower, but the pears look good enough to eat," he finally said.

"Yum," Nick said. He looked more closely at the painting. "Hey, what about the background?"

"You're right. There's a small space between the table and the back of another canvas that's intended to be off-kilter," Portia said.

"I love it." Dino's brown eyes now glistened. "How much?"

"It would be two million on the open market. I could sell it for one and a half."

"That's too much."

"What are you willing to pay?" Portia's hands felt clammy again.

"I have to think about it." She noticed that the mobster's ruddy complexion extended to his neck. He'd been calm until this moment. Now he began to squirm. "How about that Johnnie Walker? With seltzer?"

She stood up and walked to the breakfront, where she removed a bottle of Dewar's and a can of seltzer from a cabinet. Her hands shook. Somehow she managed to scoop out some ice cubes from a silver bucket with a large spoon and drop them into a glass. Then she poured the scotch and seltzer, swirling the mix exactly as her father had taught her to do when she was a teenager. Once again she wondered what he'd think if he could see her now. Would he consider her brave or a little crazy? She liked to think he'd praise her courage.

Dino downed his scotch as if it were lemonade, put the empty glass on the table, and motioned for a refill. "Good stuff," he said as she poured him another drink.

"Do you want it?" Portia asked, pointing at the painting.

"Maybe," Dino said. He sat back, and Portia followed his gaze as it moved from the elegant drapes framing the window to the wall display of black-and-white photographs of former St. Botolph presidents. "Do you think Impressionist paintings will continue to increase in value?" he asked her.

"Exceptional art is always a good investment." She had come to believe this with all her heart.

"I don't like stocks; tangible stuff excites me."

"Me too." Nick looked at Portia and winked, an agreed-upon sign that it was time to bring up the art theft.

"Hmm . . . If you're looking for another tangible investment, has anyone mentioned Vermeer as a nice acquisition? If *any* were ever on the market," she added.

Dino pushed his chair away from the table. He looked at the ceiling and corners of the room for any signs of hidden cameras. "Nothing," he said. "I know nothing. That stuff is too hot. My RISD daughter introduced me to the art world. I'm not an expert," he said, hitting the broad *a*'s of his Boston accent. "That was quite a heist," he said as his eyes widened. "I'm proud of whoever pulled it off . . . It was probably the Micks who did it." He turned to Nick and asked, "What do you think?"

"I'm only a dentist. What would I know?"

Then Dino turned to Portia. "I'm partial to pretty Italian women, as Nick here will tell you, but you've made me jumpy."

"I didn't mean to," she said. "I thought, since we're all art lovers, we could talk openly."

There was a knock on the oak door. Portia covered the small painting with the brown paper and stashed it in her bag. "I asked them not to disturb us. Who could that be?" She was terrified someone might have recognized Dino.

As she opened the door she was relieved to see William, the club's most affable young waiter.

"Oh, it's you," she said. "What do you want?"

Portia knew William must be taken aback by her abruptness. She was not acting like the Portia Malatesta who usually asked him about his family in Georgia.

"I wondered if you'd like some hors d'oeuvres, ma'am . . . Chef Gary just made them."

"No, thank you. We're fine," she said and rushed to close the door.

Dino looked at his watch and said he had to leave. Portia opened her mouth to try to keep him there just a bit longer. She decided against it when Dino banged his empty tumbler on the table. Nick escorted him downstairs.

When he returned to the President's Room, Nick sat next to her and patted her hand.

"Was Dino angry that I asked him about the stolen Vermeer?"

"Don't worry about Dino. He's cool, and you charmed him. Art is only a prestige item for him. He's into drugs and protection money. Shall we try the next person on our list?"

"Yes," she said. "Next time I won't be as nervous."

On Monday afternoon, April 2, Portia and Nick were scheduled to meet with Alan Styles in the President's Room at the St. Botolph Club. Nick asked Portia about her family as they waited for Alan to arrive.

"Alexa scored the winning soccer goal this weekend."

"Way to go, girl." Nick punched his fist in the air.

"I hope Alan will provide us with some information," she said, returning their attention to the robbery.

The previous Monday evening, as they sat in Portia's office, Nick had briefed her about Alan. He had been born into the Patriarca clan. When he was in kindergarten, his parents changed their name to something less infamous and more American. He had grown up in Roxbury on Pompei Street, an Italian American enclave. After they changed their name, his family moved to Needham. Later, they sent Alan to prep school at Groton and then on to Middlebury College. He now worked as an accountant at Price Waterhouse and wore three-piece suits. Nick made a point of telling Portia that on Saturday evenings Alan was seen at various downtown music clubs dressed in a mustard-yellow Nehru jacket.

"Gosh, Nick, don't you think Alan's inconsistent behavior fits my profile of the thief's conflicted personality?"

"It's possible."

"While Alan might work incognito in accounting, he indulges himself in a more flamboyant lifestyle outside of business hours. What's more, his interest in buying a Cézanne of questionable provenance is additional proof of a man leading a double life."

"Hmm . . . You make a good case." Nick accepted Portia's offer of a glass of Dewar's while she took a few sips of Sancerre to keep him company.

Together they agreed that Alan might have been able to put aside some money from his safe Price Waterhouse position, but not enough to buy expensive art at auctions. And if Nick's supposition was correct, Alan supplemented his earnings by facilitating a few drug deals without giving away his identity. In all likelihood, his family still maintained some Mafia contacts.

Alan walked into the President's Room. His six-foot stature and dark hair combed in a pompadour made a positive first impression. Dressed in his navy Brooks Brothers suit, he shook hands, first with Nick, patting him on the back, and then with Portia. Still holding her hand, he admired her father's signet ring. Both his trilling voice and bouncy behavior made Portia think he was gay. She had solid relationships with gay artists and art dealers, but she couldn't help wondering about Alan's family. If they were strict Catholics, they probably didn't accept his apparent homosexuality.

After some small talk about the weather and the Celtics, Nick asked Alan about Pete, his blue-and-green macaw.

"Pete's well, Doc," he said. "Nice of you to ask." On weekends, Alan put the parrot on his shoulder and brought him out for a walk around Kenmore Square, near where he lived. He told them that Pete would sometimes scare passersby with an occasional *Fuck you*, but mostly he just basked in the attention.

Portia found this hilarious. Then Alan leaned forward in his chair, put his arms on the table, and raised his hands to cup his round face. "I'd love to see that Cézanne."

Portia perspired as she unwrapped the small painting and placed it on the table. Alan picked it up with both hands and held it at arm's length. "What a gem," he said. "This Cézanne would fit nicely into my Impressionist collection."

"I'd love to hear about it."

"I have a Renoir painting of a beautiful young woman, a Courbet landscape, and two Monet watercolors of Giverny."

"I'm impressed," she said. "Do you also collect anything else, like the Dutch masters?"

"No, they're far too serious. Their dour faces remind me of my colleagues."

Portia couldn't help laughing. "Rembrandt was a genius, don't you think?"

"No question about that, but, as I said, I'm an Impressionism aficionado."

"Oh," she said. "You're focused."

"About everything."

Nick asked Alan if he knew any other Italians who collected art.

"Just the two of you," Alan said, leaning back in his chair. "Hey— what do you think about the Gardner robbery? That's all everyone's talking about."

Nick said, "I wonder where it's all hidden."

"Haven't a clue," Alan said as he patted his pompadour. "I understand the police and the FBI are stumped. Don't quote me on this, but I'm glad they're getting away with it."

Portia put one hand against her mouth as she tried hiding her disapproval. Alan's blatant praise for the thieves shocked her. "Why?" she managed to ask in her most matter-of-fact voice.

"Because why should only rich folks own the best art? They aren't any better than the rest of us."

She realized that even if Alan knew where the art was hidden, he wouldn't tell her. She sensed there was some kind of reverse snobbery at play. And he was crafty, certainly not above buying stolen art for himself.

Alan didn't like Portia's final price of $1 million for the Cézanne, reached after several attempts at negotiation. He politely thanked them for their time.

After he left, Nick and Portia remained at the mahogany table. "I'm disappointed," she said. "I had hoped Alan would know something."

"He's a character, all right. Hard to tell what motivates him."

They had now seen two Mafia-connected art collectors. Both said they knew nothing about the Gardner heist, yet each had praised it.

"Either they truly know nothing or they're afraid to implicate anyone else." Portia got up from the table to get herself and Nick each a glass of Pinot Grigio from the breakfront. She needed to calm down. Meeting the Mafia guys was more stressful than she had imagined.

"These guys buy art because status symbols make them feel important," Nick said, before taking a sip of the wine. "But in their *business* lives, they've learned to keep their mouths shut."

"The Mafia must be involved. No one else would dare to do this or would be as clever." Portia thought for a moment and remembered that the robbery had happened late in the evening of Saint Patrick's Day. "Hey, Nick, Dino suggested that the Irish Mob are suspect. Is there a rivalry between the Irish and Italian gangs?"

"You could say they're in fierce competition."

"That means if either Dino or Alan knew anything, they might have dropped a hint," she said.

"Possibly," he said.

"Do you think it's worth continuing with others on your list?"

"Portia, my dear, each Mafia guy you meet brings new risks. I admire your brains and your guts, but you're getting into FBI territory. They're trained to handle danger."

"I hear you," she replied, yet Portia was still intent on interviewing one more Mafia art collector. Perhaps he would be the one with information. She understood that by showing a forged Cézanne, her future as an art dealer might be jeopardized. Yet as much as she loved her work, the loss of Vermeer's painting outweighed everything else. For Portia, *The Concert* had become synonymous with Antonio. And although he'd died ten months ago, she still felt the warmth of his arm around her shoulders as they walked along the street. Their devotion to one another had begun as children, when they'd drive their mother crazy by tasting each other's ice cream cones. Or when they'd break branches from her prized rhododendrons while playing hide-and-seek.

Antonio, dear Antonio. I want you back beside me. If I can't have you, then please help them find The Concert.

CHAPTER EIGHT

April 2, 1990

Understanding Isabella's Choices

After dinner on Tuesday evening, Portia began reviewing her Isabella Gardner biographies. She sat on the Victorian sofa, snuggled up with the books. As part of her theft analysis, Portia planned to delve deeper into Isabella Gardner's character, exploring her considerable strengths as well as her idiosyncrasies. She wondered which of Isabella's flaws had possibly made her museum vulnerable to this robbery.

She knew that not every wealthy person was smitten with art. And not every wealthy art buyer became an avid collector. Portia thought that if she could discover what inspired Isabella's major acquisitions, she'd be able to apply similar reasoning to the crooked collector's choices.

At 10:00 p.m. Stansky came into the library and kissed Portia on the top of her head. "It's late," he whispered while putting the books down on the table next to the sofa before taking her hand to help her up.

Early the next morning, Portia took the usual route from her South End townhouse to Newbury Street. Dressed in gray sweatpants and a matching sweatshirt, she walked to the corner, past *West Canton Street Child*, a sculpture in Hayes Park by her neighbor Kahlil Gibran. As she admired the disarming work of art, she thought about Isabella, whose adventurous spirit made her seem more like a vital contemporary woman than a privileged patroness from the past. Portia wished she had known her. She imagined the two of them having exhilarating discussions about paintings while drinking afternoon tea in one of the sunlit first-floor rooms at the Gardner. For the occasion, Isabella would wear the black Worth gown that showed off her Scarlett O'Hara waist and voluptuous bosom, while Portia's tailored Armani outfit flattered her slim figure. Their mutual fondness for fashion transcended the decades between them but was far exceeded by their passion for art.

From the first time she had visited this special place fifteen years ago, Portia had embraced Isabella Gardner's aesthetic sensibility. She admired the collector's unorthodox style of integrating art with furnishings so that visitors felt more like guests in her home rather than tourists. There were no spotlights in her museum. Or captions about the art.

Over time and many perusals of the collection, Portia had discovered Chinese vases from the twelfth century, Japanese screens, Spanish altarpieces, Flemish tapestries, and illustrated Arabic texts scattered about the museum, even a black chalk drawing of Michelangelo's *Pietà* unpretentiously hung on a wall of the drawing cabinet with other Italian drawings in the Short Gallery. If she hadn't known it was there, she might have missed it. Portia had scrutinized this amazing drawing over and over again, often with Antonio. "It's so like Isabella to devise treasure hunts for her visitors," he had said. "She was as clever about displaying art as she was in acquiring it."

Later, as she led tours, Portia marveled aloud about Isabella Gardner's discerning eye, her surprising eclecticism, and the sheer beauty of her museum. She told her tour groups that Gardner's Bostonian peers had shown their lack of sophistication by making snide remarks about her character and art selections. The society scandal sheet *Town Topics* had reported on "the recently developed

fondness of the artist Whistler for the inimitable Mrs. Jack Gardner . . ."
They figured flirtation was what she had in mind when all Isabella's
energy was directed toward collecting remarkable paintings. Clearly,
they were envious of her success.

What baffled Portia was that a woman with the foresight to collect superb art hadn't thought to invest in its safety. Why did she fund
the greenhouses, but stint on security? Portia had read that a friend
of Isabella's once suggested Pinkerton men be hired to protect against
theft, but she decided to rely on Harvard undergraduates. And not just
any Harvard undergraduates. Only dean's list students manned the
halls.

On Wednesday evening, the kitchen still smelling of her favorite
spaghetti and ragú dinner, Portia shared a passage from *Mrs. Jack* with
Stansky. "As a tiny woman with flashing blue eyes, she lined Drake
de Kay up with the rest and then produced red ribbons, one of which
she personally tied to each man's arm. Looking up at him as she tied
his ribbon, she thanked him for coming and made him feel like a
knight-errant in the service of his queen."

"That sounds like our Isabella at her most charming," Stansky said
as he put an arm around Portia's shoulder.

"Yes, the students proudly guarded her museum—for a pittance."

"So Isabella began the tradition of hiring student guards, although
now it's only at night," Stansky said.

"It makes me sad," Portia said. "It's as if her lack of foresight
about security—there was no provision in her will—has come back
to haunt her."

Sitting at her writing desk before dinner on Thursday, Portia leafed
through her notebook and wondered again why none of the Italian
treasures had been taken. The Early Italian Room, on the same floor
as the Dutch Room, held priceless paintings by Piero della Francesca,
Tommaso Masaccio, Simone Martini, and Fra Angelico, all of which
had been acquired with Bernard Berenson's help. Portia was partial to
the Italian paintings, and not just because of her heritage. Each Italian
Renaissance gem deserved its masterpiece status.

After dinner, she switched gears and read a few pages of Judy Blume's *Blubber* with Alexa. They had been reading books together since her third birthday. Alexa, who tended to be a little plump, enjoyed how the author championed kids who stick up for themselves.

When they put the novel down for the night, Alexa asked, "Do you think they'll find the thief?"

"I hope so." Portia smoothed the covers on Alexa's bed and kissed her cheek.

"Maybe you'll catch him."

"Not by myself." Portia felt pleased that her young daughter was supportive.

After softly closing the door to Alexa's bedroom, with its framed posters of endangered animals, she came downstairs to spend some time with Stansky.

"How's my researcher?" he asked as she walked into the library and sat on the sofa. He was sitting close to her in a wing chair.

"I've been wondering whether Berenson's ghost was protecting his Italian Renaissance treasures," she mused.

"Your imagination runs wild. The mastermind simply had a passion for Dutch masters."

She was pleased that Stansky now bought her mastermind theory. "You could be right . . . We know collectors often follow their hearts . . . Why would stolen art be any different?"

"But value still counts. After all, three Rembrandts and the Vermeer were the Dutch Room's most valuable pieces."

"That's probably true, but then why did the robbers take the twelfth-century Chinese bronze beaker, called the *Gu*, in that room?" She got up from the sofa. Tired from the long day, she was ready to go to sleep.

"It's strange they chose something that may have been less valuable than the Zurbarán painting hanging above it." Stansky was now fully engaged with Portia's project.

Later that night, after they made love, Portia thought about how long it had been since they had been intimate. She wanted to ask Stansky about it. Instead, she chose to answer her own question. "They took the ancient Chinese beaker because they were told to do so, and it was portable."

"The robbery's never far from your thoughts," he said in a warm, teasing voice, pulling a strand of Portia's long hair across her eyes with his broad, capable hand. "I'm lucky you notice me at all."

"I love you," she said, sitting up in bed. She kissed him on the cheek. "You know I do." Then she lay on her pillow with her eyes open. "Stansky, think about the only other stolen painting, *Chez Tortoni*. Why did the mastermind find this portrait so compelling? It's beautifully painted, all right, but he didn't just love Manet. There was a small Sargent portrait, *Madame Gautreau Drinking a Toast*, in the same room. And a marvelous Degas oil painting, *Joséphine Gaujelin*, in the nearby Yellow Room. Since the thief liked Degas, they could have easily taken that. Instead, *Chez Tortoni* spoke to him."

"So one of his henchmen had to run downstairs to the Blue Room to steal it," Stansky said.

"Exactly," Portia said. "Selecting this painting from the eclectic art in those small, crowded rooms couldn't have been random. None of the choices were."

"Okay," he said, kissing her shoulder. "Now go to sleep."

"I'm going to find out why he had to have it," Portia declared, looking toward the ceiling in the dark. "While it's more contemporary than the Dutch paintings, I'm sure the thief had a reason for taking it. *Chez Tortoni* must be part of the bigger picture." She had been sure that Stansky would scoff at her if she told him about her conjecture of the mustachioed man's appeal to the thief. Now she hoped he'd understand.

"I see," Stansky said, stroking his beard. "Putting together the puzzle of why this and not that could help you create a profile of the thief."

He yawned, turned on his side, motioning for Portia to lie down next to him.

At first she complied, then she tossed and turned. She could not shut off her mind and began wondering why the mastermind had passed up Michelangelo's *Pietà*, which was located so close to the stolen Degas drawings. This prized drawing would not have been difficult to remove. "If the thief coveted the most valuable art, he would have taken the Michelangelo," she mumbled to herself in the dark.

Portia woke up the following morning still thinking about the robbery. Perhaps the two henchmen had split up on the second floor so that one could remove the Degas drawings in the Short Gallery while the other detached canvases and the Rembrandt etching from their frames in the Dutch Room. Regardless of how they worked, after removing the Degas drawings from a movable panel and taking them out of their frames, they had once again helped themselves to something nearby. This time it was a bronze finial in the shape of an eagle sitting atop a Napoleonic flag in the corner of the Short Gallery. *Was the eagle taken as a spontaneous memento, or was it an object the mastermind had specifically requested?* Portia wondered.

As she brushed her teeth, Portia peered at the bathroom mirror and imagined seeing Isabella's face with a determined look that matched her own.

On Friday, Portia and her assistants hung the Stockwell show. He had brought the framed paintings to the gallery in a rented truck. As she stood back from the canvases with Brenda, she felt awed by his talent.

"Aren't you pleased?" she asked him.

"You inspired me," he said as he gave her a hug.

Portia held on to this moment as her spirits soared.

Later that night, after giving Alexa a good-night kiss, Portia sat reading a biography of Isabella in the library. She couldn't believe it was almost three weeks since the robbery and there were still no leads. Leaning her elbows against the arms of the wing chair to comfortably hold the book, she was reminded that Isabella Gardner had the remarkable good fortune to purchase *The Concert* in 1892, at a time when Johannes Vermeer was relatively unknown and underappreciated. The book dropped to her lap as she closed her eyes. She had a vivid daydream that she was sitting next to the Gardners at the Hôtel Drouot's auction room in Paris. An old mansion that had been turned into a dealers' gallery, the Hôtel Drouot was located in the bohemian Ninth Arrondissement, a neighborhood where the audacious French novelist George Sand and her lover, Frédéric Chopin, once lived.

The small hot, windowless auction room was filled with people sitting in uncomfortable chairs. Wooden paddles lay idly on their laps until they were ready to bid, except for those who used them as fans. The air buzzed with talk. Two auctioneers stood behind a tall wooden desk,

*taking turns shouting the names of paintings as they were presented,
and then "Going, going, gone—sold to the highest bidder."*

*Isabella was dressed in a high-necked black silk dress, honoring the
occasion with her serious demeanor. Not wanting to appear overeager
to buy the Vermeer, she put her handkerchief up to her face as a sign to
the friend who would bid for her. She whispered to her husband, "That
girl with a round Dutch face isn't pretty, but her charm speaks to me."*

*Portia wanted to encourage her, so she leaned toward the art
patroness and said, "This is one of only thirty-six Vermeers in the world.
You'll never be sorry you bought it."*

*Isabella looked surprised by this unsolicited advice. Then she smiled
in appreciation. Portia believed that Isabella's admiration of Vermeer
went deeper than her identification with the Dutch girl playing the
harpsichord. She was sure that the prescient art collector had grasped
the brilliance of Vermeer's rendition of light flooding the interior of a
room. When the auctioneer pounded the gavel at Isabella's winning bid,
Portia clapped her hands in excitement.*

She opened her eyes, startled by her familiar surroundings, and
returned to her reading. Isabella Gardner had bought the painting
for $6,000, a bargain for a masterpiece, even in 1892. During her life-
time the value of the painting rose to at least $200,000. Portia knew it
was now worth more than $50 million. Clever Isabella had outbid the
Louvre in Paris and the National Gallery in London for the Vermeer.

The more she learned about Isabella, the more attached she became.
She found herself having dreams about and imaginary conversations
with Isabella. Such a rich fantasy life worried her until she realized
over the next few days how the daydreams sharpened her intuition
about why Isabella, as she became an increasingly sophisticated collector, had bought or commissioned certain paintings.

On Saturday afternoon, Aaron Stockwell's new work was shown to the
public in Portia's gallery. The opening attracted a large crowd, including her best collectors. Later that evening, Aaron told Portia he was
thrilled by the sales. "Thanks to your publicity," he said.

"Your talent," she corrected.

They hugged goodbye, and she noticed that Aaron's cheeks glowed as he left the gallery.

She was the last to leave. Before she walked out the door, Portia picked up the price list and touched each red dot that was placed next to a painting. Out of forty-five new canvases, forty had been sold, for a total of $625,000.

Now she could concentrate on helping to solve the robbery without feeling guilty.

The Sunday after her Isabella daydream, Portia returned to the Gardner to give a gallery talk on Titian. After she finished her lecture, she remained standing with four Japanese businessmen in front of the Italian Renaissance painter's *Europa* for five whole minutes.

"Isabella would have been pleased," she later told Natalie Judd, a clever art historian who worked for the museum. They were having coffee at the almost-deserted café.

She then asked Natalie, as subtly as possible, "Which of her paintings do you think Isabella loved the most?"

"Why do you want to know?" Natalie asked, examining Portia over her spectacles.

Portia knew she couldn't tell her the truth. The museum might not appreciate her independent inquiry. "For my gallery talks," she said. "I think she particularly liked portraits, both of herself and others. Don't you agree that Isabella was enchanted by the faces in Giorgio Vasari's colorful *Musicians*?"

"Yes," Natalie replied, leaning back in her chair.

Although the art historian was not exactly forthcoming, Portia engaged her in a brief discussion about the Sargent portrait, painted in 1888 when Isabella was forty-six and in her prime. Portia noted it had originally been hung in the St. Botolph Club, until Boston society went berserk over Isabella's plunging neckline, and Jack Gardner had the portrait removed.

Once again Natalie agreed. "At the same time, Jack Gardner considered his wife's portrait to be Sargent's best painting," she said, adding another sugar cube to her coffee.

They had a good laugh about that, and Portia's hypothesis about Isabella's love of portraits was confirmed.

At their steak dinner for two on Sunday evening—Alexa was at her father's house—Portia asked Stansky if he thought Jack Gardner would have eventually changed his mind about showing the Sargent portrait to the public.

"Definitely not. You know husbands are possessive louts," he said.

She laughed despite herself. "I'm sure that no thief would want to face her head-on. Maybe her imperial presence in the Gothic Room protected it from intruders."

"She certainly was formidable," he said. "Like you."

"Stop teasing. You know I'm a big softie. Hardly on the same level as Isabella." With that, she picked up their empty plates and brought them to the sink.

Stansky came over and kissed her on the back of her head. "I like my women soft," he whispered.

"Get out of here," Portia replied, but she couldn't help smiling. She wondered why her life with Stansky couldn't be this sweet all the time. Tonight he didn't mention his to-do list or complain about her spending too much time on the robbery.

Later that evening, Portia returned to her research in the library. As she took a few sips of Sancerre, she was pleased to discover that Isabella loved horses even more than she herself did. An accomplished equestrian, Isabella also enjoyed the drama of horses racing around a track. Besides, elegant horse races were one of her favorite venues for showing off her Parisian costumes and jewels.

Isabella on a cold winter day looked splendid among an array of sables and chinchillas, her hair smothered in violets from her own conservatory. She was ready to parade in her carriage at the oval-shaped Charles River Speedway in Brighton.

Isabella motioned for Portia to join her. As they headed to Faneuil Hall, she whispered in Portia's ear, suggesting that the thief chose the Degas pieces because he loved horses.

"Find out if he owns racehorses," Isabella requested.

"Yes, that's a good clue," Portia said. "What about the other stolen Degas, Program for an Artistic Soirée, *featuring ballet dancers and*

musical instruments? Wasn't Degas most appreciated for his dancers? Perhaps the thief was a Degas devotee and not a horse owner."

"I don't care, Miss Portia. Just find him!"

Portia appreciated Isabella's determination and focus. Now that she knew her love of horse racing had inspired Isabella to buy the Degas drawings of mounted jockeys, she wondered if the same passion for horses had inspired the thief.

On the second Monday in April, the day after she'd received Isabella's marching orders, Portia returned to her desk and her rigorous study of the individual pieces. She found the interplay of light and dark that so intrigued her in *The Concert* was also apparent in Degas's *La Sortie de Pesage* and in his *Three Mounted Jockeys*. While the tension between light and dark was most dramatically portrayed in *Cortège sur une Route aux Environs de Florence*, Portia had to admit that it was nonexistent in Degas's minimalist *Program for an Artistic Soirée*.

Portia reviewed her notes. She found plenty of contradictions in her heroine's temperament: Isabella was extravagant but could be frugal over small things, such as buying a tiny hot-water heater for the Gardner custodian's bath. She often behaved in an imperious manner but could be compassionate. She was mostly gracious but could be rude if someone was wasting her time. She was generally disciplined about assembling a great art collection, but some smaller purchases had been impulsive. Portia noted that while Isabella had bought paintings of people, horses, dramatic scenes, and exotic locations in her early days as a collector, Berenson raised her standards so that she then coveted Titians and Rembrandts.

Now that she finally had a clearer view of Isabella's motivations for selecting specific art, Portia was ready to turn to the thief's.

She wondered how important a painting's content was to him. Was the drama more important than a painting's value or the painter's reputation? Who would choose drawings by the prolific Degas over a great one by Michelangelo? Or a rare Vermeer over an even more priceless Giotto? In addition to the thrill of owning something everyone wanted, what meaning did the paintings have for him?

From the beginning Portia suspected the stolen art was for his own personal enjoyment. She now became convinced that if she looked hard enough she could find the overarching theme in the stolen paintings and drawings. Possibly it was the same force that reverberated in the thief's essential being.

CHAPTER NINE

April 10, 1990

Good Karma

As she walked through the Public Garden on her way to the gallery Tuesday morning, Portia spotted Paul Travigne. She recognized his Red Sox cap, and of course, Cyrus, his bulldog, who sashayed beside him, was the giveaway. She hurried to catch up.

"You're darling," she said. She crouched down to pet Cyrus under his chin. He licked her cheek, and Portia laughed with delight, her dimples flashing. "What a great dog." Portia looked up and saw Paul's appreciative smile.

"Nice to see you again," he said.

Portia was glad she happened to be wearing her pistachio-colored jacket that brought out the green in her eyes. She felt an undeniable chemistry with this man. Although she knew it was dangerous, she chose to ignore the voice in her head that warned her to be careful. What was the harm in a little flirting?

She hadn't seen him for more than two weeks, and yet she'd thought about him more than once. Perhaps there was something about their shared Italian background that made the attraction so powerful—at least for her.

"How have you been?" she asked, standing up and pulling a strand of hair behind her ear. She was annoyed with herself for being so awkward.

"Pretty well. And you?" Paul's voice sounded scratchy. He seemed to be getting over a cold.

"Obsessing about the Gardner theft," she told him in an unusual burst of openness with a virtual stranger.

"Funny—I was there yesterday," he said. "I stood in front of the empty frame where the Vermeer used to be and thought: *How dare they?* The room felt haunted."

"I know what you mean. I particularly miss the Vermeer." Portia caressed her arms as she stood facing him. An image of Antonio working in his studio streaked across her mind. He was standing with his legs apart, a resolute look in his eyes, poised to prime an oversized canvas with a brush. The pungent smell of rabbit-skin glue mixed with linseed oil permeated the room.

"That painting used to cheer me up. I swear I could hear the musicians' perfect harmony." Paul's words interrupted her memory, and she noticed his cheeks redden. She couldn't help wondering if his high color came from their shared passion for art. His appreciation of *The Concert* encouraged her to share her thoughts.

"I've been analyzing the stolen works to see if I can discover what drove the mastermind to steal them . . . I think one person was behind this, and I suspect there's an overriding theme to his choices." Portia heard how seriously she was taking herself.

"He's a selfish guy, all right," Paul said.

"I hope they catch this bastard."

"I'm angry too."

Portia couldn't help smiling at their similar reactions. Before she could speak, he interrupted her. "If you're willing to share your notes with me . . . I'd be happy to read them. It seems that the actual investigation isn't getting anywhere."

Now she couldn't believe her luck in bumping into him; but then she wondered if he had an ulterior motive.

"Of course," she said. "I'll bring them to the gallery when I'm finished." Although she was flattered by his interest in her report, she remained suspicious. Was Paul one of those guys her father used to call "a player"?

Paul asked her to let him know when he could pick up the notes. "They'll be a lot more stimulating than most of my cases. As far as I know, detectives who chase stolen art don't begin by analyzing the missing objects. You may have something special to offer."

"That's kind of you. Are you just being polite?" A gust of wind blew into her face, and Portia buttoned her jacket.

"If your notes are as good as I imagine, I'd like to tell my old college roommate, Joel Soderburgh, about your research. He's a detective with the FBI . . . I'm getting ahead of myself. Let me read them first, then we'll take this one step at a time."

"My thoughts exactly. I don't have much to offer yet, but I will . . . I hope."

At that moment they stopped walking and sat down on a bench. The daffodils were in bloom, and an occasional iris peeked out from the new grass. The squirrels ran around the lawn, looking for food scraps left by picnickers, and Cyrus growled at them. Paul tied his leash to the bench so he couldn't pursue them.

"Well, why don't I call Joel anyway, and see what he has to say."

"Thank you," she said as she held out her hand for him to shake. Paul took hold of her soft, slim hand and held on to it a little longer than necessary.

Paul's touch set off Portia's internal alarm system. "I guess I'd better be going," she said and stood up.

"I'll call you at the gallery after I speak with Joel."

As she walked away, Portia felt that her encounters with Paul Travigne could not have been accidental. It was as if they were destined to meet. Fate was, in Portia's opinion, an underrated concept in the modern world.

CHAPTER TEN

April 15, 1990

Tension between Light and Dark

Late Sunday morning, Portia sat down at her kidney-shaped desk in the townhouse library. She put a cup of Earl Grey tea on a coaster and took a magnifying glass from a drawer. Having just emerged from the shower, gardenia soap and Nivea scents encircled her.

Where to begin? she wondered, shuffling through the photocopies of the Gardner's stolen art.

For Portia it inevitably began with the Vermeer.

Studying the reproduction once again, Portia traced the light in the painting with her finger, determining how rays coming from the unseen window hit the wall, lighting up the folds of the young harpsichordist's silk gown and settling on a portion of the black-and-white tile floor in the foreground. The painting was so realistic she could just about smell the wood polish on the harpsichord.

The quiet drama of the intimate scene—portraying the harpsichordist, the woman keeping time, and a male musician with his back to the viewer—was heightened by the interplay of light and shadow.

She had already established that most of the stolen art objects possessed a similar tension between light and shadow, but today she reviewed the three Rembrandts, which markedly had the same quality. Reconsidering their imagery might well shed some new light on the thief's machinations. She planned to discuss her findings with her psychologist friend, Margot, whom she was meeting in two hours. They were driving to the Rose Art Museum in Waltham.

The most dramatic Rembrandt, an unusual seascape, *Christ in the Storm on the Sea of Galilee*, showed Jesus and his disciples facing one another as their two-mast sailboat was about to capsize. The disciples grappled with the masts while Christ, sitting alone under a patch of light streaming in from an otherwise stormy sky, appeared calm as he reminded them to keep their faith. The painter's portrayal of the scene from the Gospel of Luke was so realistic that the viewer could almost feel a spray of ocean salt hit his face.

A viewer, such as the thief, could not help being moved by the wrenching drama of this painting so skillfully conceived by the master painter, Portia had written in her notebook. *The profound strain between dark and light, between panic and calm, which is captured in the painting's narrative, dramatizes this tale of survival.*

This painting exemplifies the forces of good (light) overcoming the forces of evil (dark). If the thief was drawn to this pictorial representation of the pull between the two forces, he might want the painting near him as a reminder of how he should live his life. Despite having committed a few malevolent acts, he could still rationalize that he was a good man at heart.

I'm convinced that the master thief had to be a he. Only a man would dare to steal these paintings for himself. There were just a few historical female figures (perhaps Delilah or Medea) who have demonstrated such dangerous egotism. The spiritual subject matter tells me that this painting reveals more about the thief's character than any of the others.

Oh, and yes, Rembrandt painted his face onto the disciple who is staring at us with his cap in one hand while the other holds on to the rope. It's the same face he etched in his Portrait of the Artist as a Young Man, *the one that was stolen. Putting himself in a painting reminds me of Velázquez's inserting himself into* Las Meninas. *How I wish I could share this comparison with Antonio.*

From her open window, the fresh smell of budding trees and newly turned earth wafted into the room. These welcome signs of spring made Portia a little giddy. She felt like taking a break, to go for a short walk in the Public Garden—where she might run into Paul Travigne. Instead, she disciplined herself to analyze the other Rembrandts. She only had another hour to study these prints before Margot arrived.

She picked up the copy of the double portrait, *A Lady and Gentleman in Black,* and once more noted that the realistic portraits and somber tones made the painting worthy of its eminent status. The Dutch gentleman stands next to his wife, who sits in an armchair. Both are dressed in heavy black clothes that make their oversized white collars and the white lace cuffs on the woman's dress stand out. The man has one hand hidden inside his spacious cape. His other hand is gloved. The lady has both hands on her lap. She wears only one glove on the hand that holds the other glove. *Her ungloved pale hand points to an empty chair, creating a sense of mystery in the painting,* Portia wrote in her notebook.

On the surface, this elegant couple seems to be a perfectly matched seventeenth-century pair. Yet, on closer inspection, the empty chair that faces them takes on a certain prominence. The wife looks toward it, while the husband gazes into the distance. He appears to have some authority over his seated wife. An apparent lack of communication between the husband and wife around the empty chair indicates a more complex and tense narrative in this seemingly simple portrait. There is a tension between light and dark in this painting, too, although it is treated more subtly than in Christ in the Storm on the Sea of Galilee.

A knock on the closed door interrupted her.

"What're you doing in there?" Stansky asked. When she didn't answer, he continued, "You're wasting your time, my dear, and your daughter needs you." He was supposed to take Alexa to Cambridge for a playdate, so Portia didn't understand what he was talking about.

She tapped her foot three times before she rose to open the door and was surprised that he was still there. She pointed to her desk, full of papers. "Remember my support when all you could think about were your Roman puddles? Please let me get back to work." Not waiting for his response, she shut the door, taking care not to slam it, even though she felt like banging it in his face.

The previous evening, after dinner, Stansky had told her he wasn't pleased about Paul Travigne's interest, particularly his offer to introduce her to Joel Soderburgh. "You're taking this too far. Why are you spending so much time with these men?" he said. "Remember, you're in your second marriage and you're not even forty—"

"What does that have to do with anything?" Portia had been taken aback by Stansky's dire warning. Normally she might want to talk things over with him, but he had made her so angry she didn't want to. Besides, every day that the paintings were missing the trail grew colder, and now that the FBI, well, one person in the FBI, had expressed an interest in her research, she felt a pressing need to continue improving her analysis.

Christ in the Storm on the Sea of Galilee and *A Lady and Gentleman in Black* had been painted on canvas. The third stolen Rembrandt, *Portrait of the Artist as a Young Man*, was a postage stamp–sized etching in which the painter at age twenty-eight looked surprisingly scruffy. His unshaven face, framed by curly hair cascading down the side of his right cheek and peeking out on the left from under a soft, round hat, held her attention once again. The left side of Rembrandt's face was more distinctively etched in shadow than the right. And although etchings in general lent themselves to the interplay of light and dark, this one also told a story about a complicated artistic personality—as she had previously discovered before her docent interrogation.

Portia reviewed the passage she had written in her notebook. *I imagine that the unsmiling artist looking at the viewer through intelligent black eyes reveals that he's seen more of life's ups and downs than most men in their twenties. I find it significant that the thief stole this self-portrait when another more valuable and attractive one by the same artist hung in the same room. The other, an oil painting of a younger Rembrandt, dressed in a lush velvet cape with a jaunty feathered cap and a hefty gold chain around his neck, showed the artist as a successful young man of twenty-three. Berenson considered this painting to be "one of the most precious pictures in existence," and yet it was not taken. Why?*

True, the etching was more portable, but size didn't seem to matter. Rembrandt's portrait of the husband and wife was large (51.6 x 42.9 inches), so the size of the younger Self-Portrait *(35.3 x 28.9 inches) could not have been a deterrent. The younger portrait was oil on wood— heavy!—but so was the stolen painting by Govaert Flinck. Perhaps the Rembrandt oil painting on wood was indeed too cumbersome to carry. Or perhaps the thief selected the slightly older artist, with its dark shadows playing against the light on his face, because it portrayed a complex man. If he had reasoned beforehand that the more attractive self-portrait was not as important to him, then this etching spoke of his identification with the artist's moodiness as he wrestled with the forces of good and evil in his life.*

Portia was so immersed in her research that she lost track of the time. When Margot entered the library, Portia checked the clock on her desk and apologized for not being ready to leave.

"No problem," Margot said. "Our trip to the museum can wait." She pulled up a chair next to Portia's. "Show me your notebook. You're not the only one in Boston who's upset about our loss."

Portia handed her the notes. "What do you think of this?" she asked, pointing to the page she had just completed. Margot read the passage about the thief choosing Rembrandt's scruffy portrait.

"Rembrandt's shadowy guy must have resonated with the thief. Don't you agree?" Portia asked her friend.

"Seems to be true, given his choices." Margot smiled at Portia.

"When I first examined this self-portrait, I felt his moodiness. The thief's a tortured soul, I'm sure of it."

"Your psychological profile makes sense." Margot stretched her arms.

Portia found it hard to put the project aside, even for the pleasure of a visit to a special museum. "Are you willing to be my sounding board for the profile?"

"I'd be happy to critique its validity."

"I think the thief was familiar with the Gardner collection as a whole and went out of his way to choose the particular objects to steal."

"So you've said."

"Why do you think he stole this?" Portia pointed to a photo of *Landscape with an Obelisk*, a painting reattributed in the early 1980s to Rembrandt's pupil, Govaert Flinck. "So even with the Rembrandt provenance in question, the mastermind included this landscape on his shopping list. Isn't that strange?"

Margot skimmed through the folder until she found Portia's sheet labeled *"Landscape with an Obelisk."*

The stormy scene with a dramatically lit obelisk in the middle ground features two shadowy men. The landscape around the obelisk is immersed in light, while murky shadows cloud the rest of the scenery. The huge dark trees in the foreground, near the men, look ominous, as does the sky directly above them. The obelisk beckons as a safe place in an otherwise dangerous world.

"I see where you're going. This dark image with its beacon of light must have a special meaning for the thief. He showed audacity when he stole these paintings, but he must be afraid of something. I wonder if he's built himself a safe fortress from a scary world or at least dreams of one."

"Exactly," Portia said. "His selfishness drives me crazy."

"Me too."

To calm herself down, Portia walked over to the bay window before turning around to look at Margot. "He may have stolen this painting because it was easy to take."

"What do you mean?" Margot's eyes narrowed.

"Flinck's landscape was in the same table stand as the Vermeer, only it faced the opposite direction."

"Sure, it was right there, but why bother stealing a reattributed painting . . . I mean, who cares about Flinck when the Rembrandts, a Zurbarán, and a Van Dyck were in that room."

"My point exactly. Does my hypothesis ring true?" Portia returned to her chair.

Margot scrutinized the rest of the file, while Portia straightened up the papers on her desk.

"It's sound." She handed the manila folder to Portia. "You've shown that the shadowy dark and light tension exists in all the paintings," she said in her calm, therapeutic voice.

"Then I'm on the right track?" Portia asked, jumping up from her chair and throwing her arms around Margot.

"Yes." Margot returned the hug. "You're doing us a big favor by analyzing the stolen art."

"Good." Portia put the folder away in her desk. She was thrilled that her intelligent friend understood and approved of her detective work. Yet she knew this wasn't the right moment to celebrate when another worry lay dormant. "What about Paul?" she asked. Only her wise friend could help her deal with the power of this new attraction.

"I've been wondering about him." Margot removed a cigarette from a pack of Marlboros.

"I'm too attracted to him," Portia whispered. "Paul's gallant, and he's been helpful to me, while Stansky's been a pain in the neck. How could I even contemplate such a thing? What would happen to Alexa? She's crazy about Stansky, although she's also loyal to her dad. Do you think I'm nuts? What should I do?"

"You're moving too fast," Margot said. "Don't muddy the waters with sexual longing." She walked over to the bay and exhaled smoke through the open window. With her tall, svelte figure and soulful brown eyes, Margot could have been a model or an actress. Instead, she had chosen to be a psychologist. "Focus on this project. There may be some risk involved, but you're not easily scared. I know you'll take the proper precautions. Portia—be flattered that the FBI might be interested in you and your case."

"Believe me, I am."

"Then don't mess it up with complications."

Portia felt appropriately warned. She trusted Margot, who had been a devoted friend, calling her every morning for a month after Antonio died. She remembered telling Margot about the last time Antonio had walked her home from the gallery—how the raindrops pattering against her umbrella as they discussed Thornycroft's new work helped soothe her anxieties—and then he had stopped her and said, "You have great instincts—and not just about art."

"He's right, you know," Margot had said at the time.

"If I have such great instincts, then why didn't I know he was so depressed?"

"Don't blame yourself," Margot had said. "You were devoted to each other."

How lucky Portia was to have such a wise confidante. And one who knew her so well.

CHAPTER ELEVEN

April 16, 1990

Another Italian Connection

On Monday around 6:00 p.m., Paul stopped by the gallery as planned. He had come from his downtown office and looked very lawyerlike in his pinstriped suit. Portia was pleased to see him, but since her discussion with Margot, she promised herself that she wouldn't get carried away. After he sat down on the orange chair in her office, she handed him her file folder with everything she had gleaned about the robbery and the missing works of art.

"I'll treat your report as carefully as my aunt Constanza's will." Paul bent down to put the folder into his leather briefcase, which lay at his feet.

"I hope she was a delightful aunt," Portia teased.

"She dabbed lily-of-the-valley perfume on her wrists like someone else I know," Paul said.

"I'm old-fashioned as far as scent goes. My mom loved lily of the valley."

"She must have been special. Tell me more."

Before she could answer, the doorbell rang, and Portia excused herself to open it. "I wasn't expecting you," Portia said to Nick.

"You never do," Nick replied. "I saw the light on."

Back inside her office, Portia introduced the two men. They shook hands.

"Oh, another Italian," Nick said to Paul.

Portia understood that Nick's casual comment meant he was sizing Paul up as a potential rival for her time. He looked approvingly at Paul's conservative suit. "You don't seem Italian," he said and opened up a folding chair on the other side of Portia's desk.

Paul was taken aback. "You do," he said as he eyed the gold ring with a sizable diamond on Nick's right hand. A thin gold chain was partly visible under his open-necked shirt.

Oh no, Portia thought as she watched Paul eye Nick's jewelry. She recalled his telling her about his embarrassment when his flashy Italian American uncles stopped by Groton to watch him play soccer. She wanted the two men to get along, although she wasn't sure why this meant so much to her. She counted on Paul's getting past the superficial to see the real Nick. The Nick she cared about, with his big heart.

"Is that a compliment?" Nick asked. He sat up straight on the uncomfortable chair and appeared ready to do battle.

"Yes and no. Jewelry's not my thing. I'm a pasta aficionado."

"Enough, you guys." She turned to Nick. "Paul's offered to introduce me to a friend at the FBI."

"That's impressive. Our little gal here is one determined lady," Nick said.

"I know," Paul said. "Please keep the FBI info to yourself."

"Of course—you probably don't know that she's met some Mafia guys through me."

Portia couldn't help but notice the shocked expression on Paul's face. This was not going as she'd hoped.

"I had to meet with them," she said. "I feel sure the Mafia was involved in some way."

"I encouraged her to do this, but nothing much came of it," Nick said, in her defense. Then he turned to face Portia as if she was the only one in the room. "I stopped by to tell you that I've had those Irish Mob rumors checked out."

Portia was intrigued and wanted to know more. Before she could question him, though, Nick asked her for a glass of wine. She knew he would tell her when he was ready. He was probably being careful around Paul. She walked to a low, wooden cabinet against the opposite wall and removed a bottle of Chianti. Then the three of them sat in her office, savoring the wine's full-bodied taste as they chatted about their Italian heritage.

"Have you ever been to the Feast of San Gennaro?" Portia asked. She was trying her best to find common ground.

"Sure," Nick said. Paul shook his head no. Nick described how four men carried a statue of Naples's patron saint along New York's Mulberry Street between Canal and Houston. "The narrow streets, jammed with people, made us even more excited when we saw San Gennaro's statue approach. Under a gold crown, his sweet face looked noble."

"A perfect description," Portia said. "My dad gave Antonio and me each a dollar so that we could pin a bill on San Gennaro's chest when he passed by. Dad told us he never understood why the magic of this act had stayed with him." Portia felt warmed by this sweet memory.

"Sounds like Little Italy was a great place to grow up. Or am I projecting?" Paul asked.

"I suppose being part of a close-knit neighborhood must have been fun, although my father's family was quite poor," she said. She told them that before the procession, her family first went to three o'clock Mass at the Most Precious Blood church. "Don't you love that name?" Portia asked. "It's real."

"It's fantastic. I'm going to investigate its origins." Paul explained how much he enjoyed doing this kind of research. *So like a lawyer,* Portia thought. When he put his empty wineglass down on her desk, they all agreed to share another round.

"La bella Italia," they toasted.

Portia could feel the wine making her woozy, amplifying her nostalgic mood. In an excited voice, she told Paul and Nick that after the feast, she, Antonio, and her father used to hit duckpins at one of the arcades and then have dinner at Da Nico's on Mulberry Street with their mom and grandparents. "My mom . . . Her name was Serafina," she said. "She always ordered the fettuccine with clam sauce. She was an excellent cook, and even she said Da Nico's homemade pasta was *something special*."

"Oh, so you named your gallery after your mom," Paul said.

"Yes, she was an angel, the most loving person in the world." Portia choked up. Nick came over and put an arm around her.

Portia pulled herself together so she could continue with her story.

"The best part, the very best part, came after dinner, when we made what can only be called a pilgrimage to Ferrara's, where my dad and granddad visited old-timers who still worked there. They'd hug one another and ask about their families. Antonio and I couldn't wait for them to finish chatting. We were eager to dive into the chocolate-covered cannoli while Mom, in her ladylike fashion, dipped her biscotti in the cappuccino."

"What rich traditions," Paul said. "I envy you."

"You were lucky to have such a warmhearted childhood," Nick said.

Portia agreed, but remembering what she once had also made her sad. As a child, she felt safe to be surrounded by family. Now that her father and Antonio were gone, having Italian men in her life made a difference. No one could replace her dear ones. Never. Nick and Paul—and she was glad that they had now met—couldn't have been more different from one another, but their combined presence filled a void she hadn't realized was there.

Before Nick left, he said, "As I mentioned—there's a good chance that the Irish Mob was involved."

"Just as I thought," Portia said. "Saint Patrick's Day had to be a clue."

After he kissed Portia goodbye on the cheek, Nick whispered in her ear, "I like him more than Stansky." Then, as he shook Paul's hand, he said, "We Italian Americans need to stick together." With that, he was out the door.

Paul took his leave soon after. "What a great time," he said to Portia. "Now I'll go home and read these notes."

Paul called her early Tuesday morning. "Your analysis, especially of the three Rembrandts and *The Obelisk*, is outstanding. Joel will be impressed," he said. "If you're free for lunch tomorrow, I'll find out if he's available, so we can all meet at the Café Florian?"

"Marvelous," Portia said before she hung up. As she moved about her gallery space later that morning, she admitted to herself that she felt intimidated about meeting someone from the FBI. It was a good thing Paul would be there when she met Joel. She was willing to do whatever she could to help get the paintings back, but this was scary, new territory.

CHAPTER TWELVE

April 19, 1990

What Will the FBI Think?

Portia spotted Paul at the back corner table in the timeworn yet lively Café Florian. He was sitting across from the short, bald man with enormous eyes that he had described.

Once she was seated, Paul introduced Portia to Joel.

"I've been in your gallery," Joel said. "I like Aaron Stockwell's paintings."

"He's my star . . . Paul tells me you two met at Harvard."

"That's correct. Only, he's a preppie; I was a scholarship kid."

"Joel got the As." Paul gave his good friend a warm tap on the shoulder.

"I'm fascinated that you work for the FBI," Portia said. "What inspired you?"

"I read Superman comics as a kid."

Portia thought he was teasing her, but Joel assured her it was true.

Against the noisy backdrop of the luncheon crowd, he explained that he'd been with the FBI for fifteen years. He'd worked his way up to become an intelligence research specialist on major cases. "So my job is to gain a deep understanding of the criminal's psyche. I've built my expertise by spending a great deal of time interviewing convicted felons, playing on their egos, and learning how they fooled the police—until they were caught."

"Then you're the perfect person to talk to." Portia smiled before taking bites from her tuna salad. She hadn't expected to meet such a psychologically sophisticated man.

"Paul tells me you've been doing a little of what I do—looking for insight into a criminal's motives and patterns," Joel said. "I construct a profile based on my observations and then search through databases for people who might match the profile."

He told Portia about his more complex cases, especially the ones involving Mafia takedowns in Boston and Providence. "I made the cigarette fall out of Raymond Patriarca's lips," he said.

"He's not exaggerating." Paul clapped his friend on the back. "No one else could have nailed the guy."

"Wow," Portia exclaimed. "I remember hearing about Patriarca. He was that big, scary guy in Rhode Island."

Joel shrugged at her compliment. He moved his chair closer to the table and asked Portia to tell him how she had examined the qualities of the stolen art objects.

"I study each composition for its meaning, by analyzing both the story and the way the artist has chosen to express it." She took out a photocopy of Vermeer's painting, putting it on the table for them to examine. "For example, here we see three musicians in one room. We can't help speculating about the one musician with his back to us. Who is he? It's a mystery. Although the light falling on pearls, gold threads of a sash, a white skirt, and a Persian carpet gives us clues about their social status, there's so much more we don't know."

She went on describing what she saw in several of the other paintings.

"Interesting," Joel said. "Do you have an impression of the person behind the robbery?"

"I've become convinced the mastermind connected with the paintings and drawings that either reflected the conflicts in his life or motivated him to resolve them," she answered. To prove her point she showed them a photocopy of Manet's *Chez Tortoni*, the portrait of a well-dressed, lonely man that had hung in the first-floor Blue Room. "He stole this, while he ignored Degas's *Portrait of Joséphine Gaujelin*, another small, easy-to-carry oil painting in the nearby Yellow Room. The thief stole four Degas drawings in the Short Gallery, but this portrait by the same artist was apparently of no interest to him."

"That's riveting," Paul said after taking a sip of his cappuccino.

"His not taking this Degas remains a mystery," Portia said. "The Impressionist artist Berthe Morisot considered this solemn portrait of a dancer in her Sunday best to be subtle and distinguished."

"Can I keep your notes so I can study them?" Joel asked. "Paul used such laudatory language about them, I need to read them myself."

"I'd be honored," Portia said. Despite his apparent interest in her research, her stomach fluttered. She felt anxious about being judged.

"Have you always been an art dealer?" Joel asked.

"No, I worked for Polaroid as a marketing manager in South America during the early eighties. Three times a year I met with our distributors in Mexico, Colombia, Venezuela, Brazil, Chile, and Argentina."

"I assume you speak Spanish?"

"I'm almost fluent."

"You've been in Medellín, Colombia?"

"Yes." Portia looked puzzled. She wondered what this question had to do with the robbery. It seemed to come out of the ether.

"So you know people there?"

"Quite well, especially the Polaroid distributor and his wife. Also Colombine Muñoz, a smart, successful art dealer. She sells art to the city's most important people."

Joel's eyes widened. "Hmm. You might be able to help us even more than I thought." He told her that the FBI had a database of underground suspects who were also art collectors. "Let me try to match your profile against it. One or two people already come to mind. They happen to be from South America—but this is moving too fast. First I'll read your notes."

"Thanks," Portia said. She couldn't help wondering if he really would.

Joel leaned toward her. "I'd like to let Julian Henderson on the Art Crime Team know about you."

"Sure."

After Paul paid the bill, Joel got up to shake hands with Portia. He promised to be in touch.

"Thanks for coming," Paul said to his friend. Portia enjoyed the way the two men showed their mutual fondness by tapping each other on the back.

After Joel left, Portia and Paul lingered at the table for another cup of cappuccino.

"This is my hangout," he confided.

"Mine too." She felt the room heat up.

"Boston's such a small world, it's amazing we never ran into each other before."

Paul leaned toward Portia. The tenderness she saw in his eyes reminded her of the way Nicolas Cage stared at Cher as they watched Mimì and Rodolfo declaring their love in *La bohème*. Despite its operatic sentimentality, that scene in *Moonstruck* had stayed with her. The drama was so Italian. So romantic. It gave her goose bumps.

Portia knew she had to leave. She looked at her watch. "It's getting late."

As they got up from the table, Paul's leg accidentally rubbed against hers. She chose to ignore the tingling sensation and thanked him again for organizing this meeting. "I can't tell you how much your support means to me."

"You really know how to interpret paintings."

Portia blushed at his compliment.

He walked her back to the gallery. "I told you Joel would be impressed," he said as they reached the door. "Let me know when you hear from Henderson."

Portia rummaged in her purse, then removed a plastic bag with dog biscuits and handed it to Paul. "I hope Cyrus likes these treats."

He gave her a gallant thank-you kiss on the cheek.

When she returned to her desk in the office, Portia called Stansky to tell him about the success of her lunch.

"I'm more than a little concerned that you're getting in too deep," Stansky said.

CHAPTER THIRTEEN

April 20, 1990

Enter the Super Sleuth

The following morning, Paul called Portia at the gallery to tell her about his conversation the night before with Joel. He admitted that at first Joel didn't find her well-documented notes so useful. "The psychological profile you drew of the thief didn't ring true to him," Paul told her.

"That's too bad."

"It gets better, I promise," Paul said to reassure her.

"Let's hear it." She picked up a paper clip holder on her desk and stared at it.

"Well . . . Joel reviewed your write-up again. And this time, he found it more persuasive. So he did a search for an equivalent profile in their database. He was surprised when a match came up, and then he recognized the name of the drug-trafficking suspect, so he called Henderson, advising him to meet with you as soon as possible."

"Oh, I see." Portia played with the cord of the phone.

"Don't you think it sounds promising?" Paul asked.

"I do," she said. "I'm afraid I have to go, though. A collector just entered the gallery."

Although she had been awaiting it, Portia was startled by Joel's call, which came early that afternoon. She didn't anticipate hearing from him so soon, and had been mentally preparing herself for the worst, imagining that he was only being polite about her analysis with Paul.

"I'm fascinated by your notes," he said. "What creative sleuthing. I never would have thought of analyzing the paintings."

"Why, thank you," Portia said. She grabbed her notebook and pen and began writing down his comments on a blank page.

"When Paul recommends someone, I listen. He's a good judge of character. I just spoke with Julian Henderson about you, telling him that as a Gardner docent and an art dealer, you've just completed a full analysis of the stolen art. Why-this-and-not-that type of thing. Julian said he was interested."

"That's great," Portia said.

"I described how you had created a profile that matched ours of a drug lord's son-in-law, and Julian was impressed. He agreed that it would be a good idea to talk with you and suggested we do a background check . . . Hope this is all right with you, Portia."

"Yes, I understand the FBI works this way."

"Julian asked if you are a team player. I told him you're passionate about wanting to help find the thief. So expect a call later today from him. He's a much smoother guy than me. Those Oxford types are like that."

"He sounds like quite the expert."

"Henderson's the best we have."

Portia had already researched Julian Henderson's accomplishments. She discovered he had led the team that investigated the robbery of valuable artifacts at Grace Cathedral in San Francisco and found the culprit. Before that he'd been responsible for the conviction of the infamous Thomas J. Maloney, the circuit court judge in Cook County, Illinois, who had accepted bribes from murderers and let them go on technicalities. Henderson had also coined the term *bagman* to describe the intermediary between the receiver and the person who concocts the bribe. He sounded quirky and effective. Just her kind of person.

Julian Henderson called Portia after 6:00 p.m. Her employees had left for the day, and she was reviewing bills at her desk in her bare feet when the phone rang. Portia recognized a British accent that lent his voice a certain authority, although his manner was informal.

"Soderburgh has been telling me some impressive things about you."

"How nice," Portia said. "He also spoke highly of you."

"We must meet next week." He told her that her research had motivated them to take a closer look at a suspect in their database. "Our Colombian contact had been hearing rumors about a drug lord's son-in-law with a hidden treasure room in his villa. They've put his name on their list. Now that we've seen your research, we've double-checked this man. We've tried to get local officials to go in there and investigate, but they're all too afraid. His father-in-law the drug lord is a Pablo Escobar type of guy, a cutthroat who won't hesitate to have someone he doesn't like knocked off. Dangerous and powerful, yet beloved by the local people."

"My business trips to Colombia took place before the drug business became lucrative. I'd heard about the cartels, but back then they weren't a danger to civilian life. I can't imagine what the country is like now." She was beginning to feel a little scared.

"I know it's premature, but please give some thought to working with us . . . I promise you'll have round-the-clock protection."

"What do you have in mind?"

"Going with us to Medellín. As an art dealer you'd have a believable reason to inquire about private art collections. You could possibly gain entry into the suspected villa. No one else has been successful."

"Sure . . . I'd be happy to talk my way into the home of a drug lord on false pretenses." Portia hoped her sarcastic humor wouldn't be misunderstood. It was her way of dealing with anxiety.

Julian laughed. "I like your attitude."

"That's a good sign we'll get on just fine."

They set up a date to meet in Manhattan for afternoon tea on the following Tuesday at the St. Regis Hotel's Astor Court. Brenda could cover for her at the gallery.

After she hung up, Portia immediately called Paul. She could not believe this was happening. As soon as Paul picked up, she blurted out, "He just called. I'm meeting Julian Henderson in New York next week."

"Didn't I say you're onto something? Joel would never have contacted Henderson if he didn't think your analysis had merit."

"I'm excited and can't thank you enough."

"Let me know what happens."

Portia hesitated for a moment. "By the way, are you free for dinner tomorrow evening? My husband, Stansky, would like to meet you."

"Wish I were. I'd like to tell that man how lucky he is."

"That's kind of you." Portia could feel her cheeks flush.

"Unfortunately, I have theater tickets."

There was an awkward pause as Portia wondered *whom* Paul was taking to the theater.

"Be in touch," Paul said, and they both hung up.

Newbury Street had become dark while the lights in her office still blazed. Portia's head throbbed from the FBI phone calls until she gazed at the Gardner poster on the wall and sensed Isabella urging her on. *Show your backbone, Portia. I was a social pariah in Boston because I dared to be different. You must go to Medellín. You're clever and certainly brave enough to handle this assignment.*

It had been more than a month since the paintings had been stolen. Portia did not plan on telling anyone, except Stansky and Margot, who already knew, about her Isabella Gardner fantasies. Their "conversations" brought them closer in her mind and, she intuitively felt, made her smarter about the investigation. She knew that a purely rational organization like the FBI would look askance at any mystical information. Portia's emotions soared, then fell as she became nervous about her proposed meeting with a senior member of the FBI. She was afraid that Julian Henderson would be dismissive of her findings and put her down, like her ex, Henry, used to do. Now that she was a professional, the chances of her being treated like an amateur were slim, but the pain from Henry's belittling of her still lingered. It was a good thing that he treated Alexa well.

Despite her worries, Portia welcomed the opportunity for an adventure and decided to fly on an early flight so that she could make a day of it. She would see the new show at MoMA before meeting with Henderson. The museum was only two streets away from the St. Regis. The Picasso collection at MoMA always satisfied her thirst for classic modern art. She also liked to keep up with the latest creative breakthroughs in her field. If no innovative shows were available, she'd see whatever new exhibit was featured.

Looking at remarkable art before the FBI meeting was Portia's way of grounding herself. If she left early and visited MoMA, she'd be at her best for Julian Henderson.

CHAPTER FOURTEEN

April 25, 1990

The Art Crime Expert

Portia entered the St. Regis Hotel's Astor Court dressed in an understated Armani suit and a matching black headband. Julian stood to greet her, then held out an upholstered chair for her. She noted that he was probably in his early forties, well over six feet tall, and had chiseled features, steel-blue eyes, and a high forehead. As Portia sized him up, she was sure he was doing the same for her.

"Nice to meet you in person," Portia said, shaking his hand. Once they sat down, she beheld the soaring ceilings and then admired the Limoges china tea service and Waterford glasses on the table.

"The St. Regis is a long way from my nondescript office. I've taken the liberty of exploiting my Art Crime Team expense account." Julian motioned for a waiter, who came over to take their order.

"I love this room," Portia said, taking in the well-dressed patrons at the linen-covered tables. She silently acknowledged the dour king in Maxfield Parrish's ribald mural that spanned the length of the King

Cole Bar. Her father had once told her that inappropriate trysts sometimes took place here, making the room's ambiance even more enticing.

"What did you see at MoMA?" Julian asked. He had a knowing look in his eyes.

"Boy, you're good. How did you know I'd been there?"

He pointed to her lapel, where she still wore her button.

She laughed and then told him about the exhibit, *Matisse in Morocco*. "His odalisques speak to me—I've never forgiven myself for passing up an opportunity to buy one in London some time ago."

"A similar thing happened to me. Now I don't hesitate to buy art if I have the cash."

"Was it a Matisse?"

"No, a de Kooning. But I do like Matisse's odalisques—very sexy women, if you ask me."

The waiter brought their tea, along with slender cucumber sandwiches, some scones, and two small plates of English trifle.

"Yes, they're exotic," she said as she spread raspberry jam on a scone. "When did you become interested in art?"

"As a scrawny lad of ten, when I was on spring vacation from public school, my aunt Patricia took me to the National Gallery. I've been smitten ever since. You see, Botticelli's *Venus and Mars* was not in my school's curriculum. I'm grateful that the old dear wanted to introduce me to sex, and that she did so in such an enlightened way."

"She sounds a bit like Auntie Mame."

"Aunt Patricia's even more outrageous."

Julian Henderson turned out to be charming. His casual crew cut clashed with the Oxford elegance of his bespoke pinstriped suit. Yet somehow he pulled off a seamless integration of American earnestness and British sophistication. She was glad that he did not fit her stereotyped image of an uptight FBI agent and that he shared her love of art.

As if he were reading her mind, Julian explained that part of his job involved going undercover and that he was good at playing different roles. "I've been a priest, a race-car driver—you name it. Perhaps I should have been an actor, but my parents would never have approved. My job gives me the freedom to have a bit of fun, in addition to being serious. Besides, I feel like I'm doing some good in this world. What about your passion for art?"

"When my brother, Antonio, and I were kids, our folks would bring us to the city . . . New York, that is . . . most weekends from our Westchester home. I loved the Met, where I could sit on a bench and stare at a painting for fifteen or twenty minutes. My favorite was Pieter Brueghel's *The Harvesters*."

"I like it too."

"Don't you think Brueghel's scene of peasants working in the fields looks deceptively simple? A few farmers eat together in the foreground, while one sleeps against the tree. I always wondered how the sleeping peasant got away with avoiding his job."

Julian laughed. "That's Brueghel, all right. Did your brother share your passion?"

"Later he did. When he was young, he'd get antsy in the painting galleries and would pull on our mother's dress until she took him to the Medieval Hall. How many times can you look at knights on horseback? Whereas, for me, paintings are full of mysteries."

"Speaking of mysteries, does that fancy black briefcase contain your research?"

"Yes."

"Let's have a look."

Portia removed her carefully prepared file and handed it to him. It held xeroxed copies of the stolen art objects and her analysis neatly typed underneath each one. As Julian read through the pages, Portia tried to calm herself by sipping her tea, noting that the cup and saucer were antique Haviland Limoges, a lovely pattern. She tried to appear casual, all the time wondering what page he was on and what he was thinking.

Several times Julian let out a sigh. Portia interpreted this as his dismay about the loss of the art. As she awaited his response, she scanned the room and admired the potted palms and faux eighteenth-century murals on the ceiling, focusing on a small one of two angels with their human faces.

"Portia Malatesta," Julian said as he put the papers down and looked directly at her. "I'll admit to being dubious at first. You've now convinced me that the dramatic tension between light and dark can be found in most of the stolen paintings and drawings. I have one question: Doesn't the younger, more elegant Rembrandt *Self-Portrait* at the

Gardner show the same interplay of light and dark as the older, scruffy one?"

"Not to the same degree. In the younger *Self-Portrait*, Rembrandt's face may be lit with evocative shadows, but it lacks expression. The painting seems to be more about costume than character. In his *Portrait of the Artist as a Young Man*, the etching that was stolen, there's dramatic interplay between light and dark." Portia sat back in her chair and feared that her answer fell flat. Julian's face looked noncommittal.

She was just about to say something more when Julian interrupted her. "What does this commonality signify? The thief appears to be a man obsessed with the conflict between light and dark in art and, as you suspect, in life."

"Correct," Portia said, hoping that she had pleaded her case fully.

"You assume this person feels guilty about dark deeds he may have done in his past and, at the same time, entitled to have all the trappings of success because he's a good man at heart."

"Yes, he wants to do the right thing . . . finding the light from a kind of Catholic morality, if you will. Yet he's driven by an overpowering dark desire to get what he wants when he wants it, no matter who he may hurt . . . in the process."

"What a complicated character you've divined," Julian said. "He wants to be treated as a gentleman despite his chutzpah."

She laughed at Henderson's delightful attempt to speak colloquial New Yorkese. "That's our man."

They went back to comfortably sipping tea as if they were old friends.

As Portia sat upright in the oversized upholstered chair, her petite frame dwarfed by its dimensions, she said, "In a strange way, our villain shares similar contradictory values with Cosimo de' Medici, who, as I'm sure you know, controlled the Florentine political system from behind the scenes."

"I never thought about making a connection between the Gardner thief and Medici."

"Well, as a Renaissance patron," Portia continued, "Medici may have paid for his art, mind you, from inherited wealth and exorbitant profits made at the expense of the workers in his bank. Yet he commissioned paintings that depicted biblical morality tales."

"So you're implying that Medici's guilt about his greed can be inferred from the subject matter he commissioned."

"Yes. And please remember that one exploitative patron from the past was embraced by society, while our villain is an outsider."

"What a clever premise . . . analyzing the stolen art . . . then divining the buyer's character."

Portia sat up in her chair. Her eyes glistened when she heard Julian's acceptance of her reasoning. "Thank you," she said.

"Did Joel tell you about the false leads we've already followed?" Julian whispered as he leaned forward.

Portia nodded her head yes. "I've also read the newspaper reports. I'm intrigued by the latest suspect, the Mafia-connected Whitey Bulger, who I understand escaped from Boston to heaven knows where. I take it he hasn't been found?"

"We don't know his whereabouts," Henderson admitted. He looked dismayed. Then his expression softened. "As I told you, there's been a rumor about a hidden treasure room at a drug lord's villa in South America."

"Yes, you did." Portia put her cup and saucer back down on the table. "Do you think it's true?"

"It's worth checking out. You told Joel that you have acquaintances in Medellín from your Polaroid days."

"That's right."

"Well . . . as you know, that's one of the reasons I wanted to meet you. Tell me more about your job back then."

Portia explained that Polaroid had hired her as an advertising supervisor for South America. "It was pretty much a dream job for a twenty-nine-year-old fresh from her MBA. My boss, a British guy named Mike Phillips—"

"Ah, a fellow Brit," Julian interrupted. "He must have been outstanding."

"As a matter of fact, Mike made sure I had hands-on training in print production, public relations, and TV commercials before launching me into the South American market."

She went on to explain that all the country managers were well-educated, hospitable men, married with families, and living in comfortable, sprawling homes staffed with many servants. "Someone I think you'll find helpful is Rupert Heilbrun. He was Colombia's camera and film distributor, and he's well connected."

"He sounds like a promising source of information."

"Rupert's also kind. He accompanied me on a tour of the largest photo shops in Medellín, as well as to meetings with the principals of the city's advertising agencies. Afterward, he invited me to a sumptuous dinner at his home, where I first met his lovely wife, Luisa. Dinner was followed by a late-night chamber music concert in town."

Julian's eyes widened. "I'd call that entertaining on a pretty grand scale."

"They were grand. On that same weekend, I had been invited to Rupert's finca in the countryside, where I saw Luisa again. I had a feeling she came from money because she carried herself regally and wore designer clothes and important jewelry. There were even more servants at the finca than at their home in the city. Late Saturday afternoon Rupert and I went horseback riding. I had my pick of the horses in his stable, and I chose a honey-colored palomino. We rode along mountain trails where the vegetation grew so quickly, Rupert said, that the workers had to trim the trees every month. It was like a scene in a movie."

"Wealthy South Americans certainly know how to live. Their lifestyles may be even more luxurious than those of aristocratic Europeans," Julian commented. "Do they collect art?"

"Why, yes. They have a valuable South American art collection. In fact, they introduced me to a fabulous art dealer in Medellín, whom I met again when she exhibited in a South American art show at the Park Avenue Armory."

"What's her name?" Julian asked, laying his wire-rimmed spectacles on the table.

"Colombine Muñoz," Portia said.

"Wealthy distributors with art collections are good contacts. They may come in handy. How do you relate to ordinary South Americans?" Julian asked. "Can you win their confidence?"

"Do you have time for a story?" Portia asked. Her worries about Julian taking her seriously evaporated as she recalled those heady days in South America.

"All the time you need," he said and, at her request, ordered her a glass of prosecco from the solicitous waiter who was hovering nearby.

She told him that after she'd been working at Polaroid for a year, she met with the local photography union in Mexico City. "I learned from Raul, our Mexican distributor, that these street photographers were the biggest users of Polaroid film, and that their instant cameras, which had been bought at flea markets, were falling apart. Polaroid was pleased I'd made this connection and arranged for me to return to Mexico City with good cameras for the two hundred union members. The cameras had sturdy bodies with expensive Mamiya lenses that had been designed for news reporters, who ultimately decided they were too heavy. So they had been in storage collecting dust, and the accountants wrote them off."

"Typical corporate behavior," Julian muttered.

"José, the president of the union, and his lieutenants met me at the airport. All the men wore dark glasses and dressed in black suits with oversized shoulder pads. They looked like mobsters, but they weren't."

"How did you know?" Julian asked.

"Raul told me they were legit. Besides, they treated me like visiting royalty." She described the drive to the Floating Gardens of Xochimilco and how they asked about her family. "After walking down a dirt path to the river, we came to a small launch with an arc-shaped bower made of brightly colored flowers spelling out 'POLAROID.' You can imagine my surprise," she said, noting Julian's look of approval.

"We boarded the boat, and a gondolier with a long pole eased us into the river. Mariachi musicians in a larger boat serenaded us with blaring trumpets and violins."

"Gorgeous," Julian said. "Go on."

"I was so touched by their generosity that, for once, I was at a loss for words."

"You must have been."

Julian told Portia that her story convinced him she could get along with all kinds of people, a valued trait in his world.

"José and his men showed me more respect than some of my male colleagues at Polaroid."

"They must have appreciated your enthusiasm for their work," Julian said. "By the way, you passed the background check. You're good to go, Portia. But I must ask why you met with those two Mafia guys in Boston. What's up with that?" His piercing look made Portia nervous. She wondered how he could have found this out, and that also scared her.

"I thought they might have some leads about the stolen art." She was careful to leave Nick's name out of it.

"That's what I figured. You're feisty, and I like that."

"Thanks, Julian." She sat back in her chair, and for a moment Portia was a little concerned that she might not live up to his expectations. She hadn't considered what would happen if her private fantasy became a reality. And what would Stansky think?

Then Julian invited her to FBI headquarters in Washington. "I want you to meet my boss. We should be able to have you consult with us in an unofficial capacity."

"That's fantastic," Portia said. "If we can get the Gardner paintings back, I would be so happy."

"We will." Julian spoke with confidence as he ushered Portia outside to a waiting taxi that drove her to the airport.

On the plane back to Boston, Portia reflected on her day. *Looks like I may be traveling to Colombia. Stansky will go ballistic.*

CHAPTER FIFTEEN

April 30, 1990

Passing Muster at the FBI

On a ticket paid for by the FBI, Portia flew to Washington, DC, the following Monday morning. Julian met her at the airport in a green Jaguar convertible, which she found appropriate for the caper she was beginning. He drove her to the J. Edgar Hoover Building, where she would meet his boss and the rest of the Art Crime Team. She was expected to make a presentation of her research to them.

Worried that Stansky might object, Portia told a whopper to her husband. "Don't expect me home until nine. I'm taking a new *Globe* art critic to dinner." Lying went against Portia's better judgment, but she didn't want to go through the emotional turmoil of another confrontation with Stansky. He would have a fit if he knew what she was really doing.

The sky was cloudless and the temperature balmy. "It's not fair that warm weather comes earlier to Washington," she said to Julian as he drove.

"Our summers tend to be humid."

"So do ours." Portia opened the window to breathe in the fresh air. "Classy car. I didn't know FBI agents owned such fancy rides."

"It must be my British genes," Julian said, a little defensively. "As a senior manager I can add my own money to our car allowance and get the car I want."

"With or without the Jag, you'd never be mistaken for an FBI guy."

"I'll take that as a compliment."

Portia had dressed in a black linen suit and an elephant-patterned Hermès scarf for the meeting. She looked professional, she thought, as she smoothed her skirt. She studied her shiny new patent leather pumps. When she put them on in the morning, they produced the same fashion high as her Mary Janes had done when she wore them to third-grade assembly programs. She laughed to herself as she drew this parallel.

As they drove past the Capitol building, Julian asked about her flight, which led into another discussion of the weather. She preferred that he tell her what might be expected of her. When she asked, he said that he'd like to wait until they were in his office to discuss the Gardner robbery.

"My boss is straight-up FBI."

"Hope he finds my report interesting," Portia said, fiddling with the tortoiseshell barrette in her hair, a nervous habit from adolescence.

When they reached the parking lot, the boring architecture alone would have told Portia that they had arrived at the FBI building.

The security was endless. Portia had to show identification, of course. She also had to allow her bag and pockets to be searched. Julian had warned her that she needed to bring her passport and driver's license along, but she found herself feeling annoyed by the meticulous care with which the security guard scrutinized both her documents and her person. The process must have taken at least fifteen minutes. "They sure need to know I am who I say I am," she said to Julian in the elevator.

"Get used to it, Portia."

They got out of the elevator on the tenth floor, where Julian ushered her into his spacious corner office. It had beige wall-to-wall carpeting, beige walls, and a pleasant view of the Potomac River's Tidal Basin.

Julian pointed to a small conference table at the back of the room. "We'll use that later." He offered her a seat at one of the two brown leather chairs that faced an ample satinwood desk. He sat next to her in the other. "Don't you think sitting side by side, as opposed to across from one another, encourages collaboration?"

Portia, not sure if this was a test, nodded yes. "Your office is more welcoming than I thought," she said. "You described it as nondescript."

"All right . . . I exaggerated," he said. "As I told you, we're going to meet with my boss, Ronald Begun, and two specialists dealing with Interpol, Sheldon Till and Evan DiDonato." He picked up the phone and told Begun's secretary that they were ready.

Portia's brows knitted together.

"Don't worry. I promise they won't grill you."

Three men soon entered the room, all of them in monochromatic suits, white shirts, and ties in various shades of gray. Portia stood and shook hands with each one before they sat down at the conference table to the right of Julian while Portia sat on his left. *Now,* they *look like FBI men,* she thought.

"How was your trip?" Ronald asked.

"Uneventful."

"That's always a good thing," Ronald said. "We're ready if you are, Ms. Malatesta."

"Please, call me Portia." As she handed out copies of the pages Julian had read at the St. Regis, she smiled at them as if they were potential collectors. Then she walked the men through her observations about each piece of stolen art. There were no interruptions or questions. She was surprised that they didn't show any reactions—and was grateful when Julian gave her an encouraging nod from time to time.

When she finished, Ronald congratulated her on her report. "Your profile of the mastermind based on his choices of art is convincing."

Till and DiDonato, mumbling their approval, stood up to shake her hand.

"Why, thank you," she said. She hadn't expected it to go so smoothly but couldn't help wondering what they really thought. Her suspicion that their interest in her had to do with her Colombian contacts surfaced again.

"Writing such a detailed report shows your commitment to help find the culprit. Is that correct?" Ronald asked.

"Yes . . . I want those paintings back where they belong."

"Good. We understand you have business contacts in Colombia and speak Spanish."

"That's true."

"Julian has told you we have a suspect in Medellín?"

"Yes." Portia was relieved that Julian now stood next to her as if they were already a team.

"Are you willing to go to Colombia?" Ronald asked.

"I need to discuss it with my husband."

"Of course," Ronald said. "I can assure you that you will be safe in whatever role you agree to play. Julian will brief you on that later. You're not trained, and we will be extremely careful that you're protected."

"I'll let you know my decision tomorrow," Portia said.

Julian accompanied his colleagues to the door.

After they were gone, she sat down in one of the leather chairs and looked at Julian. "Well . . . did I pass muster?"

"I imagine they learned a few more things about art. Your notes showed them how clever you are. Besides . . . how could they not be impressed with your courage in coming here . . . as well as your commitment to finding the stolen art?" Julian sat down again next to her.

Portia hadn't realized her participation was so important. She no longer cared if they were hiring her more for her contacts than her art expertise. Although she hoped it was for both.

"We're ready to test out that rumor," he said. "We can use your help, even more than we had originally thought."

Portia leaned in conspiratorially. "I'm dying to hear how."

"About a month ago a colleague in the Drug Enforcement Administration stopped by my office. He confided that his local contact in Medellín, who tracked cartel activities, had been drinking at a popular bar and overheard a carpenter-electrician bragging about how he had been well paid to build a room hidden behind a bedroom wall. The local contact found out the villa belongs to a drug lord's son-in-law, although the property is registered in a woman's name . . . probably his wife."

"Was the carpenter drunk?" Portia asked.

"He paid for several rounds of beer."

"Now that the room's existence has been confirmed, I take it the question is what's inside."

"I like the way you think," Julian said as he looked Portia in the eye. "The carpenter continued bragging about his work and mentioned his brilliant installation of state-of-the-art track lighting. His wealthy client had asked for the lights to be positioned in a certain way."

"Wow . . . Lighting like that could only be for art."

"So here's the point."

At last, Portia thought, straightening her barrette.

"We think the art may be from the Gardner."

"How amazing." Portia's eyes widened. "Why do you suspect this?"

"The drug lord's son-in-law and his wife are known to be fond of art. Why would they need a hidden room?"

Portia could hardly sit still.

"You told us that your Polaroid contacts are also art collectors. When was the last time you saw them?"

"It was in 1981." She told Julian that, at the time, the Heilbruns had two young children and six servants. Back then, the drug cartels were small and disorganized. Yet, despite the relative tranquility, the super-rich hired guards to sit in front of their doors. "We still exchange Christmas cards."

"That's great . . . If you can revive your association with them, they would provide a legitimate cover." He told her that she would have no trouble posing as an art dealer scouting Colombian art for one of her wealthy American patrons.

"Sounds plausible." Portia showed Julian a brave face. The idea of returning to Medellín, which was now a decidedly dangerous place, scared the hell out of her. She had heard how the once-peaceful city had changed over the past nine years. It was home to the most notorious cocaine cartel in the world, and the violence associated with drugs, including drive-by shootings, was horrific. But she reminded herself that she'd be well protected and wouldn't have to go anywhere near the undesirable neighborhoods.

"I admit this is moving rather fast," Julian said. He told her that they'd been in touch with Interpol and had already laid the necessary groundwork in Colombia. "Of course, Interpol will be running the sting operation."

"Wait a minute," she interrupted him—something she almost never did. "I haven't agreed yet."

"But you must. We need you," Julian said. "You know that, right?"

"I hear you." Portia admitted to herself that Julian made a compelling argument.

He continued to brief her, telling her they'd first go to Buenos Aires for an in-depth session with Roberto Castellano, Interpol's agent on Medellín's cartel activity. After they returned, she would need to learn the FBI's most important protocols with members of the Boston branch. "You will also take karate lessons for self-defense and have target practice."

"I'm against guns."

"Please remember that Medellín is a scary place. If, god forbid, something goes wrong, you'll need to defend yourself . . . even though you'll always have a bodyguard."

"Whoa . . . Guns, bodyguards, karate . . . I'm an art dealer!"

"That's exactly why we want you to do this. You're devoted to art and the Gardner Museum. You have the motivation. And you've shown great courage in leaving an early marriage that didn't work."

Portia was stunned. How did Julian know? She was pleased he thought that way about her divorce, while she had often felt ashamed, mainly because it was against her religion. "I'm taken aback. What else have you thought of?" She sat up straight in her chair and caught a glimpse of the Tidal Basin. Water views helped calm her down.

"Your husband can take care of your daughter. The gallery will manage. You have employees you trust. You've proved that you know how to evaluate people by having the good sense to work with the Mexican street photographers." Julian looked proudly at his new protégé.

"You're the successful undercover agent. What do you have in mind?"

"Here's the bottom line. We'd like you to inveigle your way into the son-in-law's villa to see if the Gardner art is there. I'll be with you in Medellín, and you'll get all the help and protection you need." He stopped and looked at Portia. "Are you still with me?"

She returned his gaze and her eyes said yes.

"I'll be traveling undercover as an Old Masters dealer from New York wanting to diversify my art portfolio by investing in talented South American artists. At the same time, I hope to sell some of the valuable prints in my collection. Since I don't speak Spanish and have no contacts, I'm relying on you to show me around."

He sat back in the chair, waiting for her response.

"So that's the role you want me to play." Although she had been informed this was what they wanted, somehow hearing it again at the FBI office made it more real.

Julian told Portia that was part of her role. The other part was scouting art for a smart New York client. The client already collected Botero, but she wanted to own paintings by the other Colombian Expressionist artists and was willing to pay good money for them. "You'll travel to Medellín. And while you're there, you'll spend time with your former business associate Rupert Heilbrun and his wife, Luisa, as well as their friend the art dealer Colombine Muñoz."

Portia listened. Before she could say anything, Julian spoke again.

"Most importantly, you're to befriend the son-in-law's wife and charm her into inviting you to their villa. We understand she has bought Colombian art from Colombine."

"So you think I could pull this off?" Once again Portia looked at the Tidal Basin.

"I'm sure of it. Your inner strength comes through in your daring meeting with the Mafia guys, in the way you handled yourself with my boss, in your leaving a safe corporate job to become an entrepreneur and open your own gallery."

"Thanks for your vote of confidence." Portia had never considered herself that way. It was interesting how Julian put her actions together. "What's your time frame?"

"We'd leave May 22, and if all goes well, you'd return around June 7. Does that schedule work for you?"

"I'm a little concerned about going away the last week in May. I'd be leaving my daughter for two weeks toward the end of her school year. And I have preparations to make for an important new show in June. I don't want to die and miss the opening."

Julian burst out laughing. "We'll get you back safe and sound."

Portia was already imagining herself back in Colombia. Despite her fears, it seemed impossible that she could get caught in the cross fire of rival gangs. She was American and didn't have anything to do with drugs. She was beginning to feel a little excitement.

He knows he has me.

CHAPTER SIXTEEN

April 30, 1990

Homecoming

On the flight home, Portia stared out the window. She worried about how to tell Stansky that she'd be working with the FBI on a dangerous mission in Medellín. She knew he'd be against her traveling to such a violent place. *He'll think I'm out of my mind.* Not to mention that he'd be unhappy about his increased responsibilities at home, and that she'd need him to supervise her staff and answer any questions they might have. She was appreciative that Stansky was there for Alexa when she came home from school. He spent time with her precious daughter, playing board games, reading books, or taking photographs in the neighborhood. She was also grateful that he often did the grocery shopping. If the boiler needed fixing, he was there to meet with the serviceman. More than half the time, Stansky cooked dinner for the family. He was the perfect stay-at-home dad. Henry would never have helped her in this way. Her first husband had hated anything to do with housework and often stayed late at his university office.

As the plane soared toward Boston, she pushed her seat back. She left musings about Stansky behind in favor of savoring her mission. It had been quite a day at FBI headquarters. When she first began analyzing the stolen paintings, she never imagined that in a short time she would be returning to Medellín. She hadn't realized that when she met Joel Soderburgh at the Café Florian, he was dead serious about the FBI needing her. Once again she couldn't help wondering how important her analysis of the paintings had been to them, despite their telling her it had helped them confirm the persistent rumors about a hidden room. *I suppose it doesn't matter. What matters is getting the paintings back.*

As she looked out the window, she recalled that on her twentieth birthday she had made a wish that her life would be full of learning and adventure. *I guess I've gotten my wish.*

How would she be able to get inside a heavily guarded villa, and then the secret room? Yes, she was good at developing friendships. Colombine knew the married daughter of the drug lord, as she was one of her collectors, so meeting her would not be difficult. But wangling an invitation to her villa might be impossible.

Before she knew it, the plane had landed at Logan. She combed her hair and refreshed her lipstick. As she walked into the airport, she heard her father's voice inside her head. *Portia, don't let your emotions sway you.* He had been strict, setting harsher limits than her friends' fathers. She wasn't allowed to stay at their houses for sleepovers. And when home on breaks from college, she had a curfew. Portia recalled the smell of the pungent hot sauce he made for *pasta arrabbiata*, and a wave of sadness overcame her.

Now, even in her thoughts, he was still constraining her behavior. Portia had adored her father. This time she was going to rebel.

Lost in her daydream, she bumped into an older man while striding ahead of him in the airport. "I'm terribly sorry," she said.

"Slow down, young lady. There are no fires here," he said and glared at her as if she were a rambunctious teenager.

"You're right, sir," she said, slowing her pace for a moment.

"You'll find out when you're my age," he said. Portia noticed his faded blue eyes and thought they illuminated hard-earned wisdom. "That briefcase you're carrying looks pretty heavy."

"Yep," she said. "I'm going to catch a thief."

"Cary Grant's dead," the old man said. "And he wasn't really a thief."

She couldn't help laughing. It was a good reminder that thieves could pass as solid citizens. She'd need to have sharp antennae when she was in Medellín. She walked on ahead, this time being a little more careful of where she was going. She was anxious to tell Stansky the truth. She regretted lying to him.

Portia's taxi dropped her off just before 9:00 p.m., about the time she told Stansky she'd be back from her "dinner." After she greeted him with a hug, she went upstairs and gave the sleeping Alexa a soft kiss on the forehead. She looked so vulnerable lying there in her pink nightgown, holding her stuffed elephant, that it pained Portia to leave the room. They had never been apart for as long as the Medellín trip would be, and Portia would miss her daughter. After quickly changing into jeans and a black T-shirt, she went downstairs to the kitchen for a talk with Stansky. The kitchen table was where they discussed things. She pulled a bottle of champagne from the fridge and sat down.

"What are we celebrating?" Stansky asked from his preferred seat on the divan. He closed the Robert Caro book he had been reading.

"Come to the table. I have big news to share with you."

"Has Robert Rauschenberg agreed to show in your gallery?"

"I wish."

"Then it has to be the Gardner," Stansky said in an irritated voice.

"You get points for being clairvoyant." She handed him a flute of the bubbly. "This must stay between us."

"My God, Portia. We're married."

She took a deep breath. "I flew to DC today for a meeting with the FBI. They have a hot lead about the Gardner paintings." She chose not to tell him that it was only a rumor. "In Medellín."

"What?" He looked incredulous.

"They want me to renew contact with Rupert Heilbrun and Colombine Muñoz to help them and Interpol track down the stolen paintings."

"Medellín . . . What the hell, Portia . . . It's the cartel's headquarters. Kidnappings happen all the time. There's gang warfare in the streets."

"I know, but Rupert and Colombine . . . You remember me talking about them . . . They still live in the city, so there must be ways to protect yourself." She spoke rapidly, hoping to calm him down by telling him that the FBI planned to give her a crash course in undercover work. "I'll be with Julian Henderson, the head of the Art Crime Team, who'll watch out for me, and we'll both have bodyguards." She thought she'd also omit telling him that she might need to be armed.

"What do they want from you?" Stansky's eyebrows rose. His face was flushed.

"They want me to get together with the married art-collecting daughter of the drug lord. She knows Colombine, so that part's easy. And they want me to find a way to get invited to her villa."

"What . . . They want you to be in close contact with someone connected to the drug trade? You'll be in real danger, Portia. Get your head around this." Stansky's voice had gotten louder as he began pacing around the kitchen floor.

"The violence in Medellín occurs between young thugs and the police or rival gangs in Santo Domingo Savio. I'll be far away from that neighborhood, in elegant El Poblado. You know how much I loved it there. It's gorgeous. I'll be safe." She got up from the table, grabbed his hand, and tried pressing it against hers, but he resisted.

"What does Rupert Heilbrun have to do with the art theft?"

"Nothing. Part of going undercover involves having a believable story. I'm traveling there to buy Colombian art for one of my clients. Rupert and Colombine will help me. I'm also sure he'll pick me up at the airport if I ask him."

"I never expected this in a million years. You really think you can go off and play sleuth? You're not Miss Marple . . . You run a gallery." Stansky sat down and put his hands in front of his face. Portia had never seen him so upset.

"I can't quite believe it myself . . . You understand why I need to do it, don't you? Wouldn't you want to do it if you were me?" Portia asked in an excited voice.

"No, I don't court danger." His eyebrows rose.

"C'mon, that's not what this is about."

"For how long?" Stansky looked calmer for a moment.

"About seventeen days."

"Goddamn it." Now he was yelling. "How can you be so irresponsible? You're willing to risk your life and our marriage. Not to mention leaving your daughter." He got up from the table and paced around the room again. "Why can't the professionals handle this? And why did you lie? That's not like you. You should have told me you were going to Washington."

"I was afraid you'd try to talk me out of going. Please understand, Stansky . . . I'd be supportive of you, if this was what you wanted."

"It's not the same. Not even close. And just how do you propose to pull this off?" He could barely get the words out, so he sat down and glared at her.

She gave him the big picture of what she and Julian would be doing in Medellín.

"I suppose your Colombian friends will buy it, but don't get me off the subject. What about Alexa? She'll miss having her mommy at home."

"I'll miss her terribly. Leaving the two of you for more than two weeks won't be easy. Please understand . . . I must do everything possible to help get the paintings back. I'll try to speak with you every night."

"Don't ever go off like that again without telling me." Stansky picked up a plate from the table. She knew he wanted to throw it. He had told her enough stories about his Russian mother's tendency to smash plates against the wall when she was angry. Portia felt relieved as he put the plate down and looked at her.

"I need your support." She opened her hands to plead her case.

"Forget it. I've tolerated your obsession until now because it seemed harmless. You're testing my limits. You've turned selfish, even a little crazy. It's Gardner this and Gardner that every single day. Are you planning to sabotage *our* marriage too?"

Portia's right hand flew to her heart. "That's a nasty thing to say, and it's not true. You know how much you and Alexa mean to me. You know what I think, Stansky. I think you wish you were having this adventure instead of me."

She stormed out the door. Stansky chased her down the hall and grabbed her before putting his arms around her. He held her tight.

"Okay, I'm furious you lied to me," he said. "But I know I can't stop you. Just . . . please be careful."

CHAPTER SEVENTEEN

May 2, 1990

Putting on the Ritz

Two days later, Paul Travigne stopped by Portia's gallery on his way home from work. The door to her office was open, and she overheard him ask Brenda if she was available.

"What a surprise." Portia invited Paul to come inside and motioned him to sit down on her orange chair.

"I was in the neighborhood and wondered if you'd join me for a drink at the Ritz."

"How nice," Portia said. "Give me about fifteen minutes to clear my desk and I'll meet you there."

"I'll alert the bartender that a fascinating woman is about to enter his realm."

"Get out of here." Portia felt the color rise in her cheeks before Paul left. She never could handle compliments. Yet, before she left the gallery, she checked her makeup in the mirror. It was an old habit. She decided she didn't look too bad, despite the day's toll of stressful phone calls, including one from a demanding customer who wanted his new painting's frame upgraded at no cost. Portia had a little more than an hour free before she needed to be home.

The Ritz was just across the street from her gallery. In its intimate ground floor bar, Portia found Paul at one of the few tables overlooking the Public Garden. You could see out, but passersby could not see in.

"That's where we met." Paul pointed outside as he got up to offer her a chair.

"I know," she said, equally happy and uncomfortable with his reminder. She remembered how much she liked his gap-toothed smile.

The room smelled of Joy perfume and strong furniture polish on the mahogany chairs. After she sat down, a young, clean-shaven waiter brought them a bottle of Dom Pérignon in an ice bucket. "Wow," Portia said. "That's quite a treat." She realized Paul wanted to impress her, and she fiddled with the small dish of almonds on the table.

"My pleasure . . . I've been wondering about your Italian name. I used to know someone named Malatesta in high school. Doesn't it mean headache or bad head?"

Portia couldn't help laughing. In grade school she had often been teased about her name. Now she felt proud of it. As she sipped the champagne, she told Paul about discovering Piero della Francesca's portrait of Sigismondo Pandolfo Malatesta in an art book at the Cornell library. "That Malatesta later became a nobleman, the Duke of Urbino. And when I asked my dad if, by any chance, we were related to the duke, he was amused. 'Don't let that Ivy League education go to your head,' he warned. 'We're pure peasants, my darling.'"

Paul's eyes twinkled as he teased her. "Guess I'll have to call you Duchess."

"No way." She liked Paul's ease with banter.

"It's true we Italian Americans endure some ribbing about our names . . . Hey, Joel told me about your upcoming trip," he said, changing the subject. He picked up his briefcase from the table and dropped it on the floor with a dull thud.

"I'm surprised. I thought everything was hush-hush. Isn't the FBI super careful?"

"Joel trusts me."

"Of course." Now she understood why Paul had stopped by her gallery.

"I imagine your husband's on board."

"Not exactly. He's worried about my safety."

Paul settled back in his chair before he responded. "I understand his concern. Though I suspect you'll be fine in a city you know so well. And, of course, you speak Spanish."

"I'm counting on my fluency returning." Portia took another sip of champagne. Out of the corner of her eye, she noticed a man speaking loudly to the waiter. He was sitting alone at a small corner table, dressed in a tuxedo. For a moment she thought he might be her neighbor, Jules Brevard, a BSO cellist. Then she took a closer look and realized, to her great relief, he was a stranger.

"What about your daughter . . . Alexa, right?"

"How nice of you to remember." Portia was touched, but she also felt a bit defensive about the question. "She'll be fine. Alexa and Stansky get along really well." She described how they sometimes worked together in Stansky's top-floor darkroom, with its small, enclosed space reeking from developer fluid, the table covered with old contact sheets. "Stansky taught Alexa how to make pictograms . . . if you can believe it . . . by using her miniature teddy bear, an old teething ring, and a long string. He encourages my daughter's creativity."

"Lucky kid," Paul said.

"She is." Portia felt a tinge of guilt about Stansky. He was such a devoted parent. "And she'll spend more time with her father, who usually only sees her every other weekend."

"Oh . . . I didn't realize you were divorced." Portia watched Paul's forehead wrinkle. His jaw tightened as he put his glass down on the table. She sensed they had entered dangerous territory. Yet she decided to tell him about her miserable first marriage. "My first husband, Henry Bergamont, is a political science professor at Brown."

"That's funny. I studied political science." Paul explained how he'd wanted to go into the Foreign Service until his father convinced him that law was more practical. "'You can always travel,' my father said. 'Better to choose your destination, instead of being sent to some lonely outpost where you don't speak the language.'"

"Sounds like a smart man." Portia recognized a similarity between her father's outlook on life and Paul's.

"He was."

"Oh—you mean he's no longer alive."

"I'm afraid not." Portia noticed Paul now looked sad. He took out a handkerchief from his pocket and blew his nose.

"I'm so sorry," Portia said. She resisted touching his hand to show her compassion. "I know how it is. I still miss my dad."

Neither one talked for a few moments. She felt the bubbly beginning to go to her head. She was drinking on an empty stomach. Lunch had consisted of half a BLT, which she had wolfed down at noon. She sensed that Paul wasn't keen to talk about his father, or perhaps something else was bothering him.

"You must have married Henry when you were still a kid," Paul said.

"I would call twenty-five far too young to get married, but that's because I'm now a wise woman of thirty-eight."

"You mean a beautiful woman of thirty-eight." Paul's compliment made Portia blush again. She wished her emotions weren't so transparent, although Paul didn't seem to notice. "Well, at least you've tried twice. I'm gun-shy. My parents went through a nasty divorce when I was in prep school, and I swore I'd never do that to any kid of mine."

The waiter stood nearby. Paul signaled him not to interfere by holding up an open hand.

"I can only imagine how tough it must have been for you." Portia leaned forward in her chair. "Alexa was five when I left Henry, and she languished for a couple of months. Thank goodness, young children tend to be resilient." Portia knew she sounded defensive, but she was telling the truth.

Paul looked thoughtful for a moment before he said, "Why did you do it? It's none of my business, I know, but I don't approve of divorce . . . and it's not just because I'm Catholic. You might be able to help me understand my parents' decision. It seemed so selfish at the time."

Portia felt annoyed that Paul would voice his disapproval. She'd had to defend her decision to herself, her parents, and her friends. Paul's view about divorce was not unusual. Yet she believed it must be holding him back in some way. She wanted to set him straight. As a lawyer, he must know that life was never black-and-white, and some-times divorce made sense. "Henry said he adored me, but he criticized my every move, from the meals I cooked to the dresses I wore to my choice of friends. He could be downright mean. If he didn't like what I made for dinner, he'd light up his pipe and let me know what was wrong and how I could improve."

"That's awful. I guess you didn't know he was like that before you married him."

Portia liked how the sympathetic look returned to Paul's face. It encouraged her to continue. She moved her chair even closer to the table. She didn't want other people in the bar to eavesdrop. Boston was a small town.

"Henry couldn't have been more charming." She described how he used to bring her Lindt chocolates when he picked her up for a date because he knew she loved them. He often complimented Portia on her elegant style and held her hand when they walked down the street. "His fraternity brothers told me he bragged about me all the time."

"He had every reason. I know I would have. Too bad Henry changed so much once you were married."

"I'm not sure he changed. I was just too naive to recognize his nar-cissism." She took another sip of the delicious champagne. She wanted Paul to know the real Portia and not some idealized version.

"What do you mean?" he asked.

She described how Henry's intolerance of people who screwed up came out in scathing comments. They had never been directed at her, until she became his wife. "Now when I look back on those days"—she closed her eyes for a moment—"I can see how unformed we were as people . . . far too young to have made such a serious commitment."

"Henry probably wanted to make sure you wouldn't get swooped up by someone else."

"Thanks for your positive interpretation."

"I've been thinking of your upcoming trip. I imagine you must be nervous," Paul said, changing the subject again.

"I'm pretty keyed up, although this champagne's helping me relax. It was dear of you to get me out."

"Of course, that's why I stopped by. Will you call me from Medellín? I feel responsible."

Paul moved his head closer to hers and looked into her eyes.

Portia could feel the heat between them and wondered what it would be like to make love with him. She was tempted to leave the bar with Paul and go to his nearby apartment. Yet she was grateful that her more rational side prevailed. As she got ready to leave, she recalled having a similar tingle on her first date with Stansky. *Perhaps love is only exciting in the beginning.*

"That's kind of you to ask." She somehow managed to keep her cool. "I'll call if I'm allowed to. Don't you think Isabella would approve of what I'm doing?"

"Oh, you've formed a bond with her spirit?"

"Yes, she wants me to help get the paintings back, I know it."

"You're intriguing. I'd like to know you better." He reached for her hand and patted her long, graceful fingers.

"Paul, it's getting late. I'd better get back to my family." *Before the champagne makes me do something I'll regret.*

She got up from the table and gave Paul a kiss on the cheek before she turned around and walked out the door.

The following Sunday morning, Portia went to Shelley's ballet class. This time she amazed herself, and Shelley, with her performance of perfect pirouettes. "What's going on?" Shelley asked. "You're focused today. Your dance routine is flawless."

"I have a new project that's very exciting."

"I'm not going to ask. Whatever you're doing, it's working."

MEDELLÍN

CHAPTER EIGHTEEN

May 15, 1990

Red-Hot Information

On the third Tuesday in May, a week before Julian and Portia were scheduled to leave for Medellín, they flew to Buenos Aires for a briefing with Roberto Castellano, the Interpol agent, about their suspect, Carlos Alfonso, and his family, his work, his world in Colombia.

As they entered a wood-paneled room with floor-to-ceiling windows, Roberto greeted them by shaking their hands and offering them coffee or something else to drink. A glass water pitcher and matching cups were on a table in the center of the room. Portia sized up the swarthy Roberto as a no-nonsense kind of guy with a Roman nose, flecks of gray in his black hair, and a chiseled chin. She chastised herself for noticing his good looks. *No more flirtations,* she reminded herself.

Roberto led them to a plush white sofa with a table next to it on the right. He adjusted the slide projector that sat on the table. Portia found their host's behavior more direct than other South American men she knew. They tended to be polite and gracious, taking time to make a woman feel at ease. Roberto got right down to business. It made her wonder why he was different. He seemed to have a need for control. At the same time, she felt far less anxious with Roberto than she had the first time she met Julian Henderson. Perhaps she was getting used to meeting "spooks" of every persuasion.

"Let's strategize how to get Portia into the suspect's villa," Roberto began.

"Julian said that I should ask Colombine for an introduction to her friend, the married daughter of the drug lord."

"Yes, that's one way of making it happen. First let me familiarize you with the extended family and the drug world."

Roberto shut off the lights, pulled the curtains across the windows, and showed them slides of Colombia's drug kingpins, their siblings, spouses, and children, as well as other important connections they had. As he clicked through each slide, he gave the person's date of birth and schooling, whether they attended church, where they lived, and who guarded their houses. He covered the rivalries between the regional drug leaders. Carlos's father-in-law, Don Pedro Martinez, was discussed in great detail.

"Don Pedro began his career by hawking contraband cigarettes and fake lottery tickets before he sold used Cadillacs. Then he made his fortune selling cocaine and went from small-town creep to big-time crook and philanthropist. He's a wily character. And a devoted family man."

"It's hard to imagine he can be both," Portia said.

"You'll see," Roberto assured her.

As Roberto clicked through several slides of Don Pedro's vast organization, he told them that the Medellín cartel had developed its own coca plantations in Colombia's highlands. It ran protection rackets in the city and had laboratories in the north, near the Panama border, and in the remote southern regions, as well as in neighboring Bolivia and Ecuador. Don Pedro also personally invested in legitimate businesses and financed massive public works, such as bridges, schools, and highways.

"Don Pedro's shown tremendous generosity in giving back to his community. The people who live in the barrio treat him as a hero, and their appreciation is heartfelt."

"That's impressive at least," Portia said.

"Despite hearing stories about his violent activities, they don't react to murder reports as long as their families aren't the victims," he said.

"Horrible." Portia felt depressed by this. She still liked to believe that most people were honorable.

Roberto told them he had heard rumors that Don Pedro's long-term goal was to get out of cocaine trafficking and retain some of the legitimate businesses he now funded with drug money. "Then no one would be able to touch his family."

"Do you believe that?" Julian asked. "The American Mafia is stronger than ever."

"I think Don Pedro's different, although all crime syndicates were created for the purpose of making money. As you undoubtedly know, the American mob business was handed down from father to son, their roots harkening to southern Italy for at least a hundred years."

Portia acknowledged Roberto's accurate account of the Italian American Mafia.

"The Colombian drug business, taking advantage of strong demand abroad, only began in the mid-1970s, but it didn't take off until the mid-1980s. When cocaine production became a huge international business, Don Pedro made a great deal of money. He hoped to create a philanthropic legacy for his family so they could be more fully accepted by society," Roberto said.

"Wouldn't he have a hard time with that?" Julian asked as he put his glass of water down on the nearby table. "People might never forgive him."

"Yes and no. The Colombian political leaders are ambivalent about Don Pedro. They admire his philanthropy, but they don't like having the international community, particularly the United States government, on their backs because of him. They also don't like him giving them orders."

"Understandable. What about his son-in-law, Carlos Alfonso? Do the locals associate him with Don Pedro's cocaine operation?" Julian asked.

Roberto told them that most people in Medellín took the cartel for granted. They didn't bother to make a connection between Carlos's boutique hotels and the drug trade. They saw Carlos as a barrio boy who made good. They liked that he took care of his mother and that he and Don Pedro's eldest daughter, Maria, bought her a house nearby. They thought Don Pedro wanted to protect his daughter and that Carlos was a solid family man with two children and a wife.

"That's bizarre," Portia said. She thought about how most of the Italian Americans she knew, including her family, had no ambivalence about the Mafia. They were hated and feared and produced more than a little shame when they came up in discussions with friends. "Not again," her mother used to say with sorrow in her voice when there was a new story in the paper about a Mafia killing.

"You hinted at some tension between Carlos Alfonso and Don Pedro. Is that true?" Julian asked.

"There's a rumor about a rift," Roberto said. He told them he'd heard that La Gran Conchita hotels that Carlos managed were profitable, but Don Pedro also used them to launder money from cocaine production. "Our source, eavesdropping on his boss's conversations with Carlos, recently overheard Carlos objecting to the flow of illegal money into his business. One night, as my source was polishing the furniture in the hallway outside Don Pedro's office, he heard Carlos pleading with his father-in-law to keep the hotels straight. Don Pedro became angry. 'Just do what I say, and don't bring this up again,' he told him."

"I thought Don Pedro was grateful Carlos had made an honest woman of his daughter Maria," Portia said.

"That was nine years ago. Now Don Pedro might be feeling a bit envious of how easy Carlos's life has become. Or maybe it's something else. Let's return to the La Gran Conchita chain for a moment. There are five hotels. The two of you will be staying at the one in Medellín."

"It's quite beautiful," Portia had said when she saw the slide of the hotel's simple Spanish architecture and lush grounds.

"You'll have all the amenities there, and hopefully you'll also meet Carlos on his home turf."

"Sounds good," Julian said. Portia agreed.

"I'd like the two of you to observe Carlos in the course of his duties and learn about his habits and idiosyncrasies. Does he get to work early? How does he treat his employees? Although I know it's an improbable request, if either of you could uncover some dark secrets from his past we could use them . . . Portia, you might be able to pick up innuendos from his staff, his wife, or Colombine. We'd love to get more information about his wife and her routines. We understand she plays a small role in the day-to-day operations of the hotel."

"You've given me a lot of responsibility," Portia said as she squirmed in her chair. "I hope I can pull this off."

"I'll be there to help you," Julian reassured her.

"I'm sure that by staying at La Gran Conchita you will gain more knowledge of Carlos's activities. We've had our suspicions, but still need the information confirmed," Roberto said. "Carlos's hotel is part of the world that you will need to elbow your way into."

Portia sighed and Roberto walked over to pat her shoulder.

"You'll be fine. I promise you," Roberto said. Then he moved back to the slide projector and continued with his briefing. He told them that Carlos spent most of his time at this hotel. Once a month he traveled to Venezuela, where he devoted a few days to reviewing the hotel books in Caracas and meeting with the staff. In Mérida, where they had a small mountain resort, he also met with the staff, but he didn't stay as long. "Evidently, Carlos learned the importance of building employee loyalty from Don Pedro and decided that regular meetings in person were crucial to the hotels' success. Often, Maria goes to Venezuela with him. I imagine that spending a few nights together far away from the family and the cartel must be a welcome break. Also, we understand that he values her take on the people he hires."

"So we'll find a way to get into their villa when they're in Venezuela," Portia said.

"Perhaps," Roberto answered. "We're getting ahead of ourselves."

"They're an unusual couple," Julian said. "While they're classy and well spoken, Carlos isn't above getting his hands dirty when he advises his father-in-law on cartel activities . . . and Maria goes along with it."

"It seems that Carlos fits the portrait I've drawn of the thief. He's certainly troubled: wanting to be seen as honorable, while feeling entitled to material possessions as payback for helping his father-in-law with cartel operations."

"Perfect," Julian said. He looked proudly at his protégé.

"Well, yes," Roberto agreed. "Your profile made us dig deeper into Carlos's life."

Portia took this as a compliment from Roberto, although she wasn't sure.

Roberto took a few sips of water before he returned to his slideshow. He briefed them on the current social and physical landscape of Medellín, which aside from the prevalence of the cartels, did not seem very different from Portia's previous time there. Julian had never been to Colombia before and needed to understand the context in which their raid would hopefully take place.

Roberto covered the high points, telling them that downtown Medellín was a grid of narrow streets with banks, insurance companies, newspaper offices, one or two department stores, a few remaining real estate agencies, flower stores, and the Museo de Antioquia with its world-class art collection.

"Antioquia's the region's name," he said. "Julian . . . you'll want to visit the top museums there if you're going to mix with patrons of the arts."

"I've been to the Museo de Antioquia," Portia said to Julian. "And if you like Botero's work as much as I do, you'll be knocked out. We'll go together." Portia felt pleased she would see this artist's work again. Botero's imaginative world, peopled by rotund characters of exaggerated volume, always made her smile.

Roberto returned to the slideshow once again. "Sections of downtown Medellín are considered semi-dangerous, but that doesn't stop *paisas*—the local people—from going there. It's where the best restaurants are. You'll probably get an invitation to dine there, so please bring a bodyguard with you. In addition to the fancy restaurants, the downtown area has small bars and convenience stores sandwiched in between skyscrapers. There are even some open fields with a few cows tied to posts. One of my favorite experiences in Medellín, as well as in many smaller towns in Colombia, is finding a letter writer sitting at a table with a typewriter in a local café. Most locals are semiliterate, and customers need help with writing either personal or business letters. A letter writer could be a good source of local gossip, if you need the latest information."

"You're crazy, Roberto," Julian said. "Why would I talk with a letter writer?"

"Because they often know what's happening. I'll prove it to you in a moment," Roberto went on. "Like most South American countries, there's a huge difference in Colombia between the classes. The wealthy live in mansions with many servants in El Poblado, high on a hill south of the center. Armed guards sit on porch chairs in front of the doors to the houses."

"That's how my friend Rupert Heilbrun lives. He's come to accept it as a way of life." Portia felt good about contributing to the discussion.

"It's wonderful that you stayed in touch," Julian said. "One of the many reasons we value you."

Portia smiled and Roberto continued with the briefing. He told them that a mansion in Medellín is likely to be one of a wealthy person's many homes. There's probably a finca in the countryside, and possibly a beach house in Cartagena on the Caribbean coast. "This means our quarry might not always be at home, so whatever intelligence Portia gains about their comings and goings will be helpful."

Portia looked at Roberto. "If you say so," she said. Her stomach felt queasy from the pressure building up inside.

Roberto recommended that Portia and Julian spend some time at the InterContinental, which was in the heart of El Poblado. This large hotel had an outstanding restaurant, with magnificent views overlooking the city, and was an informal hub for the local high society and wealthy foreigners. It also had a business center if Portia or Julian needed to send a fax. There were other posh restaurants in the neighborhood and an active nightlife in the Zona Rosa, the commercial section of El Poblado.

"One sign of normalcy is that young couples often get up to dance after dinner. They don't let the cartel's existence in their city interfere with them enjoying themselves."

"I love the deep-toned drumming of *cumbia* music," Portia said, remembering how much fun she used to have in Colombia.

Roberto continued with the slideshow. He told them that the hopelessness found in Santo Domingo Savio was in sharp contrast to the lives of the wealthy. "The slum is on a hillside in northern Medellín, where the homes are mostly tin-roof shanties made from crumbling cinder block. Here its inhabitants barely eke out a living. The streets are poorly paved, and there are only a handful of cars. The few streetlights are often broken. I strongly advise you to avoid this neighborhood. It's dangerous, although there are certainly some good people living there."

"We'll never go there," Julian promised. "Don't worry."

"But I would like you to visit the outskirts of Medellín before you meet Maria Alfonso. She and her family live there, so it's something else to talk about when you meet her, Portia. I'll tell you more about her villa later."

Portia was impressed with Roberto's knowledge. She complimented him on his work, which he shrugged off, but his big grin told her he was pleased. Now that Roberto had finally finished the slideshow, he offered them coffee again. This time they gladly accepted. A young woman wheeled in a cart laden with drinks and canapés before she left the room.

As they sipped coffee from china mugs, Roberto handed out printouts of the slides he had shown them. "You must memorize this information. The papers can't go with you to Colombia."

"Of course," Portia said. "As an art dealer I've had lots of practice noticing and remembering important details." Her heart pounded as she grasped the danger of her role.

"Julian will be there as an Old Masters dealer to reinforce your knowledge and give you support," Roberto said. "We'll need you to take him to Colombine's gallery so that he can show her the work Colnaghi will give him on consignment."

" Wow . . . Colnaghi's the most prestigious gallery in London . . . Colombine will be impressed. I couldn't do this without Julian."

"I don't think you're giving yourself enough credit," Roberto said, his face lighting up. "Now comes the interesting part."

Portia found herself warming up to Roberto. She decided he resembled an actor in a daytime soap opera. Mexico's *The Rich Also Cry* would have been a perfect venue for him. Focusing on Roberto's self-assured expression helped calm her fears.

"Do you remember the carpenter-electrician who built the hidden room?" Roberto asked.

"Of course," Portia said.

"Well . . . we just learned he has disappeared. And, Julian, you may be interested to know, our source was a local letter writer."

Portia pulled her light summer shawl around her shoulders. She felt chilled in the same way when her grandfather, a sweet old man smelling of pipe tobacco, had told her and Antonio about the Calabrian Mafia rubbing out local people who opposed them.

"That's frightening," Julian said. "We need to come up with a fool-proof plan." She noticed for the first time that Julian had dark circles under his eyes and wondered why. He was the consummate cool guy.

"We've been working on it," Roberto said. "Portia, as you know, your role is to befriend Maria Alfonso through Luisa Heilbrun and Colombine Muñoz, who both went to school with her. Maria also happens to be Colombine's best client. You and Julian can strategize the best way of finagling an invitation to her villa."

"We'll come up with a plan after Portia and Colombine meet," Julian promised.

"Once you're inside the villa, you must look for an odd-shaped wall, one that feels out of proportion to the room and seems out of place," Roberto continued.

"That doesn't sound easy," Portia said. "I'll do my best."

Roberto told her to make sure she saw all the paintings in the villa; there was bound to be at least one in each of the many bedrooms. "Your memory about the layout and where any suspicious wall is located will have to serve you well. Also pay attention to where all the bathrooms are. That's practical information for Interpol and the local police when they raid the villa and recapture the paintings. Once you're off the grounds, we'll need you to draw a detailed map of the layout."

"This is getting scary. What if I'm found out?"

"That's not likely," Julian responded. "Most South American men would never suspect a woman was capable of espionage."

"Oh, so you're counting on a negative stereotype?"

"Not exactly. We need you, Portia. Will you do it for art? And to honor the legacy of the fabulous Mrs. Gardner?"

"Of course. Of course, I'll do it. I just didn't realize how nervous I would be."

"That's normal."

"If you say so."

"We hoped we could count on you," Roberto said. He then told them that he'd be in a rented villa on the outskirts of Medellín with two

Interpol contract workers, waiting for whatever they found out. "Rest assured, we've already cleared this with the Colombian law enforcement agency. They've wanted to break up Don Pedro's hold on cocaine trafficking for some time now." He told them the sympathetic mayor had given him a list of their finest local police, and that they planned to interview and select the best men to be part of their team. "At the right moment, we'll use a ruse to raid Carlos Alfonso's villa when he and Maria are away and retrieve the paintings . . . assuming they're there."

Roberto opened the drapes, and the sun poured into the room. "Until we meet in Colombia," he said to Portia and Julian as he led them to the door.

The next day Portia flew back to Boston feeling more confident about everything. She had been sworn to secrecy, so she couldn't tell Stansky any details of the meeting in Buenos Aires, although he knew she had met with Julian and Interpol to begin planning the sting. She was excited about her role. Nothing was going to stop her now.

She spent a lot of time with Alexa the week before she left for Colombia. She picked her up at school every day and took her for ice cream at J. P. Licks in Cambridge. The shop was always crowded with parents and kids, and on their last excursion Portia told her, "Mommy's going to be away for seventeen days."

"Why?" Alexa looked up at her mother. She had stopped eating her hot fudge sundae.

"I'm on a special assignment to find some artists in South America."

"Can Stansky and I come with you . . . like we did when you went to Rome?" Alexa asked.

"It wouldn't be right to take you out of school."

"Aww . . . Promise you'll read me stories over the phone."

"Of course, my darling." Portia threw her arms around Alexa and held her tight. She loved this little girl more than anything. What if she was stranded in Colombia, and they were separated for a long time? This thought darkened her mood. She composed herself as they walked side by side to the parked car as if it were an ordinary day. She promised herself that no matter what happened she would make it back from Colombia for Alexa's sake.

CHAPTER NINETEEN

May 18, 1990

A Fortuitous Adoption

Friday morning dawned with a spectacular sunrise as Carlos Alfonso woke up to greet the pink sky. He threw an Italian suede jacket around his narrow shoulders and went outside to survey his property. From his viewpoint at the head of the curved driveway, he looked back at his double-storied Spanish colonial home. He breathed in the fresh mountain air. His gaze fixed on the stark contrast between the dark trellised bark in front of the windows and the white stucco façade. *Simple and dramatic,* he thought. A whirring sound of birds flying overhead interrupted his ruminations about life. The man, who had grown up in the barrio and searched the trash for food, never took his good fortune for granted. *Can all this really be mine?*

The Spanish villa was surrounded by trees. A long dirt path lined with cypresses led to a country road. The track was wide enough for cars, even the occasional pickup truck. In the early mornings Carlos used the path for exercise. On this May morning, his distress about turning thirty-one made him vow to remain fit.

He walked down the path until he reached the guard, who was stationed in a small wooden structure obscured by tall trees near the road. When he arrived each morning, the guard handed him a written report of how many cars had driven by that night, including the license plate numbers of any dilapidated or slow-moving vehicles that looked suspicious. This information was important to Carlos because his finca—this large estate, which included a villa, a farm, horses for riding, and cattle—was located only thirty-five miles from downtown Medellín. He felt safer in the countryside than in town, although he could never feel safe enough anywhere in his country.

Carlos strapped a holster over his button-down shirt, with a .38 caliber long-barreled revolver in it. He wore snakeskin cowboy boots and hid a miniature silver revolver in a silk pocket of the left boot, where he could grab it quickly if necessary. He needed to take precautions. Even his bodyguards could not be trusted completely.

Nine years ago, Carlos had married Maria, Don Pedro Martinez's eldest daughter. The young couple had decided not to live at her father's compound in the exclusive El Poblado suburb. Instead, they built their own home a half hour away. The powerful drug lord had objected at first to his daughter's move away from her mother's household, but at the couple's insistence on their independence, he relented.

Like most wealthy people in Medellín, the Alfonsos had many servants: a cook, four maids, a butler, a gardener, a nanny for the children, and a chauffeur. And also like many affluent families, they employed a team of four bodyguards. Working assigned shifts, an armed guard sat to the side of the oak front door at all times. This morning, when Carlos returned to the house, he found the night guard snoring. He shook him awake and stared at him with sharp, eagle-like eyes. "You lazy bastard," Carlos said.

The front door guard had been trained to be in hourly radio communication with another guard stationed at the end of the road. Failure to carry out this duty was a serious matter. "I'm sorry," the night guard said as he rubbed his eyes.

"You're fired," Carlos said. "How dare you risk my family's safety?"
Once again the young guard muttered apologies to his boss.

Carlos fumed as he opened the heavy door and stepped into a large foyer that led to a magnificent courtyard. Bird-of-paradise plants lined the flower beds. Canaries twittered as they flew from one tree to another in their own nirvana. In the center was a fountain, where his children liked to throw coins. Carlos sat on the edge of the fountain, allowing the sound of flowing water to calm him. He remembered how hard his childhood had been and took momentary pity on the guard. He went back out front and ran after the man as he made his way down the long driveway. Carlos grabbed his arm to stop him. "Go talk with the cook. Perhaps he'll offer you a job in the kitchen," he said. His conscience was clear now, and he returned to the house.

He knew the guard would find his way to the servants' quarters, which were located in the back of the ground floor. Only Ludovico, his personal bodyguard, had a small room near the master suite and the children's rooms on the second floor. The huge kitchen and formal dining and living rooms were on the left side of the courtyard. On the right were a series of guest rooms and a library with floor-to-ceiling bookshelves modeled after Don Pedro's own book collection, which had opened up new worlds to Carlos. Wide interior loggias with undulating ceilings connected the rooms, and arched windows looked out onto the courtyard.

Carlos appreciated his grand surroundings, although they required vigilant attention to security. There was only one room where Carlos could relax: the master bath. Nothing calmed him more than soaking in his oversized bathtub. Local cumbia music was piped inside through small speakers. Potted palms around the raised tub gave him a sense of the outdoors. With the flick of a switch, the ceiling opened so that he could experience the stark beauty of the night sky or the freshness of a new day.

When he returned late at night from a business trip to Caracas, for example, he luxuriated in the bath the following morning. Sometimes on more leisurely days, he put three rubber ducks in the bath with him and pushed them through the bubbles to the faucet. It was his secret pleasure of childish play, an experience he never had in Santo Domingo Savio. His mother's cinder block shack, with its rusty tin roof, sat on a narrow, dirty pockmarked street. And like the neighbors' houses, their home did not have indoor plumbing. Infrequent bathing, mostly without soap, took place in a nearby mountain stream. This morning, he looked at his manicured hands. Once again, he reveled in his good fortune . . . moving from the barrio on the northern hillside of Medellín to a countryside villa on the outskirts of the opposite hill. There weren't that many miles between them. Yet they were worlds apart.

Back when they lived in the barrio, Mercedes Alfonso, Carlos's mother, worked long hours picking fruit in the neighboring fields. Yet there was never quite enough food for the two of them. Most nights she cooked cheese-filled *arepas* on a primitive wooden grill. Sometimes they went to bed hungry. His father had disappeared before he was three, and Carlos only had a shadowy picture of the man in his mind. At elementary school, as they walked around the playing field during recess, his friend Victor once confided he wasn't the only boy without a father. "I don't know mine," he said. "Guess it's normal for fathers to disappear." Carlos felt somewhat better, but he still longed for a dad.

His mother, who had been an attractive young woman, refused to get involved with another man. Unlike many of her peers, Mercedes Alfonso knew staying single would protect her son. For if a woman became involved with a new man, his jealousy of the previous lover would be taken out on the son. Eventually he might throw the young son out of the house, and the boy would be forced to live on the streets. Gangs of homeless boys in the large Colombian cities banded together to sleep in doorways at night. They supported themselves by begging and engaging in petty thievery.

On the weekends Carlos helped his mother wash the inside walls of their one-room home. Together they dusted the rickety table and chairs she had cobbled together from wooden crates. There was a dirt floor, which Carlos raked every evening before he went to sleep on an old army cot.

When they reached nine or ten, most of the barrio boys who still lived at home went to work in the fields or ran errands for the local pharmacist or butcher. Not Carlos. His mother insisted that he attend school. The errand boys bullied him if they found Carlos reading a book underneath a tree. He knew being literate would eventually help him escape the slum. In truth, he enjoyed learning and found himself curious about the world outside Medellín.

As Carlos reached puberty, he admitted to feeling jealous of former friends who flashed Timex watches or showed off new black leather jackets. Some of the boys were already old enough to be hired by the cartel to run dangerous errands, including dropping off cocaine and collecting protection money. They were given guns and taught to shoot. He watched one and then another of his former friends push cheap drugs in the schoolyard. Yet while these adolescent boys earned decent money, they still lived with their mothers and siblings.

When Carlos turned fifteen and had grown to six feet, he was tired of the deprivation he had endured from the paltry meals he shared with his mother. One day his resentment exploded, and he went to the local bar, where he knew he would find Rodrigo, one of the cartel's henchmen. Although he had never been inside the dark, smoky bar before, Carlos walked up to a man with a stomach that hung over his pants and narrow eyes in a full face and introduced himself. Then he asked him if he needed any help running errands. "We always have opportunities," Rodrigo said.

Carlos was careful about where and when he collected protection money from a pizza parlor, florist, pharmacy, or convenience store so that his mother would not find out what he was doing. He avoided jobs that might take him to the open market downtown because many local farmers knew his mother. He hid his weekly pay under his mattress while he managed to slip some pesos into his mother's purse. After a few weeks she confronted him, and Carlos confessed that he had earned some money after school. "I hope you're not working for the cartel," she said.

"Well, yes," he answered, looking down at the dirt floor.

"Why?" his mother asked.

Hearing the sadness in her voice, Carlos felt guilty. "Mama, I'll quit when I'm eighteen." Then he could apply for a scholarship to La Nacional, the local university.

"I'm frightened. Promise me you'll be careful," she said. Carlos realized that she now understood he wouldn't give up this chance to help them.

"Of course, Mama. You'll see. You'll be proud of me someday."

"I just want you to live."

The next day Carlos returned to the bar, which was full of noisy workers, for his weekly meeting with the portly Rodrigo. He spotted him in the corner sitting with an older man dressed in a three-piece suit. As he approached, Carlos guessed that the man must be Don Pedro Martinez. He couldn't believe his good fortune. He never expected to meet Don Pedro, and certainly not here. As he came closer, Carlos observed the man's bushy eyebrows sprouting above keen black eyes. Although the man's face had a hard-edged quality, he didn't look mean.

"Don Pedro, this is Carlos," Rodrigo said.

The drug lord stared at Carlos and then shook his hand. "Rodrigo has told me good things about you."

"I'm pleased to meet you, Don Pedro," Carlos said, looking a little diffident in front of this legendary figure. He was glad he had taken extra care that morning to wash his face and comb his hair.

"You're a handsome lad," Don Pedro said. "I like your firm handshake."

"My teacher taught us to shake hands like we mean it."

"You're still in school?"

"I love learning new things."

"Rodrigo, you're right," Don Pedro said. "This boy's special. Not like the others."

Turning back to Carlos, Don Pedro asked, "Where do you study?"

"In a corner of my mother's home."

"Is it quiet?"

"No, it's noisy. And it's dark."

"How would you like to use my library?"

"I'd be honored, Don Pedro." Carlos wanted to bow his head or put his right hand up to his forehead in a military salute. Yet he didn't feel comfortable making either gesture. Instead, he stood tall with his hands by his side.

"My library is at your disposal."

Carlos restrained himself from hugging Don Pedro. "I'm very thankful, sir."

He told Carlos that Rodrigo would accompany him to his villa until he learned the way. Although he might have been tempted to do so, Carlos didn't brag about being invited to the villa. The boys in his neighborhood would have beaten the hell out of him.

The next day he took a streetcar through noisy and crowded downtown Medellín, and as Rodrigo had instructed, he boarded a bus that dropped him off in El Poblado. He had never been there before. Rodrigo met him at the bus stop, and then the pair walked a long way down the quiet, tree-lined streets. Carlos stared at the houses, especially the huge adobe ones set back from the road, with manicured front gardens. The open-designed villas allowed him to peer into courtyards with tropical plants surrounding circular fountains.

At Don Pedro's villa, a young male servant opened the heavy oak door and welcomed Carlos and Rodrigo inside.

"Wait there," the servant said, pointing to an oversized chair in the sitting room. Rodrigo excused himself and went back outside. Carlos, half-excited and half-afraid, looked around the room, taking in the surroundings: a glass coffee table with a few glossy magazines on it, the damask drapes, the polished oak floor, the fresh roses in a crystal vase on a table across the room. Carlos had never seen such splendor.

Don Pedro came in to greet him, and Carlos stood and shook his hand. Then the drug lord led Carlos through the carpeted living room and the banquet-size dining room, telling him about the artists of the oil paintings in each room. They entered the inner courtyard, and Don Pedro put his arm around the boy as he showed him the bubbling fountains, the exotic trees, the potted plants, and the caged birds. Carlos had never imagined that people lived like this. The sensual beauty of the place contrasted with the barrio's gritty streets, where blaring motorcycle horns pierced the air.

Crossing to the other side of this lavish villa, they passed through a wooden door, where they were greeted by another young male servant, and then walked down the hall to Don Pedro's private library. Carlos gazed at the high ceiling, covered in a fresco of Saint Michael the dragon slayer kneeling on puffy clouds, and then at the bookshelves, which contained hundreds of leather-bound books. For the first time, he inhaled the buttery smell of fine leather. A large globe stood on an antique desk, waiting to be touched, across from a refectory table with high-backed chairs.

"You can come here whenever you like," Don Pedro said to Carlos.

"Thank you for your kindness," Carlos said, wondering anew why he was being given this honor. He would learn later that Don Pedro's younger brother had died when he was only ten, and there was something about Carlos that reminded Don Pedro of little Juan Luis.

When he got home, Carlos told his mother about the wonders he had seen at Don Pedro's villa.

"I don't like Don Pedro, but if he can get you a good job, I'll go along with it." She embraced Carlos and held him close for a few moments.

"Thank you, Mama," he said. "One day soon, you'll never have to work in the fields again."

Mercedes Alfonso looked at her son's smiling face. "I'm glad something good is happening to you, but I fear we'll never escape the cartel."

"Don't worry."

Carlos made frequent use of the library, despite the long trip from the barrio. He was afraid that one of Don Pedro's neighbors might call the police if they noticed a young man in a frayed shirt and pants with tattered cuffs walking down the street. Yet, despite feeling intimidated, he arrived at Don Pedro's villa each afternoon without mishap. The drug lord's men had heard that Carlos was indeed a reliable kid, so he was given a key on a silk cord that enabled him to enter the villa whenever he wished.

Monday through Friday, Carlos could be found in the library for at least two hours after school. He loved sitting in a high-backed leather chair at the old desk. And every day a maid set out a plate of warm *empanadas* stuffed with various meats for him. On Fridays, Don Pedro left an envelope for Carlos with money inside and a note that said, "Your reward for studying." He never asked him to run errands for the cartel again. Carlos gave the money to his mother, and she handed a small allowance back to him. He understood that he was being groomed for a position in the business, and he was thankful for the opportunity.

Mercedes Alfonso became used to the arrangement. She bought roasted chickens at the local market and even purchased her first new dress in years. She tried to persuade Carlos to go to church with her, but he refused. He did not believe in God. What deity would allow such disparity between the rich and the poor in his city? Yet his lack of belief did not stop him from placing orange peels at the feet of the small clay Madonna that had stood on a table by the door of their home for as long as he could remember. According to family lore, the Madonna would bring them good luck. Carlos knew that similar Madonnas lived inside his friends' homes as well, and as a child he had wondered how her spirit could be everywhere at once.

One night while Carlos was studying, he heard the hard-rock music played by his neighbors on a nearby roof. The rat-a-tat-tat drumbeat beckoned, and he stood outside in the shadows, watching three teenage boys and one girl in an aggressive dance. They banged into each other's shoulders, as if they were jousting on horseback, and then retreated a few paces. They repeated the same routine over and over again. Born of the street, this hostile style of dancing had none of the joy of the traditional cumbia he knew from the country dances he occasionally attended with his mother.

The next afternoon at the villa he thumbed through Don Pedro's massive dictionary, which had a special place on the refectory table, searching for a word that captured the adolescents' dark play. When he read the definitions for *despair* and *hopelessness*, the word *nihilism* jumped out at him. He checked its meaning. "Yes," he said. "A belief that existence is senseless and useless; a rejection of traditional values." *That pretty much sums it up.* Carlos was relieved that he wasn't like them. He had a future. They did not.

At the same time he admitted that the adolescents' scorn for the world held a strange attraction for him. He sometimes feared he was too much of a mama's boy. A teacher's pet. A book lover. He knew his amiable personality did not play well in the barrio. Outside school, he had no friends. Fortunately, his height and his place in Don Pedro's world kept him safe.

In August of 1975, after Carlos turned sixteen, Don Pedro greeted him in the library and told him that he had a surprise. He led Carlos to the servants' quarters and then opened the door to a small, square room with bookcases along one wall. The simple furnishings included a single wooden bed, a silver cross on the wall, and an antique oak dresser with a matching night table. "It's time you had your own room. The hours you spend traveling back and forth can be put to better use."

"Thank you." Carlos was overwhelmed by Don Pedro's generosity.

"We need to toughen you up," he said. "I've hired a martial arts coach."

"How thoughtful," Carlos said to his host. He understood that as Don Pedro's protégé he was expected to go into the cocaine business and therefore needed to learn self-defense. Yet he secretly thought the hours he'd spend practicing these skills were unnecessary. He hoped to become a lawyer and use his brains. Besides, he could always hire a bodyguard to protect himself and his future family. He understood Don Pedro might not approve of his desire to become a lawyer, but he'd deal with that at the appropriate time. Meanwhile, he could not have been more grateful for everything Don Pedro had done for him.

This arrangement continued for two years, and on June 21, 1977, Carlos graduated from high school, the first in his family to do so. Mercedes Alfonso and Don Pedro and his wife, Lucia, attended the ceremony. The photograph that was taken afterward, now in a frame on his bureau, showed Carlos as a serious youth. His aquiline nose and soulful eyes made him handsome, although an open-collar shirt exposed a prominent Adam's apple. After a celebratory dinner, the drug lord presented his protégé with a proposition.

"Carlos, I've been impressed with you for a long time," he said. "I'll pay all your tuition and expenses at La Nacional. Someday I'm going to need a smart young man to help me."

"Don Pedro, you're wonderful." Carlos held his hand to his heart. He had hoped to go to a university, but he didn't know if he could win a scholarship. Only a few were available each year.

Carlos watched his mother approach the drug lord. "Thank you for taking such good care of my son," she said. He thought his mother looked especially pretty that day. She wore her long hair down to her shoulders and a red dress that brought out the color in her cheeks.

Both Carlos and his mother knew that if it hadn't been for Don Pedro's protection, he might well have been dead by now, killed in a drive-by shooting. Anyone could get caught in the cross fire as two armed boys on a motorcycle fired wildly into the barrio hideout of a rival gang as they rode by. One of his childhood friends, Tomas, who had worn his hair slicked back like Elvis Presley, had been killed this way. He was only fourteen. In Santo Domingo Savio, a shiny new motorbike was the object of desire, and a teenage boy might kill to get one.

Don Pedro didn't have any sons. But he did have three beautiful daughters—Julia, who was thirteen; Concetta, fifteen; and Maria, seventeen. Maria was closest in age to Carlos at eighteen, and she was also the daughter who interested him the most. Her intelligent black eyes matched his own in intensity, and she could beat him at tennis. Maria had taken lessons since she was eight and taught him how to play. She made a pretty sight on the court, with her suntanned body offsetting a white tennis dress. Despite a slight limp from a childhood skiing accident, her moves were as graceful as a dancer's. Carlos had never had a girlfriend, so he tended to be shy around Maria.

Ever since he had moved into the villa, he was invited to dine with the family, even when Don Pedro was away on business. He learned to keep up a lively conversation, later using his university experiences to entertain the family. He had taken an art history course, and Maria was interested in what he was learning. One night after dinner, while they were sitting together in the library, their hands almost touched as they pored over a book of Dutch masters. When he turned to a double-page spread of Rembrandt's *The Night Watch*, Maria's cheeks burned with enthusiasm. "It's so dramatic—I feel we've been invited to go with the men," she said.

"Yes, they're ready to march."

Lucia, Don Pedro's wife, made a point of asking Carlos about his day. In turn, he complimented her on the evening's meal. Although Lucia did not cook the food herself, she supervised the kitchen activities and planned the menus.

It was apparent that Lucia came from a middle-class family. Carlos had learned from Rodrigo that her parents had been unhappy when she fell in love with Don Pedro, who worked at that time as a salesman in a car dealership. They thought their future son-in-law talked too fast and was socially inferior to their attractive daughter. Yet they ultimately gave in to her wishes.

Carlos enjoyed dining with the Martinez daughters. He often teased them about a new hairstyle and loved that they could not suppress some giggles when he gave a hyperbolic account of a puppy he had seen in the neighborhood. A stranger at the table would never have guessed that this respectable and lighthearted place was the home of a drug lord.

Four years later, Don Pedro took Carlos on a day trip to one of his cocaine laboratories in the verdant countryside, just beyond the prosperous gold-mining town of Frontino, on the far side of the Cordillera Occidental, heading toward the Panamanian border.

When their chauffeur-driven car stopped at a fork in a dirt road, Carlos spotted a low cinder block structure with a corrugated roof up ahead. Don Pedro told him it was "the laboratory." Hay was piled on either side of the entrance, and bricks were strewn around the building. A goat was tied to a tree, and a few chickens paraded around the yard. The area was known for its working farms, and this place gave the illusion of being a small-scale example.

Don Pedro led the way into the building. He opened one of the strips of heavy floor-to-ceiling plastic that curtained the large room. The middle-aged manager rushed over to shake Don Pedro's hand. Then he turned to the sweating workers in the room. He raised his arms as a signal for the men to cheer their illustrious boss, who was honoring them with a visit. Don Pedro nodded his head in appreciation. "I'm proud of your hard work," he said, and they applauded. He introduced Carlos, and they politely smiled. At first Carlos thought their faces were friendlier and their stances less aggressive than the vengeful street dealers in Medellín.

"These men are happy because I pay them in one day what they'd make in four months on a neighboring farm," Don Pedro said to Carlos as they stood behind the workers.

Then they walked around the room, and Don Pedro made a point of greeting each worker individually. The manager gave the visitors rubber gloves to wear as protection. The heat from the overhead lighting beat down on them; the whirring from the ceiling fans made a deafening noise. This oppressive factory unsettled Carlos. He knew these men must have been desperate to work there. The workers looked up from spinning large wooden sticks inside the huge wooden vats on the floor and smiled at the boss and the young man in the yellow polo shirt and khaki pants who accompanied him. The manager explained that they were busy mixing pulverized coca leaves and chemicals. First a potassium-water solution was added to the leaves, then hydrochloric acid and acetone or ether, causing the cocaine to crystallize before it was dried under heat lamps or inside microwave ovens. The pungent chemicals together with the men's perspiration produced a rancid smell that permeated the room.

Don Pedro dipped his gloved hand into one of the vats and brought out particles of shiny white cocaine on his fingers. "You see the high-quality stuff I cook," he bragged to Carlos. "This pearly substance is in more demand than our emeralds." Wide-eyed, Carlos absorbed the scene. He feared he might faint.

Despite their apparent warmth toward Don Pedro, Carlos sensed the workers' hostility toward him. He felt their bad vibes penetrate the back of his shirt as he and Don Pedro left the lab to return to the car. Fortunately, the noise from the chauffeur starting the car muted Carlos's sigh of relief.

As the car drove on, and the lush scenery of Santa Fe de Antioquia began to fade, Carlos confessed to Don Pedro: "Cocaine trafficking scares me." He didn't want to have anything to do with it, though he couldn't say that.

"Don't worry." Don Pedro patted his future son-in-law's arm. "You won't have to get your hands dirty. And I'll make you rich." Carlos certainly liked the trappings of success. He looked forward to the time when he would become a wealthy man like Don Pedro. He didn't grasp the contradiction of not wanting to do what would make him rich. And he denied any connection between accumulating money and the violence of the business.

CHAPTER TWENTY

May 22, 1990

North Meets South

Portia flew to Miami, and from there to Medellín, Colombia, on Tuesday morning, about two months after the robbery at the Isabella Stewart Gardner Museum, less than a month since she'd told Stansky that she had agreed to go, and a week after her trip to Buenos Aires. It had all happened so quickly. Once she had committed to participating in the sting, she was on a fast track.

Back in 1981, when she had traveled to a more tranquil Colombia for Polaroid, Medellín's airport was in a valley encircled by the rugged peaks of the Cordillera Central. On approach, planes had to make several hair-raising U-turns. It always seemed to Portia that the plane just missed hitting a mountain before they landed. The descent had been terrifying and thrilling, like riding a roller coaster. *How crazy to be risking my life for instant film,* she had thought each time.

To Portia's great relief, a new international airport, built in 1985, was about thirty minutes outside Medellín in an open location. Not having to go through a scary landing was a blessing. There would be enough tension when she was on the ground. She had called Rupert and told him that she now owned a gallery in Boston and wanted to buy Colombian art for a client. He told her he'd be delighted to pick her up. She also called Colombine, who said she'd be thrilled to see her again. They arranged to meet at her gallery the morning after Portia arrived.

As she pushed her seat back on the plane, she felt a wave of sadness. The tears falling down Alexa's cheeks when they said goodbye made her choke up. She almost changed her mind about leaving, but the pull of the lost paintings overpowered her.

The flight turned out to be uneventful. In the morning, the sun streaming into the windows and the loud announcements from the stewardess woke her up. After the plane landed, she raced through the glass-and-steel airport, following the Spanish signs to baggage claim. As she passed a shop with folkloric gifts, she was tempted to buy a Colombian doll with a smiling face for Alexa. She made a mental note to do this on her return. The aroma of Colombian coffee emanating from the food arcade tempted her as well. She pushed on to baggage claim, where she was thankful to see her black suitcase with the large red ribbon come around the bend of the conveyor belt.

When Rupert met Portia outside the baggage claim area, she laughed at how each one lied politely, telling the other that they looked the same as nine years before. He now had a large shock of gray in his jet-black hair.

"Welcome back," he said, shaking her hand and then taking her bag. "Luisa wants you to come to dinner tomorrow evening."

"With pleasure." Rupert's friendly, familiar face comforted her. She was grateful that he didn't ask about the dark circles under her eyes. She had been staying up late every night the week before, making lists for Stansky and Brenda. She wanted to be sure that everything ran smoothly in her office, her home, and her life while she was away.

"I remember how much you loved art. What kind of artists do you represent?"

Portia filled him in on how she had begun her gallery and described Stockwell's and Thornycroft's contemporary paintings.

As Rupert drove his Mercedes through the narrow streets to her hotel, Portia reveled in the splendid Spanish colonial architecture and the purple bougainvillea that cascaded down the whitewashed houses.

"Gorgeous," she said.

"Yes, El Poblado is still beautiful, but our city suffers from the cartels." He told Portia that his children remained safely at their country estate outside Medellín, where they were taught by private tutors and guarded around the clock. "Every day I pray our government will stop these drug wars. Did I write you that we've even thought about moving to Paris?"

"No, you never mentioned Paris. I don't know how you can live with constant danger."

"Luisa is devoted to her parents, and they don't want us to leave. You know, Portia, I never imagined when my parents and I fled the Communists in Leipzig . . . I was ten at the time . . . that Colombia would someday become equally dangerous. Instead of the Stasi watching our every move, the cartels' drive-by shootings terrorize us."

"It's sad. Your city was intoxicating; I recall paisas saying that life was as sweet as your homemade honey."

"It's brave of you to come." Rupert told Portia that tourism was almost nonexistent, and his camera and film business had fallen off. "I'm lucky I can also work in my father-in-law's bank."

"My father often took the long view of a crisis," Portia said.

"He sounds very much like mine. When the drug cartels first expanded their operations, my father assured us their power wouldn't last."

Despite the seriousness of their discussion, Portia enjoyed sharing the similarity between their respective fathers' positive attitudes. "Maybe we should call them naive," she said. Rupert agreed.

"So a New York client commissioned you to buy contemporary Colombian art? That's unusual." Rupert pushed his Armani sunglasses, which had fallen down his nose, back over his eyes.

"My collector's adventurous. She's appointed me curator of her art, and now she wants me to find exceptional South American artists. I'm beginning in Colombia because I already know Colombine—through you, of course."

Portia noticed the afternoon light shimmering on the Cordillera Central in the distance. Although the mountain's beauty gave her a momentary sense of peace, it didn't assuage the guilt she felt about deceiving Rupert.

"Luisa and I appreciate Colombine's eye for talent. As you know, we've bought many paintings from her. We're also grateful that she's given our best artists international exposure. The outside world needs to know that Medellín is a center for the arts and not just the headquarters of dangerous cartels," Rupert said in his most eloquent voice.

"I can't wait to see her again."

They pulled up to the whitewashed stucco hotel on Calle 10 in El Poblado and kissed each other goodbye on both cheeks. He told her he would pick her up the following evening at eight for dinner. "I'm sure you recall that we Colombians dine late."

"You're so kind," Portia said. She knew she was in for a treat. Luisa was a fabulous hostess.

A petite woman with a thick chignon greeted her at the concierge's desk. Her English was almost as flawless as her translucent skin. Portia wondered if this was the Maria she had heard so much about, but she didn't feel up to asking her. She was still tired from the flight and the emotional strain of saying goodbye to Alexa and Stansky. After she was checked in, the woman called for a porter to take her bags.

Portia noticed a framed photo of a handsome, dark-haired man to the right of the concierge's desk and wondered if that was Carlos and if he was as attractive in person. She would have liked to look him in the eye to determine if she saw any guilt or remorse.

Once she stepped inside her room, Portia felt comforted by its ambiance. She noted how the colorful Oriental rugs were scattered over the plain Saltillo floors. She inhaled the sweet aroma from a huge bouquet of long-stem roses on the dresser, recalling the pleasure of rose-filled summers spent on Martha's Vineyard. Then she lay down on the ivory brocade bedspread of the four-poster bed and put her head on one of the lush silk pillows that complemented the red in the room's multicolored drapes. If she weren't on such a dangerous mission, she could relish being in this space. She closed her eyes and took a few more deep breaths before getting up and heading into the bathroom. Decorated from floor to ceiling with antique blue-and-white Spanish tiles, the room reminded Portia of a luxurious spa. She picked up one of the plush towels from the surface of a porcelain sink and held its softness against her cheek.

After Portia washed her face and hands, she called the receptionist and asked for a wake-up call at seven in the morning so she could walk around the grounds before the sun became too strong. "It's how I keep fit," she explained.

"Me too," the receptionist replied. "You can count on that call."

Once she was unpacked and settled in, Portia called Colombine. They confirmed their meeting at her gallery near the Museo de Arte Moderne for late the following morning.

Then Portia went outside to call Ronald Begun, Julian Henderson's boss in Washington, from the enclosed phone booth in a café across the street. She needed to let him know she had arrived safely. She had been advised by Julian not to call from her room in case all the hotel phones were tapped. He told her that one couldn't be too careful in a drug culture. This way, she could use her AT&T international calling card, and she would be assured of privacy. She crammed herself into the stuffy booth and dialed the number she had been given. Begun explained that Julian's plane would be late because of mechanical difficulties in Miami. Portia convinced him that she would be all right on her own for a day. After all, she knew local people, she spoke the language, and Roberto Castellano was not far away. She could always call him if she needed anything. At the same time, Portia felt annoyed that she would now need to lie to Stansky, who would be furious if he knew Julian was not with her.

The day before they were scheduled to leave the United States, Portia had followed Begun's instructions to call Julian. He wanted them to practice conversing using Julian's cover as Sean Findlay, the private Old Masters dealer from New York in search of Botero's early drawings and paintings. As Sean Findlay, he also hoped to sell the galleries the Old Masters drawings that he had on consignment from Colnaghi. "See you tomorrow. Can't wait to meet the art dealers," Sean had said.

Opening the phone booth door for some air, Portia noticed that the café was practically empty. Closing the door again, she braced herself for a call with Stansky.

"I'm still angry you left," he said.

She wanted to tell him how frustrated he made her feel. Instead, she asked about Alexa.

"She's fine," he said. "But you going off for more than two weeks to an unsafe place is not my idea of marriage."

"Stansky, if you can't be supportive of me, I'm going to get off the phone."

He hung up.

Portia was so upset by the conversation that she called Margot. Even her best friend was not supposed to know about her trip, but Portia trusted her and had told her about it anyway.

"What's wrong?" Margot asked.

"Medellín's beautiful. Rupert is as sweet as ever, but I'm upset about Stansky. He just yelled at me. Questioned our marriage. He even hung up on me. Why can't he understand I'm doing something important?"

"Doesn't he remember when you supported his dreams?"

"Evidently not. He knows I need to be smart and positive while I'm here."

"Don't let Stansky's bad mood get in your way." Margot told Portia that she imagined he was behaving that way because he was afraid for her. "I know I'll be relieved when you're safely home. In the meantime, think about Antonio and the Vermeer. Think about Isabella Gardner."

Shortly after they hung up, Portia took another deep breath—she had learned to calm herself this way in yoga classes—and entered the café bar, where she ordered an espresso. After a few sips, her sleepy eyes opened wide. "I've forgotten how delicious your coffee tastes," she told the bartender. He gave her a big smile. On her walk from the bar back to her room she decided to turn around and call Paul Travigne. He, too, had been sworn to secrecy about her trip. She figured that Paul could be trusted because his good friend Joel's reputation was on the line. She needed moral support, and she knew he would give it to her. Luckily, she found him at home.

"How's my favorite sleuth?" he asked.

"Waiting for Julian to arrive tomorrow."

"Oh, I thought he was traveling with you."

"His plane was delayed. There's no need to worry. I know my way around."

"I hear sleigh bells ringing when you speak. Must be the long-distance connection," he said. "I have faith in your competence, but please take good care of yourself."

That was all she needed to hear, although she wondered about his sleigh bell metaphor. She'd had a difficult time sleeping several nights before she left, and now that she was in a precarious situation, she feared her sleep would be fitful.

The following morning, Portia was dressed in her black running clothes and Gucci sunglasses that hid the dark circles under her eyes.

As she strode along the dirt path that wound around the hotel, she noticed a tall, thin man wearing an Italian leather jacket and khaki pants coming toward her from the other direction. He said good morning to her in Spanish. She made a mental note that he was an early riser.

"*Tenga buen dia,*" she said.

"You speak our language," he said. "Most of our foreign visitors don't."

Portia introduced herself in Spanish and waited for him to respond.

"An Italian who speaks Spanish?" he said.

"I'm Italian American."

"And I'm Carlos Alfonso," he said. "The owner of this hotel."

"Nice to meet you." As she extended her hand, which he shook heartily, she noted that Carlos had sharp, eagle-like eyes while he stared at her in an intense, but not unfriendly, way.

"What a beautiful hotel," she said as they made their way into the lobby. The large room was painted off-white and had high, wood-beamed ceilings. "When was it built?"

"About five years ago we modernized this eighteenth-century hacienda."

"It must be wonderful to own such a fine place."

Carlos nodded his head yes. "My wife and I had such a good time when we attended a friend's son's Harvard graduation last year. We like your country."

"I'm delighted to hear that," Portia said.

"Do you have some time to talk with me?"

When she said yes, he led her to a corner, where they sat in chairs covered in a white cotton fabric and placed around a small coffee table. He ordered iced coffee for both of them. Aside from the waiter, no one else was nearby this early in the morning.

Carlos told Portia about his chain of three hotels in Colombia and two in Venezuela. He mentioned the other locations—Caracas, Mérida, Bogotá, and Cartagena—and Portia told him that she had visited all those cities when she'd worked for Polaroid in the early eighties.

"How interesting. Then you must know Rupert Heilbrun. He's Medellín's best camera distributor."

"He's an old friend . . . He recommended I stay at your hotel."

"What a charming man, and he has a lovely family. I'm impressed that you worked with Rupert."

"He is a special person." Portia sipped her iced coffee. She felt fortunate to know Rupert.

"Rupert is a successful foreigner. I wish I knew him better," he said. "We're honored to have you here. Please let me know if you need anything special. Just leave your request with the front desk."

"That's so kind," she replied. Portia had no intention of taking him up on his offer. She felt both fascinated and a little on edge to meet the son-in-law of the nefarious Don Pedro Martinez on his own turf.

"How long are you staying with us?" he asked.

"Almost three weeks."

"Great. You must have dinner here at least one night. We have an excellent Italian chef."

"Oh, I'll be sure to take advantage of that."

Carlos looked pleased. He admitted to Portia how much he enjoyed stopping by the kitchen to confer with Gianfranco about menus. "He knows how much I like good food, so he offers me tastes of the day's offerings. I'm almost as fond of Gianfranco as I am of the man's culinary talents. If I had more time, we'd shoot baskets together during his breaks."

"You sound like an enlightened manager." Portia wondered where Carlos got his leadership skills.

"We both like basketball . . . a sport we imported from your country," he said with his boyish grin.

"My husband's a big basketball fan."

"I'm surprised he didn't come with you."

"He's home with our daughter."

"Oh, I forgot that most Americans don't have nannies."

"That's right."

Carlos looked into Portia's eyes, and once more she noted their sharpness. There was an awkward pause in their conversation until he asked her what city she lived in.

"Boston," she replied, as matter-of-factly as possible.

"Last year, when I attended Pablo Augustin's Harvard graduation, I also visited your sophisticated city," he said.

"I'd like to think that Boston has panache." She knew she was getting into dangerous territory by mentioning Boston. There were not many American tourists in Colombia right now, and the fact that she showed up here might make Carlos wonder about her. But if she dared to lie about where she lived, she risked being found out. He could always ask his staff about her passport.

"You're certainly far from home. And courageous to visit. What brings you here?"

"I'm buying Colombian art for a wealthy New York collector."

"My wife loves art. She's a docent at our Museo de Antioquia. You must meet her."

"I'd love to." Of course Portia didn't tell Carlos Alfonso that she, too, was a docent, at the Gardner Museum.

"How come your collector wants Colombian art? There's so much great art in the world, and we're only a small country. Guess you heard we're having a small Renaissance right now," Carlos said and gave Portia a friendly wink.

"My collectors are shrewd. They adore Botero's paintings and know that he's your native son. They wanted me to check out his fellow Expressionists' work. I've been informing them about the artists in the Big Five."

"Now you're talking about my favorite Colombian artist, Alejandro Obregón. I own a lot of his work. His political passion jumps off his canvases."

"They're definitely interested in Obregóns, and Colombine Muñoz promised to show me some later today."

"You know Colombine Muñoz?" Carlos's eyes widened.

"Yes."

"She's my wife's best friend."

"That's great. Then I really hope I meet your wife."

"I'm pleased you're my guest," Carlos said.

They continued to chat until Carlos glanced at his watch. "I must go to a meeting with my staff." He excused himself, and as he rose to leave, he shook her hand. "I hope we can talk again soon. I'd love to hear what you think of Obregón's work."

Amazed that her quarry was so polite, Portia remembered that evil comes in many guises. In *The Godfather*, Michael Corleone, the American Mafia son who graduated from Dartmouth, had been awarded the Navy Cross for his bravery in World War II. Later in life, he took over his father's nefarious business and became a ruthless killer.

Around nine that morning, after Portia had showered and dressed, a maid knocked on the door.

"Come in," Portia said in Spanish.

"I didn't mean to disturb you," the maid said. "I'll come back later."

"Please . . . I can write at my desk while you clean the room."

"That's kind of you," the maid said. "Our boss is strict about keeping the rooms clean every day."

"It's a beautiful place. How long have you worked here?"

Portia learned that the maid's name was Dolores. She had been working at La Gran Conchita for the past four years. She had grown up in the Santo Domingo Savio barrio and was pleased to have found such a well-paying job. "I support my mother and my own family," she said as she took off the sheets and replaced them with freshly laundered ones.

"Oh . . . you have children?" Portia asked.

"Yes, a boy and a girl."

Portia asked Dolores about them and learned that her son was five and her daughter three.

"I'm also a mother, and I'd love to see photos of your children. Can you bring some tomorrow morning?"

Dolores beamed. "I've heard that Americans are nice."

"I think the same of Colombians," Portia said as she put her makeup bag in her purse. She was impressed that as Dolores went about her housekeeping chores she was efficient and graceful.

When Dolores went into the bathroom to replace the towels and clean the sink, Portia opened the windows in her room. Medellín had a springlike climate most of the year, and the smell of gardenias wafting in the breeze was heady. Before Dolores left, Portia gave her a hundred-peso tip.

"I look forward to seeing you tomorrow," Portia said. "You can leave the door open when you leave. Perhaps there's another breeze coming from the open room across the hall. I love El Poblado's fresh air."

Just as she hoped, Portia overheard the maids talking in the hallway as they filled their trolleys with soap, shampoo, and fresh towels. They were discussing their boss and how he could be so generous to give them birthday presents. Yet sometimes he was hard on them, docking their pay and chastising them if they forgot to do something on the list.

"I don't like his superior attitude. He was born in the barrio—just like us," one of the housemaids said.

"He's not to be trusted. Remember when he cornered me in the laundry closet and fondled me?" another housemaid said in an angry voice.

"Did you report it?" the first one asked.

"*Por supuesto* . . . When I complained to the supervisor, he threatened to fire me if I made this public."

"Horrible. Truly horrible," the first one said.

Portia gathered that the maids had formed a pact so that now they only went to the linen closet in pairs when Carlos was on the premises. She strained to hear the rest of the conversation. Evidently, the housemaids were talking freely because Carlos had just left for his Cartagena beach house.

She had figured that Carlos must be egotistical, but she hadn't been prepared for his predatory behavior with female employees. Portia thought he probably didn't know what to make of her, a married woman on her own, visiting Colombia to buy art for wealthy collectors. Good thing "Sean" was due to arrive tomorrow.

Later that morning, Portia took a taxi to Colombine's gallery. From the photo, it looked like an attractive stucco building in the leafy suburb of Carlos E. Restrepo. She had always taken taxis in the past when she visited Medellín on business. The concierge called a taxi service the hotel frequently used. Unfortunately, it turned out that this particular driver, although well groomed and polite, lacked experience. As they circled the same streets, Portia realized he must be lost. Speaking in Spanish, she asked him to stop on one, and then another, street corner to ask directions, but he still couldn't find the gallery's neighborhood.

When she no longer recognized the streets and then saw gritty sidewalks, she grimaced. There was loose garbage strewn about the road. What appeared to be bullet holes in some of the facades added to her anxiety. Roberto Castellano had warned her about not going near Santo Domingo Savio, and she feared they had accidently landed there. She checked the gas gauge on the taxi and saw that it was hovering near empty. She began to hiccup and perspire. She needed to find a telephone to call Colombine or Rupert and ask for help. The driver was finally able to locate an old gas station with one pump, where Portia got out. The air smelled fetid. The shifty-looking service attendant pointed her to a pay phone with broken glass doors. She called Colombine, described where they were, and wrote down directions to the gallery as fast as she could while keeping an eye on the unfriendly streets. She noticed two shabbily dressed men who were shouting profanities as they lurched toward one another on the broken sidewalk.

Hanging up the phone, she ran back to the taxi and jumped in. She must have still been tired from travel when she assumed the driver would know how to get to the gallery. Considering the dire warnings about dangers in Medellín, she realized she had behaved foolishly. One by one she called out the street names she had written down to the driver, praying that he would not get a flat tire—she had noticed two were bald when she returned from making the call—before they arrived at her friend's place. The light-blue linen dress she had put on that morning began to feel sticky under her arms. She hoped the sweat would not leave a stain, although she knew that perspiration was the small stuff. What mattered was getting to Colombine's.

As the taxi finally parked in front of the gallery, Portia nearly cried. She bounded out of the back seat and rang the bell. She heard Colombine's footsteps clacking on the tile floor and remembered that her tall acquaintance loved to wear high heels, even though she towered over most Colombian men in her bare feet. When her friend opened the door, Portia forgot her distress as she admired Colombine's white Chanel suit and three-inch pumps.

"Manolo Blahnik would approve," Portia teased, pointing to the shoes.

The two women hugged in the doorway.

"Come in, my dear. You sounded terrible on the phone."

"I'm afraid we lost our way in a bad neighborhood . . . possibly Santo Domingo Savio . . . terrifying." Portia fiddled with the tortoise-shell barrette in her hair. "I'm still a little shaky."

"Well, you're safe now," her friend said, giving Portia another hug as she led her into an all-white office next to a well-lit gallery. She motioned for Portia to sit down on a comfortable Eames chair across from her Empire desk. "You may feel disheveled, but you still look beautiful," Colombine said. "I always envied your green eyes."

"And I always envied your tall elegance," Portia replied.

After she sat down, Portia realized that the memory of her friend's natural beauty had not done it justice. She recalled that Colombine's mother had been born in Naples, where she met her Colombian husband, who traveled to Italy on business. *You combine the best features of your dual heritage,* she'd often complimented her friend. When they met again, this time in New York at the Armory Show five years ago, Portia had told Colombine that her brown eyes "shone with a luminous quality often found in Renaissance portraits." At the time she wondered if her description was a little over the top. Now she knew she hadn't exaggerated at all.

"You're so kind. Would you like some *aguardiente*?" Colombine asked.

"I could sure use a drink after that frightening drive."

From a walnut cabinet behind her desk, Colombine took out two small glasses and a bottle. There was a plate of canapés on the coffee table. She poured the drinks and toasted Portia's arrival. She told her friend that she had organized a lunch on Friday in her honor, "with some of my best clients, who are also my friends."

"That's so dear of you," Portia said.

"After meeting you, they'll be compelled to visit your gallery when they travel to the States. And, of course, they'll happily share their views on our Colombian artists."

"You're marvelous."

"No. You are."

The 80-proof alcohol made them laugh like college girls. Although Portia felt a little woozy from the strong drink, she wouldn't let anything interfere with her focus on the mission. She told Colombine that she was staying at La Gran Conchita.

"That's my friend Maria's husband's hotel."

"Actually, I met Carlos Alfonso early this morning. He told me his wife is a docent at the Museo del Antioquia, and that you and Maria have been friends since you were children."

"We go back to grade school. In high school we were in and out of each other's homes every day. We're both fond of American films, so we often went to the cinema together. Later, I was her maid of honor. Maria's wedding was the talk of Medellín for quite some time."

"I'd love to hear more about it," Portia said as innocently as possible.

"My copy of the wedding album is right here."

"Can we look at the photos?"

Portia couldn't believe her luck as Colombine walked to a bookshelf in her office and removed a black leather album. She carried it with her to the sofa and motioned for Portia to join her there. Turning to the first page, she pointed to a photograph of the bride and groom. "Aren't they gorgeous? Carlos was twenty-two and Maria was a year younger."

"They look like movie stars."

"In a way they are. They're our local celebrities."

Portia excused herself to use the gallery's bathroom. It had been an awful morning, and she needed to freshen up. She patted her face with cold water, put some cover-up under her eyes, and reapplied her lipstick. Being in the presence of such unusual beauty made her awkward. She had never considered herself superficial before, but here she was, longing to be presentable.

After she returned to her place on the sofa, Colombine showed Portia a photograph of the Metropolitana Cathedral's interior, where the wedding took place. "I know how much you appreciate beautiful locations," she said.

"Wow! Those rose-and-lily bouquets decorating the altar are sumptuous," Portia said.

"And every aisle in our vast church was festooned with garlands."

Portia remembered that Medellín had been known as the flower city . . . before it became the drug capital of the world.

Colombine told Portia that this photo evoked the flowers' heady aroma and how perfectly its sweetness had commingled with the priest's incense, the women's expensive perfumes, and the musty odor of the cathedral's fifty-year-old walls.

"Although this was an 'underworld' wedding, it was a major social event that couldn't be ignored. Photographers, constantly clicking their cameras, and society reporters busy scribbling notes were interspersed among the wedding guests," Colombine said.

"The photos tell it all. You look amazing in that navy satin gown," Portia said as they turned a page.

Portia pointed to the place where Colombine stood in the middle of six bridesmaids and groomsmen. Colombine explained that the attendants were mostly parochial school friends and their older brothers. "They look great despite the tension in the room." She told Portia that while she had been pleased to be the maid of honor, her parents were upset by her remaining close with their local kingpin's daughter. "I begged them to come to the wedding, but they refused. This hurt both Maria and me."

"That must have been awful." Portia was flattered that Colombine would confide in her. When they first met in Medellín with Rupert, they had connected. Now it was as if they had known each other forever. Perhaps Colombine's Italian lineage from her mother fostered their bond, but their fondness for one another was solidified by their mutual love of art.

"It was terrible. The other young women—don't you love their powder-blue silk gowns?—whispered in each other's ears whenever there was a gap in the wedding Mass." Colombine told Portia that when they were getting dressed she had overheard them gossiping about Maria's pregnancy with another man's child. "I didn't know how to stop them."

"You were all so young," Portia said as she took a bite of one of the canapés.

"I knew that Carlos's best friend had tried to discourage him from going ahead with the obligatory wedding, but Carlos told him he didn't care because he loved Maria . . . Although Carlos was Don Pedro's protégé, he believed their marriage would be successful . . . They both wanted children and were good friends."

"All important things for a husband and wife to share," Portia said. "From the pictures, they look like they have a real zest for life. Is that true?"

Colombine described how Maria excelled at putting on a good show. "I'm proud of her for having braved those nasty rumors back then. I hope you understand that I'm not betraying her by telling you about this now. Everyone knows and now no one cares. Thank God."

"I get it," Portia said. "Maria sounds *simpatica*."

Colombine offered Portia an espresso that she brewed in a small machine on a table, and Portia accepted. After Colombine gave her a cup, she picked up the photo album again, opening it to the photo where Don Pedro and Maria walked down the aisle.

Portia gasped. "So that's what a drug lord looks like . . . He's quite suave. And Maria looks like an angel."

"Maria personifies Latin beauty: her translucent skin offsets those flashing dark eyes."

"The regal way she stands reminds me of Grace Kelly when she married Prince Rainier."

"Yes, and her Empire gown could not have been more stunning."

"So Don Pedro's protégé and his eldest daughter end up married." Portia put her coffee cup down and looked at Colombine, hoping that her friend would give her some clues about the Alfonsos' relationship.

"From what I understand, once Carlos recovered from his shock over Maria's condition—he had always seen her in an idealized light—he realized that Don Pedro was bestowing a great honor by giving his daughter to him." Colombine told Portia that she had imagined Carlos might have felt disappointed his bride wasn't the virgin so highly touted in their culture. Yet his gratitude for everything Don Pedro had done for him probably outweighed any possible misgivings.

"Makes sense to me," Portia said.

"My guess is that he never dared think that Maria might one day become his wife," Colombine said. She told Portia that Maria had always made it clear in the past that she thought of him as a brother. Perhaps he was afraid she might hate him for coming to her rescue. Instead, his compassionate response to her crisis deepened her fondness for him. "By agreeing to marry Maria, Carlos was getting what he always wanted."

"So romantic," Portia said.

"I see where you might get that idea," Colombine said. "After they returned from their honeymoon, she stood right here in this room—she was seven months pregnant with Toto—and complained about being treated as a puppet. She described her father as the puppeteer who pulled the strings, while her mother served her nourishing soup in their elegant prison."

"What imagery," Portia said.

"Our Maria can be quite poetic," Colombine said.

"She must be charming."

"You'll see. She's a joy to be with."

Portia detected some tears on Colombine's cheeks as she put the wedding album down on the table. "Maria was fortunate that her father chose Carlos for her."

"That's true." Colombine told Portia that Maria's other choices had included her father's burly men with their foul-mouthed speech and cigarettes dangling from their lips. "I always thought the gold jewelry spoke more about their narcissism than their greed. Maria once confided that when one of these so-called business associates happened to walk into a room, she would find any excuse to leave."

"So Carlos was her only choice. Guess it's not so romantic after all."

"Perhaps," Colombine said. "Don Pedro knows a lot of people. He might have found someone else."

"Does Maria understand the extent of her father's power?" Portia asked.

"Not really," Colombine said. "Despite seeing some unsavory men around the place, Don Pedro's daughters led a protected life. Up until her marriage, Maria was only marginally aware of her father's cocaine business."

"I don't get it. How is that possible?" Portia said.

"Thanks to Maria's classy mother, her daughters were protected." Colombine described how Señora Martinez made daily life as normal as possible inside the villa. Business was never discussed at the dinner table. Maria and her sisters were kept so busy with homework and their friends that they often missed the comings and goings of strangers in their home. Since most middle- and upper-class Colombians hired guards to protect their houses, Maria had little reason to think it was unusual for armed men to sit outside the door of her parents' villa.

"I'll bet she's learned a lot since she married Carlos," Portia said. Her heart skipped a beat. She worried, not for the first time, if she could handle the dangerous situation she had volunteered for.

Colombine told Portia that she imagined Don Pedro had been counting on this elaborate wedding to camouflage his beloved daughter's crisis. "Another Colombian father might have disowned such a daughter, treating her as a social outcast. Don Pedro adores his daughters, and nothing was going to get in the way of his family."

"Believe me, I understand the meaning of family loyalty." Portia thought about her grandfather's tales. During his childhood in Calabria, the Mafia men didn't hesitate to kill, yet those very same men would do anything for their families.

Colombine picked up the album again, turning the pages to a photo of the couple leaning forward from the back seat of the limousine as they waved to the clamoring crowd through the closed window. She explained how the crowd had disbanded once the bulletproof cars drove off to the wedding banquet at Don Pedro's estate in El Poblado. "We fortunate guests went on to the glamorous reception, while the onlookers returned to work. I wonder how many were envious, even angry about the elaborate display?"

"Some of the workers must have felt jealous."

"That's right. I expect that more than one person there was ready to attack," Colombine said.

Portia crossed her arms in front of her chest at the thought of such violence.

Colombine turned to the final photo in the album, one of the couple taken the following day, just before they left for a Parisian honeymoon. "Carlos told me how excited he was to visit the Louvre, where he could immerse himself in their great paintings. I had visited Paris with my parents when I was sixteen, so I was able to give them lots of tips. Carlos confided that he hoped to win Maria's affection through their mutual love of art."

As Colombine closed the album, Portia thanked her for sharing the Alfonso wedding. "Maria sounds vibrant and interesting."

"Actually, you two have a lot in common. She's also a devoted mother and an art lover."

Portia felt like saying that the difference was her husband didn't engage in nefarious activities, but she kept her mouth shut.

"Now let's look at some art."

"Wonderful," Portia said.

Colombine arose from the sofa and knocked on the back door. Her young assistant opened it and began carrying the paintings that Colombine had preselected into the office. One by one, Colombine showed Portia a dozen imaginative Expressionist works by Edgar Negret, Enrique Grau, Eduardo Ramírez Villamizar, and Alejandro Obregón, who had first become a star in the 1950s. Portia was grateful that Colombine remembered she had been drawn to Obregón's colorful canvases, which often featured South American flowers, buildings, animals, and landscapes. She had first seen Obregón's work at the Armory Show in New York. Now, as she looked at his paintings in Colombine's gallery, she responded viscerally to the images that captured disturbing events.

Obregón's *La Violencia*, a portrait of a woman lying on her back with her facial skin torn up, held her in thrall. After studying the painting for several minutes, she mentioned that the fear it evoked reminded her of Francisco Goya's scary series of nineteenth-century prints called *The Disasters of War*. Goya was one of Portia's most beloved painters, and she asked Colombine if she had seen his paintings at the Metropolitan Museum of Art.

"I've spent hours looking at their outstanding Goya collection," Colombine said.

"Do you agree *The Third of May* is Goya's most memorable drawing because it's so politically charged?"

"He was a master," Colombine said.

After an hour or so of looking at oil paintings and listening to Colombine's stories about each one, the two women leaned back in their chairs. Portia couldn't help wondering which ones Isabella Gardner would have bought. Probably her flamboyant nature would have been drawn to Obregón's political scenes. Portia thanked Colombine for showing her so many wonderful pieces. "I'll need to consult with my client about what to choose."

"Take your time . . . Now, please show me some photographs of Alexa."

Portia took three recent photographs from her purse and handed them to her friend. Colombine commented on how much Alexa had grown.

Then she asked Portia if she would like to have a private tour of the Museo de Antioquia.

"That would be a special treat," Portia said. Talking about art had brought her back to her enthusiastic self. "Sean is arriving later today, and we'd love to see the collection through your eyes."

"I can arrange it for a week from tomorrow, next Thursday, if that works for you."

"Sounds perfect."

It was getting late, and Sean was due to arrive from New York that night. Portia also needed time to shower before her dinner with the Heilbruns. Colombine insisted that her driver take Portia back to the hotel. She was most grateful that this ride turned out to be uneventful.

Rupert picked her up promptly at eight. She had learned during her Polaroid days that South Americans never arrive on time. Rupert's German upbringing made him one of the few exceptions. She enjoyed a delicious dinner with Luisa and Rupert at their elegant finca, and they reminisced about how much fun it had been to work for Polaroid in its heyday. They remembered how Dr. Land had chartered a plane from Amsterdam with bushels of fresh tulips to decorate the stockholders' meeting room. Afterward, the international employees would meet at the Hyatt hotel's spinning bar for drinks.

That night, Portia fell into a deep sleep.

CHAPTER TWENTY-ONE

May 24, 1990

Digging In

Portia awoke at 9:00 a.m. When Dolores came to clean her room an hour later she showed Portia the photographs of her adorable children. Portia asked a few more questions about Dolores's family, which the housemaid was only too happy to answer. When she wondered aloud who had decorated the hotel so beautifully, Dolores told her about Maria Martinez Alfonso, the boss's wife.

"Oh, she's rich, kind of snobbish. Sure, she pretends to be interested in our lives, even works here sometimes when our receptionist isn't feeling well, but we know what she's like."

"What's she like?" Portia asked.

At this point, Dolores dropped her voice so no one else could hear. "Her wedding was the largest Medellín had ever seen. People talked about it for weeks. Although she dressed like a princess, we guessed Maria was pregnant and that Carlos might not have been the father. Their son, Toto, doesn't look at all like him. She likes to come here and arrange the flowers. We see her as Pedro Martinez's troubled daughter. Some would call her a whore."

Portia's eyes widened. She covered her mouth to suppress a gasp. "I'm shocked," Portia said.

"I shouldn't have said that. It was mean of me," Dolores said.

"Never mind. Let's pretend it never happened," Portia said.

Dolores agreed. She finished fluffing the pillows on the bed before she said goodbye to Portia.

After hearing such a positive report from Colombine, Portia was shaken by the housemaid's harsh opinion. Of course she knew that Don Pedro Martinez was the feared drug lord and that his daughter would have a difficult time being accepted by ordinary people. She wondered if the animosity toward Maria occurred as a result of the drugs and violence that were destroying her country or because Dolores felt angry at Carlos's trying to take advantage of one of their own.

Portia also figured that the extravagant display of finery she had seen in their wedding album stirred up jealousy among the locals, who struggled to earn a living in the barrio. She had heard about Don Pedro's generosity to the poor people of Medellín from Roberto. She recalled how he gave out free food after Sunday Mass in all the churches in Santo Domingo Savio; he built a football stadium; and he hired the young boys to do errands for the cartel so that their mothers could buy food and pay their rent. While they must have felt grateful to him, perhaps they hated the way he showed off.

At 10:30 a.m. she spoke with Roberto from the café phone. "I met your friend at the hotel," she said in code. "I also went to visit the gallery and had a delicious dinner with the Heilbruns." She also told him about the upcoming luncheon with the gallery owner and her friends on Friday. He congratulated her on how quickly she had reestablished her contacts and was pleased that she had already met "his friend."

"What's your impression?"

"He's intelligent and charming."

"Did he tell you his favorite time to travel?"

"No, why should I care?"

"He enjoys talking about his travels and brags about his work in the hospitality business," Roberto said in code.

"I'll ask him next time."

"Did you meet his wife? I think she also works at the hotel. I understand he worships her—do you think that's true?"

"I'll make sure to meet her." Portia was annoyed with Roberto. Didn't he realize that getting into the villa would be hard enough? Gauging the level of closeness between the couple was impossible. He should be more concerned about her safety.

As if he already sensed her fears, Roberto then told Portia he had hired a bodyguard named Jaime and that he would arrive at her hotel before lunch. "Everyone has a bodyguard in Colombia," he said.

While she appreciated the protection, Portia also valued her independence. She was glad to have some free time in her room. She wanted to practice yoga and write a long letter to Alexa before she met with Jaime.

After she sealed the envelope, the phone rang. It was Sean. He had called her the night before when he first arrived and told her he needed to sleep.

"I'm now wide awake and can come to your room."

When he arrived ten minutes later, he looked super preppy in a khaki-colored suit. His calm face and big grin made her tension evaporate.

"I hear you had an incompetent taxi driver who got lost in Santo Domingo Savio."

"I managed," she said, trying to sound brave. But yesterday's harrowing journey had unnerved her.

"Sorry my flight got screwed up. I fear I put you at risk."

"Don't worry," she said. "We finally reached our destination." She asked him if he had any difficulty getting the art through customs.

"No problem at all," he said. He told her that he had brought ten Old Master drawings. "After much explaining, Lloyd's of London finally insured them."

"I can't wait to see them myself."

"You will. At Colombine's gallery this afternoon."

Portia gave Sean a cup of mint tea to drink as they sat around the small table in her room and chatted about yesterday's fruitful visit to Colombine's. "The sun was very bright yesterday," she said in code. "Probably warmer than usual. It's clear Roberto's friend's wife loves art, her children, and her husband—not necessarily in that order."

"I knew you would find the best art," Sean said. "That's why I was comfortable putting my job on the line for you." He took a sip of his tea.

"What are you talking about?" Portia sat up straight in her chair.

"Before you came to my office, I told my boss you knew more about art than anyone else."

"You're really something," Portia said. "Thanks for your confidence."

About twenty minutes later there was a knock on the door, and Portia greeted a tall, lanky man in his early twenties. He introduced himself as Jaime, and after they were inside her room, he opened his suit jacket, showing Portia and Sean the slim handgun he wore in a shoulder holster. "I promise to protect you," he said.

"Good." Portia prayed that Jaime would never have to use the gun in her presence.

The three of them sat around talking about cars. "I always use my business car, a white Ford Taurus, although I prefer driving my souped-up Falcon," Jaime said.

"We're fine with the business car," she said. Sean agreed.

Then Jaime asked them about American jazz.

"I love Coltrane. Do you?" he asked.

"Ellington's my man," Sean said.

"They're both cool." Portia was relieved when Jaime left to grab a sandwich from the hotel bar. "He's awfully young," she said to Sean. "Hope he doesn't always feel the need to talk. But, hey, Roberto must know what he's doing."

"He'd better," Sean said. "Give me a half hour to dress for the elegant Colombine, and we'll meet in the lobby."

When Sean, dressed in a white tropical suit and Panama hat, met Portia downstairs, she told him his outfit reminded her of the writer Tom Wolfe. "You're only missing his dapper cane."

"I warned you . . . I should have been an actor."

They found Jaime's white Ford in the parking lot. Fortunately, Jaime knew the neighborhood near Colombine's gallery so that day's journey was blessedly calm. The receptionist showed them into the office, and they waited in the Eames chairs for Colombine to finish her phone conversation. As soon as she hung up, she rose from her chair and kissed Portia. Then she shook Sean's hand as Portia made the introductions.

"Colombine, this is Sean Findlay, the private New York art consultant I told you about. Sean, this is Colombine Muñoz, the best dealer in contemporary South American art."

Sean, who had also risen, took off his hat and gave Colombine a dashing bow.

"I'm pleased to meet you. Portia told me you have a great eye," he said. "I have a lot to learn about your artists."

"You couldn't have a better teacher," Portia said. "We're going to the Museo de Antioquia next Thursday. I hope you can join us."

"I'd love to," Sean said. Portia caught his look of admiration for Colombine. She felt proud that they were friends. She also acknowledged a twinge of envy at how often men fell for the glamorous Colombine.

A petite secretary with bleached blond hair piled high on her head brought them clear glasses of aromatic Colombian coffee, and they all sat down to drink together.

"Juan Valdez couldn't have made a tastier brew," Sean said.

Portia moaned. "Sean, that's so corny. Didn't you sleep well last night?"

"Actually, I did. This mountain air is superb. Medellín has an undeservedly bad reputation. I hope people in Bogotá and Caracas are half as friendly."

"Oh, so you're traveling to other South American cities as well?" Colombine asked.

"Yes, that's my plan. Do you think I'm crazy to be here?"

"I don't," Colombine replied. "It's refreshing that an established New York art dealer knows enough to visit us."

"When great art is involved, I'm willing to go . . . well . . . just about anywhere."

Sean had brought a large, leather portfolio with him, which he'd placed on the floor as the coffee was served.

"If this were Italy, we'd *blah blah blah* about our lives for an hour or more," Colombine said. "In South America we're pretty relaxed as well. I'm honored that you're here and look forward to getting to know you."

"What she means is," Portia said, getting up to put an arm around Colombine, "she's dying to see your *gems*."

"Oh, that," Sean said. "You mean contemporary art dealers still appreciate the Old Masters?"

"Didn't Portia tell you?" Colombine asked. "I especially love the seventeenth-century Dutch painters—Rembrandt, Hans Holbein, even the genre painter David Teniers the Younger."

"Teniers . . . Now, he's an acquired taste," Sean said.

"I suppose he is. I saw his work at the Louvre on my first trip to Paris." She smiled at some private thought. "Some of my happiest hours have been spent walking around the European museums. Now, let's see what you brought."

Sean put on white cotton gloves before removing the drawings from his portfolio. As he placed them, one at a time, on an easel near her desk, Colombine's eyes sparkled. "Rembrandt, Bronzino, Goya," she murmured as he displayed each one. "I'm in heaven."

Sean pointed out the subtleties in each work, playing his role with confidence but without arrogance.

Portia was amused by the ease with which Sean inched his way into her friend's good graces. He had done the same with her when they had first met in New York. *What a charmer. No wonder he relished the opportunity to go undercover.*

"I may have a buyer for the Rembrandt," Colombine said. "I'll call him tomorrow and let you know."

"Great," Sean said. He carefully put the drawings back into the leather portfolio, and after putting on his hat, he tipped it as a gesture of respect.

Portia and Sean said goodbye to Colombine and met Jaime outside. He whisked them back to the hotel.

Later, Portia and Sean met for a drink at the café across the street. Exercising caution, they only talked about Colombian art. Portia knew that Sean was planning to spend the next day with Roberto Castellano, while she was at the luncheon with Colombine's friends. "What fun," he said, once again taking off his hat and extending it toward her as they said good night in the lobby.

CHAPTER TWENTY-TWO

May 25, 1990

Ladies Who Lunch

The Friday luncheon was at Salón Versalles on Paseo Junín in downtown Medellín. A wood-paneled restaurant with figurative murals and photographs of renowned Latin American philosophers on the walls, it was as famous for its avuncular waiters as it was for its Argentine-style cuisine. The waiters, who had begun working there when they were svelte busboys, now wore long black aprons to camouflage their portly dimensions. The air was redolent of an intoxicating aroma of grilled meat from the kitchen and pink lilies on every table.

When Portia arrived with Jaime, one of the kindly waiters led her to a large round table covered in a white tablecloth, while another escorted her bodyguard to the bar, where he joined several other young men in the same profession.

Colombian women wearing designer dresses in a variety of colors were seated around the table. Their pre-Columbian gold jewelry lit up the room. Portia could not take her eyes off Colombine's large gold earrings, which were in the shape of ancient frogs.

Portia kissed her hostess on both cheeks. "Those earrings are fabulous . . . and the frogs have green eyes."

Colombine took an earring off so that Portia could study it more closely.

"The eyes are real," Colombine said. She told Portia that her jeweler had bought them from a taxidermist who then had them shrunk and glossed over with silicone. "I can have a pair made for you."

"They look stunning on you, but they'd overpower me," Portia said.

"Nonsense. Boston would go wild over the frogs. They're totems of abundance and fertility in our indigenous Muisca culture."

"What fun . . . They'd look great on my tall friend Margot."

"Let me introduce you to my closest friends. Of course, you already know Luisa."

As the two women exchanged kisses, the others stopped chatting.

Colombine went on, "This is Angelica, and that's Mariana."

Portia smiled at the women and shook their hands. She noticed that the two women—she later learned they were rivals—had cloche hats, one in baby blue and the other in pastel pink, that matched their dresses.

"And this is Maria," Colombine said.

Portia recognized the petite woman with her thick dark hair worn in a chignon as the nice concierge at La Gran Conchita. She looked more professional than the breathtaking twenty-one-year-old bride she had seen in the photo album. They were to be seated next to one another.

"Welcome," Maria said.

"What a pleasure to meet you again."

"I hope you're enjoying my husband's hotel."

"It's charming, and the staff is *muy simpatico*. Are you the one with the excellent taste, making sure every detail is perfect?"

Maria blushed. "I'm glad you're comfortable there," she said, giving Portia a radiant smile.

During lunch, Portia learned about Maria's passion for art, and not just Colombian art but the Old Masters as well.

"An acquaintance from New York, an Old Masters dealer, is here on business. He is hoping to buy some Botero drawings. He also brought a few Old Master drawings to sell. Would you like to meet him?" Her heart hammered so powerfully that she was afraid Maria could hear it thumping.

"I'd be delighted." She told Portia that she had spent her honeymoon in Paris, going to all the fabulous museums. "We appreciate the Old Masters, although we mainly collect contemporary Colombian art."

"Colombine told me that your collection is first-rate, particularly your Obregóns."

"Oh, you know about Obregón?"

"Yes, I love his political paintings."

"You must come see ours," Maria graciously offered.

"That would be wonderful," Portia said.

Maria told Portia that she would call her to arrange a visit to her villa sometime the following week. "And you can bring your friend, if you wish."

"How kind of you," Portia responded, hiding her hands under the table to stop them from shaking.

Maria changed the subject. She told Portia about her two children and hiring an English nanny so the kids could learn to speak the language. "Toto and Diana mean everything to me," she said.

"I understand. I'm the same way about Alexa. Your husband told me you're a docent at the Museo de Antioquia."

"It's my most enjoyable nonprofit work. Every Tuesday afternoon I'm at that marvelous museum." Maria then told Portia about Fernando Botero's generous donation of ninety-two pieces of his work and also twenty-two pieces from his collection of modern and contemporary art, including works by Picasso. "I usually give a gallery talk on contemporary South American artists, including anecdotes about the artists' lives. From what I understand, it's popular with out-of-town visitors. You must visit the museum while you're here."

"Colombine's planning to take me."

"That's great," Maria said. "She taught me everything I know."

"I think you're being modest." Portia took a bite of a delicious rice salad.

"Colombine's the expert. I'm only a docent. If I can give back to the community, I'm happy."

"That's admirable." Portia beamed at Maria. She was impressed with her values.

Maria told Portia that she also volunteered at the Estación Hospital. "On Monday afternoons, my bodyguard, Luis, drives me there, and I arrange bouquets of freshly cut flowers for the hospital wards. My aunt Emilia taught me how to use the rough texture of long grasses and horsetails to offset the smooth petals of the flowers."

"They sound gorgeous."

"Volunteer work is very rewarding."

"Wish I had time to give back," Portia admitted. "Running a gallery is much too demanding."

"I can imagine it must be," Maria said. She told Portia that she also liked helping her husband at the hotel. "Carlos told me he met you. Don't you think he's special? Not at all egotistical . . . like many of our men."

"He was most gracious. What do you do at the hotel, if I may ask?"

Maria told Portia that on Wednesday afternoons Luis brought her there and waited while she arranged the flowers for the rooms. "Security is very tight, so Luis doesn't need to hover as much as he does at the museum or the hospital. I'm glad he has the good sense to make himself fit into the background, although he's also never far from me."

"I can't imagine living with bodyguards; unfortunately, I know they're needed."

"As you can see"—she pointed to all the men waiting at the bar, including her Luis, a tall, attractive man around forty-five years old with an expressionless face—"bodyguards are a fact of life in Medellín. And yet each bodyguard's employer needs a certain amount of freedom to be socially adept."

"It's all so interesting." Portia wanted to be compassionate, but knew she'd never accept such an invasion of privacy on a regular basis.

"It's a tricky relationship at best, but a bodyguard's generous salary virtually guarantees his loyalty," Maria said. She excused herself to go to the ladies' room, and Portia turned her attention to the rest of the table.

The women engaged in lively chatter about children, husbands, and art while they ate their delicious lunch of grilled chicken and rice salad.

When Maria returned, she invited Portia to her home on Tuesday afternoon for tea. "I was thinking, you're here for only a short time, so let's arrange it now."

"I'd be delighted."

"Colombine can give you the directions."

"I look forward to seeing you again."

After they all finished their coffee and caramel flan, the women rose to leave. The bodyguards met with their respective charges in the lobby and then they walked down the flagstone path out of the restaurant to the car park. The women chatted near the entrance. A few minutes later one of them opened the door so they could all walk outside. The quiet street changed in a matter of seconds at the sound of rapid gunshots. A female voice screaming for help pierced the air.

Maria, in her confusion, ran into the street. Portia instinctively followed her. A motorcycle roared down the road and veered straight toward Maria. Portia saw it coming. She leapt toward Maria and pulled her out of the way, seconds before she might have been hit.

Luis rushed back from the parking lot to Maria after the shots rang out. He was only a hundred or so feet away from Portia when the motorcycle almost hit his precious charge. Portia grasped that the frightened look on Luis's face came from Maria's near brush with death. Maria burst into tears as Luis put an arm around her. Portia overheard him telling her she was fine and that no one was hurt. After she pulled herself together, Maria turned to Portia, who was still in shock from the close call.

"I can't thank you enough," Maria said.

"I'm just relieved you're all right." Portia squeezed Maria's hand. She was touched by Maria's gratitude. She didn't know her well enough to put her arms around the woman, although she wanted to do just that.

Now that the danger appeared to be over, the women and their bodyguards hurried toward their cars, which were parked in the opposite direction from the shooting. As Jaime drove away from the screeching police sirens, Portia understood the fear of living in a drug-riddled city. Although she no longer felt as scared, her hands still trembled. Jaime pressed the button on the dashboard for a Coltrane tape, and the soulful notes from his saxophone helped Portia regain her composure. She couldn't wait to take a long, hot bath. Then she'd call Sean to set up a time to meet that evening so she could tell him about her day. While he'd be horrified about the drive-by shooting, he'd be pleased that she had already secured an invitation to Maria's villa for both of them.

She was playing the game just right so far and was proud of herself for managing on her own. Her fluency in Spanish had returned, giving her confidence a boost. Later, she'd go to the now-familiar phone booth in the café to call home and then speak with Paul. She wanted to tell him in sketchy coded words about her harrowing, but fruitful, day. Stansky would have a fit if he knew how close she had been to a drive-by shooting, while Paul would be proud of her for rescuing Maria. She still felt shaky from their narrow escape.

CHAPTER TWENTY-THREE

May 25, 1990

The Mysterious Sean Findlay

Portia met Sean—she was getting used to calling him that—downstairs in the lobby of the hotel later that evening. "Let's go for a walk," he said. "It's balmy outside." They chose the path along the rim of the lush grounds behind the hotel. Shaded by the overhanging tropical vegetation, and with no one else in sight, it seemed a safe place for Portia to catch him up on the day's events. Although they were out of earshot of any passerby, they whispered to each other.

Portia told him about meeting Maria Alfonso at the ladies' luncheon, including Maria's brush with death and their invitation to the villa at her finca next Tuesday. He was impressed with the progress she had already made. He was equally impressed when he heard about the note and the two dozen red roses that Carlos had sent Portia to thank her for saving his wife's life. *I am forever grateful. Please come to our villa for dinner at your convenience,* the card said.

"I'm confused. Which invitation should I respond to first?" Portia asked.

"Meet Maria," Sean said. "You already agreed on a date, and you must gain her trust."

"Of course."

"You know how to talk with someone who's as passionate about art as you are. Just keep the discussion on South American artists."

"I get it." She wished he gave her more credit for having good instincts.

Sean warned Portia that if Maria met with both of them, instead of just her, Carlos might become suspicious if they asked for a tour of their art. She realized that, despite her earlier annoyance, his FBI training was invaluable.

He paused to pull a branch from an acacia tree out of their way. "So I won't join you at Maria's villa. I don't want to interfere with your bond. I can always meet her at a later time."

"You're right . . . She's already called, asking me to join her here for breakfast tomorrow . . . so I'll mention that you won't join us on Tuesday."

Portia felt grateful that Sean was there to advise her. The situation was even more complicated than she had imagined. She thought about Stansky. Once again she realized he was right to be worried, although *his* nervousness didn't help her manage her own.

After Sean left, Portia walked to the café to call home. There was something comforting about the smell of freshly brewed coffee, the bubbling milk, the steam from hot water. To her delight, Alexa answered the phone.

"How are you, darling?" she asked. "I miss you terribly."

"We miss you too. Stansky doesn't make lasagna the way you do."

"You're so sweet, angel. How's school? And soccer?"

"I scored a goal yesterday."

"That's wonderful. I'm proud of you. When I come home, we'll go bowling together."

"Thanks, Mama . . . Stansky wants to speak with you."

She heard Alexa handing the phone to him.

"How's Medellín?" he asked. She could tell from his voice that he was trying to hide his irritation in front of Alexa.

"I met a lovely woman today. Everything's going well."

"I hope Sean will check out those Obregóns with you."

"Of course . . . We'll see those gems together." She knew she had to speak in code just in case someone was listening.

"While we're on the phone, I can't find the plumber's number. Do you have it?"

"No, it's not with me. Why don't you ask the Gibrans? You know I've got a lot on my mind." She knew she sounded irritated.

"Sorry to bother you, princess," he said and hung up on her.

So Portia called Paul. She told him in code about her exciting day, including Carlos's thank-you note and dinner invitation.

"When do you think you'll go?"

"I don't know . . . Must admit I feel skittish staying here."

"That's understandable. I know you'll be all right with your friend watching out for you."

Portia felt grateful for Paul's support. "How's Cyrus?" she asked.

"Well, he misses you almost as much as I do," Paul said. Portia realized she was getting into dangerous territory again.

"I'd better go."

"Please let me know how you're doing. Promise to call tomorrow."

"If I can."

Then Portia called Margot.

"I'm in trouble. Paul's sounding romantic on the phone."

"I'm sure he misses you. We all do. We want you back home."

"Although I want to right now . . . I can't divorce Stansky. It would be traumatic for Alexa."

"Portia, you're a wonderful mom. You'll do what's right for both of you."

"I love you, Margot."

"And I love you, Portia."

As Portia left the phone booth to return to the hotel, she sensed she was being followed. She had noticed a man sitting at the bar. His boxy suit overpowered his slight figure, and his butch haircut made him look more like a marine than a paisa. Hearing his steps behind her, she quickened her pace. He caught her arm and whispered in her ear that she had better be careful. Then he walked away.

Back in her room Portia felt frightened. She called Sean and asked him to come see her right away.

"He's probably a local thug," Sean said. He promised to have Castellano investigate this man with the police . . . just in case. "Next time you go to the café you should bring Jaime with you."

"I will."

"Make sure your conversations are purely personal."

Portia gulped. "I may have crossed the line. I promise to be more careful."

"I know this is all new to you."

"I get it. Don't worry, Sean."

"I trust you, Portia. Now get some sleep."

The following evening, Portia had dinner at Colombine's home in El Poblado. The walls of the reception area, where she waited for her hostess, were covered in a beige silk fabric. Four Botero drawings, featuring his signature style of voluminous women, graced the walls. Colombine came down the long winding staircase to greet her. She looked stunning in a red knee-length Valentino dress with matching silk shoes. Her husband was out of town on a business trip, so just the two of them were dining in that night. As they entered the midnight-blue dining room with tiny stars painted on the ceiling, Portia couldn't help exhaling. "Wow."

"So glad you like the decor," Colombine said. "What would you like to drink?"

"A glass of white wine," she answered.

As the two women sipped Pinot Grigio, they walked around the dining room and discussed the art on the walls. When Portia stood in front of the Dutch paintings, she said, "What a rich mixture of Frans Hals portraits, Jan Davidsz. de Heem still lifes, and Jacob van Ruisdael landscapes. You have the best of the best."

"You are one of the few people who could appreciate my small collection," her hostess said.

Eschewing the large dining table in the middle of the room, Colombine had chosen a small corner table covered with a dark-blue tablecloth, matching napkins, and blue-and-white Delft plates. "In case you can't tell, I'm partial to blue."

"What a dramatic space," Portia said. "Its ambiance is worthy of an exceptional art dealer."

"You are most gracious," Colombine said.

After they sat down, servants entered the room to pour water, refill their wineglasses, and bring freshly baked bread. As she listened to the soothing sounds of Julio Iglesias's music coming through the speakers, Portia felt disappointed in herself at how quickly she was getting used to the presence of servants in her friends' homes.

"I'm so happy that you and Maria hit it off. I can't wait for you to see her Obregóns."

"Yes, my dear . . . thanks to you."

"As I told you, Maria and I go way back." Colombine confided that she was the only friend who understood the real Maria. She told Portia that in high school Maria used to fantasize about traveling around the world as a tennis champion, growing taller, and, most of all, being able to walk without a limp. "You might have noticed at the luncheon that she's self-conscious about her disability."

"I did at first . . . but she's so engaging, I forgot about it."

"You may, but she never forgets." Colombine told Portia how they managed to remain friends, even after their marriages. "My husband and his banker colleagues have always been horrified about the way the drug cartels have damaged our city's reputation. However, I never let their animosity get in the way of my friendship with Maria."

"That kind of loyalty is rare," Portia said.

"Our friends often say we make a strange pair. And they're not just referring to my being tall while she is petite. We find it amusing that they can't get past our physical and familial differences."

"I like your attitude." Portia sipped her wine and nibbled on crispy crackers.

"As co-chairs of A Better Life, our nonprofit organization that raises money for impoverished children who need serious medical attention, Maria and I often meet. I may be the public face, yet it's Maria who works hard behind the scenes."

"You're a terrific team."

"Yes, we are." Colombine told Portia that they had also established a sister organization, which trained volunteers to play educational games with the kids and teach their mothers about the need for healthy diets and exercise. "Each child goes home with gifts of games and clothes. You can imagine how satisfying this project is for us."

"I'm impressed. From the way Maria spoke at the luncheon, I could tell she was pleased by the results."

Dinner was served, and Portia complimented Colombine on the roast pork cooked in cognac.

"As you know, Maria is my biggest collector," Colombine said. "While I'm grateful for her patronage, being her friend is not always so easy. A few weeks ago, when we were having tea at my gallery, I broke down in tears. I had just received a phone call telling me that a local hoodlum had gunned down Emilio, our friend Marta's adolescent son."

Portia stopped eating and put her knife and fork down beside her plate.

"I was as horrified then as you are now," Colombine said. "Maria hadn't heard about the incident and was shocked to learn the news . . . I didn't hide my angry feelings when I confronted her."

Portia had been enjoying her dinner until this moment. She looked at Colombine with compassion and asked how Maria had responded.

"She felt terrible. At the same time, Maria didn't know what she could do to change things. I remember how she closed her eyes before she admitted to dreaming about moving to Europe with Carlos and her children."

"How can she live like this?" Portia asked.

"That's exactly what I asked. Maria shrugged her shoulders. She told me that she prayed this hoodlum wasn't associated with her father. When I said that it was her father who had caused Emilio's death, she didn't believe me until I assured her I wouldn't accuse Don Pedro of anything unless I was certain."

Two male servants came into the dining room to remove the dinner plates. Colombine waited until they left before she continued. "Maria told me how much she despises the violence associated with the drug trade. She wishes it would stop. Safety is all she thinks about these days. Not just the safety of her children and husband, but everyone else's safety as well."

"It seems that Maria's generosity of spirit resides deep inside her," Portia said. She couldn't tell Colombine that she was beginning to feel concerned about her own safety. Instead, she said, "Maria has a tough life."

"Not everyone shares your insight."

While they drank after-dinner coffee together, Colombine assured Portia that Maria was indeed a good person. Portia would be safe having tea in her home.

Jaime drove Portia back to the hotel late that night. After her encounter with the shadowy man, and now hearing Colombine's story about the young man's death, she felt doubly scared, despite Sean's assurances and Jaime's presence. Before she left Boston, she had taken the precaution of packing some Valium in case she had difficulty sleeping. She knew that without a good night's sleep she would be more likely to make mistakes. After washing up in her room, she took a pill. She was against drugs of all kinds. Yet she had to allow herself this one indulgence. Colombia had changed so much since she had traveled there for Polaroid. She could feel the constant tension in the cafés, the hotel, the restaurants. *Damn it, Stansky was right,* she admitted. But her commitment to their mission remained strong.

CHAPTER TWENTY-FOUR

May 27, 1990

The Unexpected Happens

Portia couldn't help liking Maria Alfonso. She hadn't expected to care about a woman connected to the cocaine trade. Yet when Maria had revealed her warm, generous nature at Colombine's luncheon, her kindred spirit was hard to resist. Portia's positive feelings for Carlos's wife made the sting operation even more challenging than she had anticipated.

The women met at La Gran Conchita's ground floor breakfast room. The glass doors opened onto the lush garden outside, and sun poured into the room. Portia appreciated the calming choice of simple rattan wallpaper for the interior. It contrasted with the hazards of her mission. As they sipped coffee from white china cups, Portia's fluency in Spanish allowed the conversation to flow, and they talked nonstop about their two passions—children and art. Maria told her new friend about her honeymoon visit to the Louvre and how that experience had influenced her desire to become a serious collector.

"We almost lived at the Denon Wing, where the skylit gallery containing Delacroix's huge canvases astounded us, especially *Liberty Leading the People*. His canvases were the largest we had ever seen." Maria's wide eyes reflected her excitement.

"I share your appreciation for Delacroix," Portia said.

Maria told Portia how Carlos had noticed that the dark-red walls of the room and the light from above made the paintings even more dramatic. "I watched him shiver as he stared at the scary faces of the crowd breaking through the barricades and the dead bodies sprawled on the ground . . . My husband's reaction made the painting even more meaningful for me."

"The presentation of those huge paintings in that big room is overpowering." Portia put her coffee cup down on the table while recalling the Delacroix images.

"Don't you think Liberté, holding the French flag in one hand and brandishing a rifle in the other, is the strongest female image you've ever seen?" Maria said.

"I wouldn't want to get in her way," Portia said. "Liberté is imposing."

Maria described how they sat on a low bench in the room and scrutinized the canvas from a short distance away. "The imagery became so compelling that we felt the painter was standing behind us, listening to our comments."

"I've had that mystical sensation once or twice myself," Portia said.

"Don't you love being alone in a museum room?"

"It's a luxury."

"That morning only a handful of visitors drifted around the gallery, so Carlos and I could discuss the paintings without risking someone asking us to be quiet."

"Don't you hate being shushed?"

Maria laughed. She told Portia that after they left the Louvre they stopped to drink hot chocolate doused with whipped cream at Angelina's. "Have you ever been there?"

"Yes," Portia said. "The best hot chocolate in the world."

"We sat at one of Angelina's . . . you must remember their marble-topped tables . . . for a long time. I couldn't get Liberté out of my head. It's as if she followed us into the café," Maria said.

"I've had that same experience with certain paintings." Portia told Maria how Velázquez's *Las Meninas* continued to haunt her. "What a fabulous honeymoon you must have had. Don't you love Paris?"

"Colombine helped make our trip exciting." Maria told Portia that Colombine had advised them to pace themselves at the Louvre so that they would not be overwhelmed by the art.

"You mean only spend one or two hours there each day," Portia said.

"Exactly," Maria said.

"Colombine's a treasure. Now I'm dying to hear how you assembled your South American art collection."

As a waiter stood nearby, Maria told Portia that she preferred to purchase the work of talented, but not yet internationally known, artists. "I feel good when I can make a difference in their lives. Our collection features Obregón, Caballero, Negret, and Grau. They're contemporaries of our famous Botero."

"We share the same values. My gallery shows emerging artists." Portia relaxed in her chair and took the last sip of her coffee. She was pleased that they could truly bond over this. Then she opened her oversized bag and removed several glossy color reproductions of Aaron Stockwell's, Sterling Mulbry's, and Ann Thornycroft's paintings.

Maria held the photos carefully at the edges, displaying her professionalism. After examining the images for several minutes, she told Portia that she particularly liked Thornycroft's Color Field style and geometric design. She asked Portia about the artist's life.

"Well. She's British. Studied painting in London, where she met David Hockney and is now married to an American painter. They live in Los Angeles, where Ann says the light's extraordinary almost every day."

"You have a discerning eye," Maria said. "I hope Thornycroft will be famous someday."

Portia was flattered, finding it more and more difficult to remember she was playing a role. "Thank you," she said. "Your praise means a lot to me."

She was enjoying her *arepas* (corn cakes oozing luscious cheese) and *lulo* (a mixed fruit juice) almost as much as the conversation, and the coffee at the hotel was the best she had tasted in Medellín . . . which meant that it was superb. Maria only nibbled on a piece of toast. Portia wondered if her hostess was not feeling well or if this meager breakfast was her usual morning fare. She noted that everything Maria did she did with grace, even the delicate way she held her coffee cup with two fingers.

When the conversation moved toward their families, Portia showed Maria photographs of her townhouse in the South End, of Alexa and Stansky dressed up as Robin and Batman for Halloween as they posed in front of their yellow door, and some of Alexa playing soccer on her school's athletic field.

"I didn't know girls in America play football . . . That's what we call it here. In Colombia, only boys and men play the game."

"It used to be like that in Boston, but ten years ago many schools decided it was important for girls to play team sports. Alexa really enjoys it." Portia described how the girls practiced every afternoon during soccer season so that her daughter had become a good forward. "She's connected with her teammates, and the sport reinforces her confidence. Her grades too." Portia hoped she wasn't bragging too much.

"Diana plays tennis, but that's not the same as a team sport."

"I agree." She sensed that Maria was enjoying their conversation.

"I wish Diana could participate on a team. She's such a vivacious girl; she'd be a natural. Unfortunately, it's too risky for her to attend a school outside the villa."

"I'm sorry to hear that. Being confined must be difficult for the children. I suppose you have lots of family. Don't some cousins visit?" Portia hoped she wasn't getting too personal.

"Yes, young cousins stop by. Alas, they don't come often. When they do it's joyous. There's nothing sweeter than hearing my children shouting as they play volleyball on the lawn."

"That's a wonderful sound," Portia said, suddenly feeling homesick. She could hear Alexa's infectious laugh as she and her friends played that very same sport at Lucy Vincent Beach on Martha's Vineyard.

As the two women sat at the breakfast table, enjoying their second cups of aromatic espresso, Maria told Portia about how different her education had been. When she was six, her parents had enrolled her in a convent school, where she had formed lifelong friendships with other girls her age. "That's where I met Colombine and Luisa. The nuns were outstanding teachers."

"Hopefully life in Medellín will get back to normal someday," Portia said.

"Next time you must bring your family to Colombia. We'll take you to Cartagena."

"I promise. In the meantime I look forward to seeing your Obregóns, if Tuesday still works for you."

"Come to tea around 3:30 p.m., and I'll show them to you and Sean with pleasure," Maria said.

"The pleasure will be mine." Portia's dimpled smile revealed her satisfaction with the way things were going. "Unfortunately, Sean won't be able to join us, but he thanks you for the kind invitation."

Before they said goodbye in the lobby, Maria asked the concierge if Carlos was available. He was not. Portia thought it was just as well. She wasn't sure she could handle more tension.

That evening, Sean and Portia met for dinner at the Inter-Continental's open-air restaurant, and she told him in their code about her productive breakfast with Maria. He was pleased to hear that their relationship had been strengthened and that the date of her visit to the villa had been confirmed. He promised her he would inform Roberto. As they slowly savored their *sancocho de gallina* soup, Sean weighed the pros and cons of making an earlier visit to the Museo de Antioquia with Colombine. Maybe this experience would give Portia even more to talk about when she visited Maria at her villa.

"I wouldn't dare change the date," Portia said as she sipped her wine. "I plan to spend Monday researching contemporary Colombian artists at La Nacional's library. I already know something about their lives from Colombine. I want to ask Maria good questions."

"You're so diligent."

"Isn't that why you hired me?"

CHAPTER TWENTY-FIVE

May 29, 1990

Casing the Alfonso Villa

On that sunny Tuesday morning, Portia was driven to Roberto Castellano's villa, where he supervised her being wired. He wanted two Interpol contract workers, who would be in a car a short distance from the guardhouse, to be able to hear her conversation with Maria. In a worst-case scenario, if Portia seemed to be in any danger, they could rush into the villa to protect her, even shoot the guard if they had to.

At 3:00 p.m., Jaime drove her to the Alfonso finca with the contract workers and Sean following close behind. The peaceful beauty of the crystalline sky did not soothe her nerves.

As her car approached the villa, Portia wasn't surprised to see an armed guard sitting on the veranda. Roberto had briefed her this was de rigueur. Yet when Portia came up close and gave her name to the guard at the open porch, his squashed face and rifle scared her. Somehow she managed to tell him in her best Spanish that Señora Alfonso was expecting her. Evidently, Maria had already informed the guard about her American visitor because he motioned her to the door. As she walked by him, Portia noted a large key ring loaded with keys dangling from his belt.

Portia rang the bell, and a pretty, young maid wearing a black uniform with a white lace apron answered the door. She led Portia to the large living room, which was filled with overstuffed sofas and chairs.

A few minutes later, Maria appeared, looking elegant in a pale-pink silk tunic over white silk pants. The two women sat down at an antique oak table that had been set with Christofle silver, Baccarat crystal water glasses, Spode china teacups and saucers, and pale-pink cocktail napkins embroidered with flowers. A ceiling fan created a welcome breeze. Portia could not take her eyes off the large painting of a brashly colorful and oversized condor that hung over the massive stone fireplace.

"That majestic bird dominates the room," she said. "It must be an Obregón."

"In our country, the condor is a symbol of health and power. He's associated with the sun god and is believed to be the ruler of the upper world. Don't you think Obregón has captured this?"

"Yes, it's a powerful image and must bring good luck. Obregón's cubist works also intrigue me. I read that he was influenced by Picasso, which is not surprising, but also by the British painter Graham Sutherland."

"Portia, you clearly know your stuff."

"Thanks, Maria. May I take a photograph of you in front of the painting for my New York collectors?"

"I'd be honored."

As Portia was taking the photo with her small Nikon, Toto bounded into the room and ran over to kiss his mother. "Meet my darling son. Toto, this is Portia Malatesta. She lives near Harvard."

"Have you been there?" Portia asked Maria. She hoped her voice sounded natural.

"A friend's son graduated from Harvard last year, so I made my first trip to the States." Maria beamed with remembered pleasure. "Boston's a vibrant town. So many fun things to do. Like Filene's Basement."

"Isn't that place a hoot?" Portia asked. She tried her best to translate *hoot* for Maria. At the same time she made a mental note that

Maria had accompanied Carlos on their recent trip to Boston. Then she turned to face Toto.

"I hear you're a good student. What are you studying?"

"Ancient Rome."

"The Romans created great art and good government."

"I kind of like Julius Caesar. He was a hero, wasn't he?" Toto asked in a low voice, trying to sound more grown up than his nine-year-old self.

"Why, yes," she said. Her look conveyed approval of this intelligent young boy, who looked more like a nearsighted scholar than a drug lord's grandson. She realized that he was only one year younger than Alexa. His knowledge of ancient history, from his private tutoring, made him seem older. He sat with them and ate a few sandwiches before returning to his studies. She was impressed that Toto was so well behaved.

Moments later, Diana appeared. She curtsied in front of Portia before giving her mother a kiss. She, too, nibbled on a few sandwiches. "Mama, can I help the cook today?" she asked.

"Of course," Maria said. "What dessert will you make?"

"*Pan de yucca*," Diana said, rubbing her stomach. "It's yummy."

"Enjoy, my little one," Maria said before Diana left the room with Clare, her nanny, who had come to fetch her.

"They're darling," Portia said.

"I like to think so."

After they finished tea, Maria asked if she was ready to see the rest of her collection.

Off the living room was a perfectly proportioned square space that Maria called her study. It could have served as a reception area as well. Above an oversized glass table, Portia saw three framed Botero drawings of plump, dark-eyed women hung on a red silk wall. She noted these drawings were similar to the ones she had seen in the reception area at Colombine's villa.

"Botero's nudes are compelling." For the first time Portia realized that Botero must have been influenced by Picasso's classical period when the body's volume mattered most.

"Wait until you see his paintings at the Museo."

"I'm looking forward to seeing them on Thursday," Portia said.

"You must report back."

"I promise."

On the opposite wall, Portia saw a small still life of tulips and snap-dragons in a yellow vase. She walked up close to the painting, and in the bottom right-hand corner she saw the signature of an artist named Edouard Darc.

"Oh, Carlos bought that for me in Paris. We were strolling along the Rue Napoleon on our way back from the Louvre, and this bright-colored painting in the window of a dimly-lit gallery spoke to me."

"How thoughtful." Portia could see from the painting that Carlos and Maria had good taste in art . . . even early on. So what if Darc wasn't legendary? Portia knew all too well that not every talented artist was destined to become famous.

"Carlos is generous," Maria said. "I'm grateful."

Then Portia moved closer to an early Obregón portrait of a young boy called *El Caballero Mateo*.

"This was painted after his cubist period. The boy's innocence reminds me of Toto," Maria said.

"And his white clown collar makes me think of Picasso's young *Harlequin*."

"Wish I were so perceptive."

"You flatter me." Portia felt pleased at how well this was going.

As they sauntered from room to room, Portia complimented Maria on her exquisite furnishings, in particular the Spanish oak antiques. "It's not only me. My husband likes interior design."

"Mine too."

With Maria's cheerful assent, Portia took several photographs of the magnificent courtyard and its fountain and some of the pyrami-dal trees. Portia wanted Maria to become comfortable with her tak-ing photographs in her mansion, so she purposely chose some settings that were more picturesque than informative. She asked Maria to pose in front of one of the palm trees. Maria stood near the trunk, her hands down by her side, a relaxed smile on her face.

"Having you in the photo will make the images more meaningful for my family."

They returned inside and continued their tour of the downstairs rooms. While she was conversing with Maria, Portia looked at the walls for any signs of a hidden room.

"Carlos particularly likes Obregón's political paintings," Maria said as she showed Portia into a dark room smelling of cigar smoke, not far from the kitchen. She stopped in front of *Massacre of April 10*, which hung above a sturdy oak desk. It had been painted in 1948 in the artist's cubist style. The painting, illuminated by a brass picture light, was strewn with broken legs, a brown baby lying facedown against a headless white woman, and grotesque African masks scattered around the edges of the canvas.

"It's disturbing," Portia said. "I recognize Picasso's influence. Yet the artist has his own style."

"I know."

The two women left the room in a somber mood.

"Lastly," Maria said as she turned to face Portia, "I'd like you to see his masterpiece, *The Dead Student*. It's in our bedroom. Normally I don't take visitors there, but you have such a genuine appreciation of Obregón's talent that I must show it to you."

"I would dearly love to see it."

"Be prepared for even more violence."

"Picasso's *Guernica* is one of my favorite paintings. Nothing can be more violent than that." Portia recalled how Antonio used to drag her to MoMA to see this painting. A wave of sadness from this memory, like a fading photograph, held her for a few moments. Then she refocused on her mission.

"Follow me." Maria led Portia up a short flight of stairs, then down a long whitewashed hallway until they reached the enormous master suite.

Portia noted that the bedroom did not have much furniture. A four-poster bed and sleek built-ins took up minimal space. The large canvas overwhelmed the room, although there were a few smaller Obregón paintings on the opposite wall.

"What a dramatic scene." Portia pointed to the painter's large canvas in a gilt frame. "That red is the color of blood. And the altar-like table feels eerie. It's a spectacular stage setting for death."

"Obregón painted this in 1956, during a tragic period of social unrest in my country, when far too many university students lost their lives."

"Now I understand . . . why Carlos prefers Obregón's political canvases."

"He captured our country's despair."

"It was courageous to place such a sad painting in the bedroom," Portia said.

Maria told her, "The painter's personal bravery inspires me each day."

Portia walked up to the painting to take a closer look, and that's when she noticed the seam of the wall above the painting was not plumb. *This must be it*, she thought, and her heart began racing. She almost dropped her camera but caught it before it fell to the floor. She had to quickly recover and quietly took a few breaths.

"Can I get a shot of you in front of this extraordinary painting?"

"Well, yes. If you like."

Maria stood proudly, while Portia focused her Nikon.

"You look like the beautiful and beneficent patron you are."

They left the bedroom and went back along the corridor. This time Portia noted a sparse bedroom on the left before they returned to the living room. Maria told her this was Ludovico's room. "He's my husband's bodyguard."

Portia was pretty sure that she had discovered the location of the hidden room, although it could be some time before she would know if her assumption was correct. She had begun to perspire and feared that Maria might detect the change in her demeanor.

Somehow she managed to regain her cool. She looked at her watch. "You have been so welcoming, I forgot about the time." She told her hostess that she had to get back to the hotel to freshen up before dinner.

"I would like to see you again . . . perhaps at Colombine's gallery or the hotel, or maybe in Boston . . . hopefully before Toto goes to Harvard."

"Oh, we must definitely meet somewhere."

They made their way back to the entryway and said their goodbyes in the hall. When Maria closed the front door behind her, Portia nodded to the fierce-looking guard and walked as calmly as possible to the white Ford.

Jaime was waiting. She felt uplifted by Charlie Parker's "Moose the Mooche" as Jaime drove her back to the hotel, where she called Sean and told him in code about her day. They arranged to have dinner later that night at the InterContinental's outdoor restaurant again. The dinner tables there were placed far apart from one another, offering guests a little privacy.

That evening, as Jaime drove them along El Poblado's wide avenues, Portia and Sean sat in the back seat, listening to Coltrane's "Central Park West."

"Doesn't it make you want to be in New York?" she asked.

"I'm there," Sean said.

Portia rolled down her window to breathe in the delicious night air. A few moments later she opened her large bag and handed Sean an envelope with her map of the rooms. She also gave him a roll of film with the photographs she had taken at the villa.

"Well done," he said to her as he pocketed her gifts.

"I found that star in the sky."

"I knew you would."

Despite the relative privacy at the restaurant, they still spoke in code as she told him more about her exciting day at the villa. "I saw several amazing Obregóns and some wonderful Botero drawings. I was so inspired, I made sketches as soon as I returned," she said, referring to the map.

"That's fabulous," Sean said, patting her arm. "I'll let Castellano know. I'm sure he'll want to invest in some Obregóns."

At dinner that night in their villa, Carlos asked his wife about her day. "Portia, Colombine's friend, came for tea. She wanted to see our Obregóns."

"Oh yes, Portia Malatesta, the Italian American. I met her at the hotel, and she seemed quite nice. What did she think?" Carlos asked.

"She was impressed by his paintings and will probably buy some of his smaller pieces for her New York client. She's *muy simpatica*. I'd love you to meet her again before she leaves."

"I sent her a thank-you note inviting her to dinner, but I didn't specify a date," Carlos said. "Please see if she's free tomorrow evening."

Without saying anything to disturb his wife, Carlos decided to investigate this American art dealer who was buying Colombian art. He was indeed grateful to her for saving his wife. At the same time, he also wondered how she had managed to get invited so quickly to his home. He wasn't pleased that she had been in their master bedroom.

The next morning, Maria called Portia to see if she was available for dinner that evening.

"My husband wants to thank you in person for saving my life."

"I'd be delighted," Portia said, sounding cool, while her heart catapulted. After she hung up the phone, she ran down the hall to Sean's room and knocked on his door.

A sleepy-eyed Sean opened the door. "I delivered your drawings last night," he said in code.

"Great. Maria just invited me to dinner this evening at the villa," she said once she was inside his room.

"That's wonderful."

"I'm a little nauseous," she said in code.

"Remember what I told you."

"Of course." Portia reminded him that they were supposed to go to the Museo with Colombine the next day, but "I know your friend needed you," she said in code. She was sitting at the desk in his room, munching on a pear. She got up from her chair and paced around the room.

Sean held her by her shoulders. "Calm down, Portia. I'm here for you." She sat down again. "Can you reschedule the museum?" Sean asked.

Portia promised to call Colombine, hoping that she could change their date to the following Monday . . . a few days before she was scheduled to leave. Sean would arrange tomorrow's get-together with his friend, Mr. C. He assured her that this would not be a problem.

Jaime drove a wired Portia to the Alfonso villa on May 30 around 8:00 p.m. and waited for her in his parked car to the right of the curved driveway. Castellano and two of his men waited in another car about a half mile down the road from the guardhouse. This time Portia was not going to mention the Obregóns, for the men didn't want her to take any more risks. She only needed to enjoy herself and try to gain a little more understanding of Carlos.

Portia briefly saw Toto and Diana before they went to bed. Clare, their nanny, brought them into the room, and each one bowed in recognition of her before kissing their parents good night.

Maria oohed and aahed over the beautiful bouquet of flowers Portia brought. "How thoughtful. You know how much I love tulips and snapdragons."

After they entered the dining room, Carlos stood behind his wife. The table was formally set with candelabras and gleaming silver. Carlos held Portia's chair for her and made sure that her wineglass remained full. Servants scurried around with platters of cheese, cold meats, and salad. As they dined, Portia observed once again that Carlos's eyes were sharp and clear. She felt him sizing her up. Dressed in a black Gucci suit, he looked even more attractive than the first time she had met him, at the hotel. His serious expression conferred dignity on his bearing.

"I understand you admire Obregón's paintings and that you connect with his political messages. He portrayed our country's pain during the student revolution."

"His message appeals to me. In my country, I'm called a liberal."

"That must be good," Carlos said. "As I recall you're also passionate about art, something we three share in common."

"Who's your favorite artist?" Portia asked.

"Botero, of course."

"Not Maillol?" Maria asked with an ironic tone in her voice. She winked at her husband.

Carlos told Portia that during the honeymoon their only argument had been inspired by Maillol's chubby sculptures that were scattered around the Tuileries. "Maria insisted that Botero's oversized women— some people call them fat—were more beautiful than Maillol's. I've come to agree with her."

"I'd never seen his nude drawings before. His women do seem strangely delicate, although they are indeed large," Portia said.

"I agree," Carlos said. "When I discovered that Botero grew up in the barrio with a destitute mother like me, I admired him even more."

"Fascinating," Portia said. "How did he become an artist?"

"You won't believe this," Carlos said. "Botero's rich uncle enrolled him in a training school for bullfighters. But it turned out that Botero was more interested in drawing bulls than fighting them."

"That makes him very human," she said. "I like that."

Maria told Portia that Botero spent a year in Madrid copying the Old Masters at the Prado before he moved to Paris.

"You must have been awed by the European art you saw in Paris," Portia said.

Carlos nodded his head yes. "Delacroix's large-scale, revolutionary paintings made my heart race. He made me believe life in Colombia could become better for everyone." He told Portia that after their return he and Maria began haunting the local galleries. Although the European masterpieces in the Louvre could not have been more different from their native Colombian art, they had developed an eye for composition and painterly expression. He explained that his ideal was to live surrounded by beauty and culture . . . a clear sign of having an illustrious place in the world. "Owning art has made me feel that I'm far from my humble childhood. Don't you think great art represents something eternal?" he asked.

"I'm not sure what you mean by eternal," Portia said. She thought his inconsistent values about art revealed a deep schism in his personality.

"I do get carried away sometimes," he said.

"I completely understand," Portia said. "What other European artists capture your imagination?" Portia asked.

"Vermeer," he said, without any hesitation.

"He's so talented, and there are only thirty-six of his paintings in the world."

"They are precious." Carlos told Portia that ever since he saw *The Astronomer* and *The Lacemaker* at the Louvre, Vermeer's use of light pouring into interiors made him feel like he was inside the space. "Besides, the tension between his hopeful light and foreboding dark shapes speaks to me," Carlos said. His cheeks were flushed from the wine. He rose from his seat to refill Portia's glass.

"What do you mean?" Portia asked. She wondered what Isabella Gardner would think of this man. She knew Stansky would find him pretentious.

"There's good and evil in all of us, whether we care to admit it or not."

"That's true," Portia said.

"We're all tempted by evil of some sort, whether it's lusting after someone else's wife or husband, or merely their car, or being jealous of someone else's life. Why can't *I* live in the tropics and paint like Gauguin? Why can't *I* be famous and enjoy a crowd's adulation? Envy is my biggest flaw," Carlos said. "When I was young, I sometimes stole food from the market and, once or twice, clothes from a big store downtown."

"I imagine that many barrio kids stole," Portia said.

"Maybe. It was still wrong."

"Honesty becomes you, Carlos. Is that why you were able to come so far?"

The servants had removed the dinner plates and were now serving flan for dessert, along with coffee and chocolates.

"No, it was because my kind father-in-law took a special interest in me." Carlos looked at Maria and gave her a smile that was just shy of seductive.

She blew a kiss to him across the table. "I don't understand why Carlos talks like this when we now have everything we ever wanted. Yet he still has nightmares," Maria said. "My heart goes out to him."

"Maria, you're embarrassing me."

"Oh, I'm sorry. Portia's so simpatica—she understands, don't you?" Maria asked, a little tipsy.

"Nightmares are pretty normal," Portia lied.

They chatted about their children as they shared brandy nightcaps in the living room. Portia looked at her watch and realized it was time to leave. She thanked her hosts for a marvelous evening.

Carlos told her that it was always a pleasure to make the acquaintance of Americans. "I admire your country's entrepreneurial spirit.

And you, Portia, are even more appealing because I recognize that you, like me, are a slave to art."

"Why, thank you," she said, silently acknowledging the truth of his statement.

Before Portia was escorted out the door, Carlos gave her a small white box tied with a red ribbon. "In honor of Obregón's reds," he said, pointing to the ribbon. "Please don't open it until you get to the hotel."

As Jaime's car drove off, Portia sat upright in the back seat, holding the white box in her lap. After they passed Castellano's parked car alongside the road, she reviewed the evening's events, and the full impact of her mistake in mentioning the thirty-six Vermeers hit her. Carlos could have pulled a gun on her if he perceived that she was a threat. It was stupid to put herself in such danger. Yet she had not felt threatened when she was there. She had to admit she enjoyed Carlos and Maria's company. They really knew how to make a guest feel special. Listening in the car to Duke Ellington's "Take the 'A' Train" reinforced her good mood.

When she got to her room and opened the white box, she found a small pair of emerald earrings set in gold with a handwritten note: *I can't thank you enough for saving my wife.* Portia knew that emeralds were mined in Colombia and did not cost as much as in the States. Still, she was stunned by such an expensive gift and wondered if on some level, he was trying to bribe her.

Portia found Carlos to be an intelligent, caring, and generous man. She couldn't believe he was a thief, although sadly she now knew he had been in Boston a year before the Gardner robbery and that he admired Vermeer. And Maria was so sweet and gracious. She didn't want any harm to come to them. Yet she had promised Isabella she would help catch the thief. She must keep her priorities straight.

At the hotel, she called Sean, who had just returned from his dinner with Castellano. Portia and Sean agreed to meet for a quick walk around the grounds. She spoke with him in code about her dinner and the facts she had learned about Carlos. Once again he congratulated Portia on her abilities. "You're a natural," he said. He told her that they were meeting his friend the following day at his villa and she should be ready at 9:00 a.m. She let him know that Colombine was fine with Monday, June 4, for their museum visit.

On a whim she decided to call Paul again. She needed support for her difficult role, and Stansky would be outraged that she had risked her life by meeting the suspect at his home. Jaime accompanied her to the phone booth and waited at the bar until she finished.

"I'm jealous," Paul said after she described the tall, attractive, and well-mannered Carlos. "How could a man like that be a baseball player?" he asked in code. "Why didn't he just buy some new uniforms and be done with it?"

"This man's complicated. I'm sure I've barely scratched the surface of his personality, but we better not talk about him."

"Good night, dear Portia. Please call me when you're home next week."

"I promise," she said.

Back at the hotel, she fell asleep without washing up or changing her clothes. She had never been more exhausted.

The phone rang at 8:00 the following morning. It was Julio, Portia's intern, who told her about hanging the Stockwell show at the gallery the night before. She hid her annoyance with him for waking her up. It wasn't his fault that she felt so far away from her Boston life. She surprised herself when she realized that she no longer cared if Stockwell left for another gallery.

The day after he learned about Portia's visit to see the Obregóns, Carlos had his most trusted maid, Dolores, search Portia's room for personal papers, as well as the room of the other American art dealer, Sean Findlay. If she saw any official-looking documents, she was to make copies of them for him. He wanted to know if they worked for the FBI or CIA.

Portia Malatesta's room was extremely neat. Dolores found some sleeping pills inside a drawer in her night table and a paperback version of Marquez's *Love in the Time of Cholera*, but nothing else. Under the bed was a crumbled Post-it note with Colombine's name and number.

Sean Findlay's room was messy. Soiled underwear lay on the floor. Nothing was inside his night table. There was an oversized leather case in the closet containing signed drawings. His bathroom had two open tubes of toothpaste and a can of shaving cream. There were no papers or official documents. When Dolores called Carlos on his private line, he was relieved to learn this. *I was overly suspicious,* he thought. *Working for Don Pedro has made me paranoid. So what if she's from Boston? It's only a coincidence. Besides, Colombine can vouch for her.*

Carlos was pretty convinced that he was wrong to be mistrustful, but he had difficulty sleeping at night.

CHAPTER TWENTY-SIX

May 30, 1990

Hiring the Front Man

As Carlos drank coffee at his office desk, he removed a notebook from a locked drawer and reviewed his detailed description of the trip to Boston when he and Diego Augustin had hired a new front man for their Mafia connection. The previous evening with Portia made him nostalgic for Boston, and he wanted to remember every moment of his first trip there. He had written everything down so that he could share his experiences with Maria and brief Don Pedro.

Carlos put his feet up on the desk as he read his first entry.

> I flew to Boston on November 6, 1988. Diego had arrived three days earlier in order to visit his son, Pablo, who was expected to graduate from Harvard the following June. When Diego called, he admitted that while he was pleased to spend time with Pablo, he

was nervous about this assignment. He hoped I would approve of the new man.

The plan was for both of us to meet the cartel's new liaison. The previous one, Rigoberto Espinosa, often clashed with Mafia boss Doc Reilly. When Rigoberto pulled a knife on Doc, Diego had rushed the scrappy street fighter back to Bogotá before Doc's henchmen came after him. Diego told me that he had to act fast to find a replacement for Rigoberto. "This failure with the local Mafia puts us in a precarious position," he said.

We both knew the cartel could not afford to make another mistake. "I'm not pleased about this assignment," I confided to Diego. "I don't like showing my face to strangers, particularly in the United States. Our current government is committed to destroying Colombian drug production and wants to extradite the cartel leaders for prosecution. It scares me."

The cocaine business between Colombia and the United States had tripled over the past few years. Don Pedro told me that Boston's Mafia men were the main buyers and distributors of our product. My father-in-law made it clear he needed someone he could trust to collect money for the purchases, tell the Boston contacts about safe drop-off points, and make sure the cocaine arrived on time and the Boston police didn't catch on.

I get it. It's a complicated situation and I was relieved that Diego was with me, Carlos had scribbled in the margin.

I often heard that Diego's academic friends were shocked when he joined the cartel as a technical resource. He was hired to teach our employees about the chemical properties of coca production and business math so that our manufacturing operations could run more efficiently. Like many Colombians, Diego wanted to earn enough money to send his only son to be educated in the United States. He once confided that "the fallout from the drug wars is becoming worse, making Medellín a dangerous place to live. And Pablo will have opportunities in Boston he would never get in Colombia."

We met in the lobby at the Copley Square hotel, Carlos wrote in the margin. *After we were settled in my comfortable suite, I asked about Pablo.*

"I bet your son's getting straight As," I said, opening the door to the minibar before removing two Cokes. I could picture Diego's gangly kid greeting me with a big smile.

"He's doing exceptionally well," Diego replied with obvious pride. "And how are Maria and the kids?"

"They're wonderful." I handed Diego a package of homegrown coffee beans. "Maria's heard Boston coffee tastes vile. She didn't want you to suffer, even if you're here for just a short time."

"I can barely drink the stuff. Please thank her," Diego said.

"Tell me about our new guy." I sat down in one of the cushy chairs and motioned for Diego to do the same.

"His name's Guillermo Malecon," Diego said. "He's in his early twenties and was brought up in Medellín. He comes from a pretty good family, but they've fallen on hard times. He's single, so he has time for an extra job. He's a bit on the studious side, which is a good cover, and at the same time, he's got street smarts. A rare combination," Diego said in his raspy voice. "His references checked out."

"Don Pedro will be pleased that he's from Medellín and is educated."

Diego told me that Guillermo is a simultaneous translator in the Boston court system and has been living at Esmeralda's, a Colombian rooming house in Brookline, for the past ten months. "I'm sure we can trust this guy. His uncle Tomas helped us out in Medellín, risking his life during the early days of the cartel by hiding Don Pedro in the barrio when the police were after him."

"That's a good reason to hire him."

"Guillermo's not a bully. While many men in the Irish Mafia are tough, he knows how to get along with them . . . Like you, Carlos."

"Thanks," I said. "You mean, he won't make the Irish guys feel they're beneath him?"

"Never. Guillermo's smooth, and he's also strong. He was a boxer in high school and also studied karate. Yet he comes across as a calm, confident person, not easily ruffled. He won't be manipulated. He meets plenty of unsavory characters in the courts, so he's familiar with their many deceptions."

"I'm pleased to hear about Guillermo's skills," I said.

"And after I introduced them, Doc Reilly said he's worthy of the job."

"That's a good first step," I said.

Diego had filled me in on how tricky it was to work with Boston's Irish Mafia. When Doc Reilly went out, the underworld boss dressed in a suit and tie. His nails were always manicured, and he used pomade on his black hair. Although he had grown up in a rough South Boston housing project, he had graduated from high school and learned carpentry skills. He never married and employed a full-time housekeeper. Diego also told me he'd been surprised that the man, who wouldn't hesitate to have someone's throat cut, also loves opera. It's damn unlikely, Carlos wrote in the margin.

"Doc Reilly may have gentlemanly pretensions, but I know his gang, who also grew up in Southie's poorest projects, are thugs."

"Not too different from some of our guys," I said.

Diego didn't agree. "Our men, at least the ones in my finance and science classes, are smarter and speak better. Every other word out of the Southie guys' mouths is 'Fuckin' this' and 'Fuckin' that.'"

"Pretty much everything goes through Doc Reilly, right?"

"Right, and Guillermo will know how to deal with them if he has to."

"And Esmeralda is as innocent as ever?" I asked.

"Oh yes," Diego assured me. "As long as the monthly rent's paid, she doesn't ask too many questions."

As I hung up my clothes and unpacked my toiletries in the quaint bathroom, Diego called Esmeralda.

"How are you?" he asked. "I hope your arthritis is under control."

"I recognize your raspy voice. So when will I see you?" I could overhear Esmeralda's response on the speakerphone.

"In an hour. A Colombian friend is visiting, and his mother's a friend of Guillermo's mother. Is he there?"

"He's at the courthouse now and should return soon."

"Good, we'll wait for Guillermo."

We drove out of Boston proper in Diego's rented Lincoln Town Car and onto the tree-lined streets of Brookline.

"This city's unruly street design couldn't be more different from the grid-like pattern of downtown Medellín," Diego said.

"I'd get lost," I admitted. "How did you ever learn your way around?"

"Remember, I stay in Lexington with my brother and had to find my way."

"Why'd they choose Lexington?"

"Life is quiet there, but they're also close to Cambridge."

"Their high school certainly served Pablo well." I gazed out the car window and commented on the row upon row of two-family wooden houses, most of which were in need of repainting. "Is this a working-class neighborhood? I thought Brookline was wealthy."

"It's mainly full of rich people. This is a more affordable area," Diego said.

"We're almost at Kent Street near Esmeralda's rooming house." After I looked up from the map, I changed the subject. "So why does Guillermo want to work with us?"

"He wants to make lots of money so he can buy a small finca in Colombia."

"Yes, life comes down to that, owning a finca in the countryside, away from the chaos of Medellín or Bogotá," I said. "I once had the same dream."

Sure, I'm grateful that Don Pedro set me up in a legitimate business in Colombia, yet with this new assignment, my father-in-law's using me to solidify the Boston drug connection. This was not the life I had imagined for myself. I'm a family man and a lover of art and beauty. Now, each day when I awake, I have to decide which world I need to heed first. Unfortunately, my behind-the-scenes obligations often take precedence over my hotel management work. My dream has turned into a some-times-dangerous reality.

Diego found a parking space in front of Esmeralda's boardinghouse. It was an unadorned three-story wooden structure with a pitched roof and a small front yard. Although its blue paint was peeling a little, it was a respectable building, not far from Brookline Village. I rang the doorbell.

A heavy-set, middle-aged woman in her fifties answered the door. She gave us a big smile. "You must be the gentlemen from Medellín," she said in a deep voice. Esmeralda was from Bogotá, and for as long as anyone could remember, there had been a rivalry between our two Colombian cities.

"I'm from the city of eternal spring," I said, with a friendly wink.

Diego gave her a bear hug.

"Come in, come in," she said. "Would you like aguardiente? Or do you prefer tea?"

"Tea with milk in this chilly fall weather."

"The same," Diego said.

We sat in comfortable chairs in Esmeralda's living room, waiting for Guillermo, making small talk about Cartagena's beautiful beaches, the growing number of poor Latinos in the Boston area, who were mainly from Puerto Rico, and the chances of the Red Sox winning the pennant, a pretty unavoidable topic in that town.

I could imagine myself living there happily, taking evening courses at one of the many local colleges, having a simple day job, such as working as a Spanish instructor at Berlitz, and returning in the late evening to Mama Esmeralda's warm hospitality.

A key rattling in the door's lock roused me from my fantasy. Guillermo walked into the room, greeting Esmeralda with a kiss on both cheeks and shaking hands with Diego and me. He was tall and thin and had fine features. His thick, dark hair with its slight cowlick and his silver-framed glasses disguised the fun-loving part of his personality.

When Diego had told me that Guillermo loved to dance the salsa, spending at least one evening a week at a Cuban nightclub in nearby Jamaica Plain, I felt envious of his freedom.

Esmeralda left to get Guillermo a cup of tea. She brought it back with fresh pastries from the New Paris Bakery on Cypress Street, and we ate and drank companionably for a short time until Esmeralda excused herself to cook the evening meal.

We went to Guillermo's room to talk privately. He offered us the two straight-backed chairs that faced his narrow bed.

"How's Don Pedro?" he asked. He told us that he had grown up hearing his uncle Tomas rave about the man's generosity.

"In good health," I replied. "He sends his greetings." Then I got straight to business. "Don Pedro needs to raise the wholesale price of cocaine. Fighting against the American-sponsored crackdown has been costly. How will Doc Reilly react to a 10 percent increase?"

Guillermo looked surprised and squirmed in his chair. "I'll have to ask him."

"No, it's not negotiable," I said.

I could feel my Adam's apple moving up and down, as it often did when I'm under pressure.

"You must find a way to tell Doc that he's sure to accept. We've worked with him for a long time, and we don't want him looking for other suppliers."

"I see," Guillermo said. "I'll need your help. Doc Reilly's a brutal guy underneath his suave posture."

"That's why we're here," Diego said.

Guillermo listened while I recited the facts and figures pertaining to the cartel's increased security needs, as well as bribes and payoffs.

"Now I understand why you need to raise the price. Without revealing the facts, I'll tell Doc Reilly this is serious."

Diego and I gave each other a thumbs-up. It was clear that Guillermo was trustworthy, largely because of his uncle Tomas. It also helped that this young man presented himself well.

We began to hatch a plan.

"I hear he enjoys being with the Boston elite," Diego said.

"That's true," Guillermo responded.

"So why don't you take Doc to dinner at Locke-Ober?" I told Guillermo that I'd heard it was where Boston establishment's most influential businessmen dined. "You can discuss our need to raise the price of 'oil,' giving a broad overview of the facts and figures. The street price is low right now, so you can remind him there won't be any buyer resistance. You can also allude to a generous gift Don Pedro has sent for him, a small antique gun."

"I think he'll go for it," Guillermo said.

"On the drive home, you can give Doc his present if an agreement has been reached," I said.

"I understand he enjoys expensive presents, just like a kid," Guillermo said.

"If you need help, call Diego," I said. "He'll be here for another two weeks, while I must leave tomorrow." I asked him to set up the dinner for next week and report back to Diego when he secured Doc's compliance. "Remember, he needs us as much as we need him."

Carlos put his feet back down on the floor before returning his notes to the top drawer of his desk. He felt good about his collaboration with Diego. Guillermo worked out well. He had persuaded Doc Reilly to agree to the new price.

Carlos brushed two pieces of lint off the sleeve of his navy blazer and left his office to meet with the staff at La Gran Conchita's conference room.

THE STING

CHAPTER TWENTY-SEVEN

June 2, 1990

Planning the Sting

On Saturday morning at 9:00 a.m., Jaime drove Portia from the hotel to a daylong meeting with Sean and Roberto Castellano at Castellano's place. After Sean's phone call the morning before, Roberto had agreed that Portia should definitely be present at this sensitive meeting, although having a confidential informant there didn't follow normal protocol. Besides, Roberto had told Julian that he had come to respect her integrity and intelligence. "She's a damn smart woman," he said. Portia was flattered when she learned about this. At the same time, she was annoyed that Roberto could call Julian by his real name when she needed to call him Sean while they were in Medellín.

Portia wondered about the planning session as the verdant scenery of cultivated hills bursting with coffee and tomato plants caught her eye. She gazed out the car window and her mind went back to the frustrating conversation she had earlier that morning with Julio. He had told her that Aaron Stockwell wasn't happy with the frames for his new pieces. She would need to find the time to call Aaron and try to placate him. She knew she could not ask Stansky to do this for her. He was still angry. Besides, Aaron would want to hear from her.

Portia settled back in her seat and allowed Dizzy Gillespie's mellow rendition of "I Can't Get Started" to invade her thoughts.

At Castellano's villa, the three of them sat around the mahogany dining table. With the sun streaming into the room through the villa's picture windows, a stranger might have mistaken the scene for a friendly get-together, instead of a tense meeting for a sting operation.

After thanking her for taking the photos and for drawing the map that showed the out-of-plumb wall in the bedroom, Roberto told Portia, "We want you out of the country before the raid takes place."

"I appreciate your concern for my safety," she said. "But I'd like to be there. I've come this far—why not let me see it through?"

"Portia, we couldn't have done this without you. You must understand that we're responsible for you." Roberto crossed himself. "What if . . . heaven forbid . . . something were to go wrong?"

"All right, I get it. When will it be? I'd like to keep our new museum date with Colombine on Monday afternoon. We need to be authentic and show our commitment to becoming experts in Colombian art."

"No problem. The raid will take place after that date."

"It's a relief that our cover still holds. By the way, Colombine's invited me for dinner at the Restaurante Hatoviejo tomorrow evening."

"Portia, are you crazy?" Roberto asked, his eyebrows arched in disbelief. "Why would you risk dining in downtown Medellín?"

"I can't say no. She's helped me so much."

"We've managed to get through this without an incident. Why not have dinner at your hotel?" Roberto looked at Julian for support, but Julian shrugged his shoulders.

"Colombine wants me to experience the local cuisine. She says the food's outstanding. Besides, I have a bodyguard."

"We've pushed our luck with getting you into the villa. I'm not happy about this unnecessary risk."

"I'll be fine," she said. "Promise, I'll be fine."

"Okay, Portia, you win." Roberto calmed down and turned his attention to the raid. "We'll organize the break-in at Carlos Alfonso's finca with the help of Pepé, one of his former house guards. Julian will be in charge of getting the paintings out of Colombia and onto a cargo flight to Boston. And he will also handle the paperwork and be the liaison with the Colombian customs officials."

"How did you manage to lure Pepé to your side? I'm even more impressed with your skills than when we first met in Buenos Aires," Portia said.

"After fifteen years of investigative work and hanging out in more bars than I care to remember, I've become pretty good at sizing up talent," Roberto said. He told them that he had also learned how to make offers that couldn't be refused. He briefed Julian and Portia on how he had met Pepé downtown in the Berlin bar two weeks ago. "After three Dos Equis and a generous offer of $100,000, Pepé agreed to work with us. He told me that Gianfranco, the chef, confided in him about all the activities at the finca. That's how he found out Maria and Carlos were scheduled to fly to Caracas next Thursday, June 7, for a two-day business trip."

"Wow," Portia said.

"Well done," Julian said.

"We can execute our raid the day after they leave," Roberto said. "Pepé, along with two of the police, will also help contain the house staff once the police are inside the villa. I gave him $10,000 to show our good faith. The rest will be delivered to him by one of our agents when he's safely out of the country."

"Are you sure he's really working for us?" Julian asked.

"Pepé was relegated to the kitchen as a dishwasher after Carlos found him asleep beside the front door," Roberto said. "His demotion hurt his pride and his wallet. I'm convinced we've given him enough motivation to help us succeed. In addition, he has an exit plan. He intends to live with a close cousin in Puerto Rico."

"He had better come through. Who's paying for this?" Portia asked.

"The Gardner Museum," Julian replied. "When you consider the paintings are worth at least $300 million, a hundred grand isn't an unreasonable amount."

Roberto continued the briefing, explaining that Carlos and Maria usually went to Caracas at the end of the month, but this trip was planned to coincide with their children's summer vacation. Maria's mother would take some of the Alfonso servants and spend a week with Toto and Diana at their beach house in Cartagena. "Their travel plans are perfect for us . . . Portia, you should leave on June 7, one day before the raid."

"I'll ask Rupert to drive me to the airport." Portia still hoped to convince Roberto to let her participate in the raid, but she thought it best to acquiesce for the moment.

Roberto walked to a flip chart on an easel nearby and pulled up the cover, revealing a photo. He pointed to a blowup of the aerial view of the Alfonso finca, which Interpol had taken a few days ago from a helicopter.

"As you can see, there's a dirt road through the woods to the right of the main road, which leads to the patio off the front door. The road is wide enough for a van. If all goes according to plan, my assistant and I will drive the van inside after the local police have subdued the guard at the entrance right off the country road."

"How will the police be able to restrain the guard? Won't he be suspicious when a police car drives up?"

"Good questions, Henderson." Roberto explained that the raid would occur at 5:00 a.m., when the night guard would be sleepy. One of the policemen would tell him they had received an emergency call from Carlos in Venezuela. He will tell the guard that his boss was upset that a valuable pre-Columbian object, a gold bird, had been stolen from the villa. Suspecting the robbery was an inside job, Carlos had asked the police to interview the staff at once.

"Will he fall for that?" Portia asked.

"We think so. We're counting on surprise. If they can't engage him in conversation, they'll handcuff him right away and shove a sedative down his throat to make him quiet. Then they'll proceed to the villa, where they'll repeat the same procedure with the guard at the front door. A second police car will follow once they hear the radio confirmation from the first."

"Can you trust the local police?" Julian took off his wire-rimmed spectacles and rubbed his eyes.

"As you know, Interpol often works with the local police, and fortunately I have a good relationship with the police chief. I interviewed their best men last week."

He told Portia and Julian that, for a long time, the police had been trying to find a legitimate excuse to arrest Carlos Alfonso for his role in drug trafficking. "Frankly, the police chief would have preferred to target Don Pedro, a much bigger prize. But, as I said before, he's considered a hero in the barrio, and the chief was afraid of inciting a riot if they arrested him."

"Isn't it possible Don Pedro has been bribing him for years?" Julian asked.

Roberto agreed that Don Pedro had probably tried, but so far this chief hadn't seemed too interested in money. "You see, a nephew of his was killed by one of Don Pedro's henchmen, and he has a personal vendetta against him. He's also a good friend of the new mayor, who wants to rid Medellín of corruption. Both officials must be aware of the American commitment to stopping the drug war in Colombia, although we can't be sure of their feelings about Americans. They might be ambivalent about your country's involvement, but I'm Argentinian," he said.

Before Roberto could discuss the next page in the flip chart, Julian interrupted him. "Will the guard believe Carlos called the police from Caracas? Perhaps the police should say they received a call from Ludovico," Julian suggested.

"No," Roberto said. "We need Carlos's name to open that front door. The police will move quickly, before the guard has a chance to think."

Now Roberto turned to the next page, which featured a crude drawing of two cars and one van. Names of the Interpol contractors were listed beneath each car.

He told them there would be two police cars and a van driven by his assistant. The first police car would be driven by the two cops who would subdue the guards. The second police car, followed by the van, would drive through the road in the woods. This car would have three cops and two Interpol contractors, including one who was a master locksmith. "Sounds pretty straightforward, doesn't it?" he asked, before turning to the next illustration, an enlarged photo of Portia's map of the Alfonso villa.

"Once the guard at the front door is drugged, we'll have his keys. Thanks to Portia, we know where he keeps them. My team and the five local police will use his keys to enter the villa. The police will go upstairs to Ludovico's room, here," Roberto said, pointing to a green star on the map. "Once again we'll have surprise on our side, and five cops, so it shouldn't be too difficult to overpower Ludovico, sedate him, and then seal his mouth with duct tape."

"What about the other servants?" Portia asked.

He pointed to a red star on Portia's map, indicating the servants' quarters. "At the same time the cops are sedating Ludovico, two Interpol contractors will go here, to the other side of the villa, where they'll meet Pepé. Together they'll gather the four remaining staff and put them in a large bedroom with an adjoining bath. The servants will be left with food and water before the bedroom door is locked. The other hired help will have been given the weekend off to spend time with their families because the Alfonsos will be out of town, or they will have accompanied Lucia Martinez and her grandchildren to Cartagena. After Carlos and Maria have been apprehended in Caracas, the police will release the servants. Of course, they'll ask for their cooperation."

"There's certainly no need for them to suffer," Portia said.

"They won't dare cooperate. Don Pedro will have them killed if they do," Julian said. "They probably know this already, but you'd better remind the police to wear ski masks, Roberto."

"The servants will have no choice." Roberto got back to the briefing. "While three police officers drive Ludovico to the police station, where he will be questioned about Carlos, Pepé, with the help of the remaining officer, will be standing guard over the servants. At the same time, our Interpol contractors, including the locksmith, will look for hidden electronic devices in the master suite. The locksmith uses a handheld instrument that's something like a metal detector. There has to be a buzzer somewhere near the painting that will make one of the walls slide open to reveal the hidden room, possibly behind that painting, *The Dead Student*. Hopefully, the paintings will be in the hidden room. I trust Portia's profile of the thief, so once we locate the paintings, my two Interpol contractors will bring them down to the foyer, where they'll cover each one with a plain white sheet and tape the corners. Then they'll carry them to the waiting van. I have two heavy canvas bags, and our contractors will put the bronze eagle in one bag and the bronze Chinese beaker in the other to protect them from possible damage. I'll keep watch from the van with a pair of high-powered binoculars in case there's any unexpected trouble. I figure the whole operation shouldn't take much more than two hours."

"I hope that's all the time it takes," Portia said. She couldn't help feeling nervous.

Roberto stared at her. "We are Interpol, and when I say two hours, it's two hours."

"Okay, Roberto, don't be so touchy."

"I'll rendezvous with Julian at my villa, where we'll assemble the crates to hold the paintings. After the crates are carefully loaded, Julian will board the prearranged cargo plane and accompany them home. Henderson, have you already filled out the paperwork?"

"Yes."

"Sean, please keep in touch with me," Portia said. "I'll be a wreck until I hear from you."

"I will."

Portia noticed that the sun streaming into the room illuminated the silver streaks in Roberto's black hair, making him look even more distinguished.

"If by some chance the paintings aren't there, we will quickly leave and I'll explain everything to the local police. We'll all get on the next plane out of here."

Portia gasped. "Oh my God, I hadn't thought about that."

"We always have a plan B." Roberto spoke with confidence as he looked at Portia. "But as I said, I have faith in Portia's work, so after the operation is completed, I'll call the police in Caracas, and Carlos and Maria will be apprehended before the plane boards."

"Well done, Roberto," Portia said with a sigh of relief. "Thank you for your belief in me. Please call and let me know how the raid went and what happens after that."

"It would be best if Julian calls. I must remain in the shadows."

CHAPTER TWENTY-EIGHT

June 3, 1990

Risking Another Downtown Dinner

On the drive back to La Gran Conchita the previous evening, Portia had asked Sean if he could convince Roberto to give her a role in the raid . . . no matter how small.

"It's impossible," he said.

"Does this have anything to do with my being a woman?"

"No," he said. "It's that you haven't had experience in the field. Something could go wrong."

"Okay, I get it." Portia looked down at her folded hands and realized how much she hated leaving before their work was finished. At the same time, though, she missed Alexa and Stansky.

Sean asked about her upcoming dinner date with Colombine.

"It's at 8:00 p.m., and I'll be back at the hotel around 10:30 p.m."

"Promise you'll call as soon as you return," he said. "We're concerned."

"Promise."

Portia's flight was scheduled for the morning of June 7, leaving her four more days in the city. At dinner she would ask Colombine for ideas on how she might spend her time, aside from her personal tour of the museum. They would need to arrange a meeting where Portia could give her the final list of Colombian paintings she wanted to show her New York client. Portia planned to bring back slides of those paintings and a price list. And while she focused on activities that strengthened her ruse, Portia would have dropped everything if Sean and Roberto had asked for her input before the raid.

As she entered the restaurant that Sunday evening, the high decibel level in the dimly lit room told Portia that an exuberant crowd was inside. This was not the kind of place she would have picked for dinner, but she wanted to honor her friend's request. She looked around and saw Colombine waving to her from the back. As Portia threaded her way around the tables, Jaime headed toward the bar, where he promised to nurse only one beer, or maybe two, until she was ready to leave.

Colombine rose, and they traded kisses on both cheeks. After Portia sat down, she leaned over to smell the white roses in a crystal vase on the table. This gesture soothed her. She hated deceiving Colombine and Maria, but if her work could help recover the Gardner paintings and apprehend the criminals, it would far outweigh any guilt she might have.

"Colombine, you're a dear. I've so enjoyed getting to know you better on this trip."

"The pleasure's mine." Colombine told Portia that Obregón and Caballero were both happy that Portia's New York client might want to buy at least one of their paintings. "They're thrilled you're taking some of their drawings on consignment as well as slides of their paintings. By the way, Sean is charming. He's so knowledgeable about art. Much more than I ever imagined. I'm looking forward to our private tour."

Our ruse has worked, Portia thought.

"Thanks to you and your art connections, our trip has been marvelous. Sean and I can't wait to visit the museum with you."

"Your appreciation means everything to me." Colombine handed Portia a menu.

"Thank you for going out of your way with the museum staff so that we can be there on Monday when no one else is around."

As Colombine ordered the restaurant's specialty—*plato montañero*, a mixture of ground beef, eggs, and fried pork skin—for both of them, the waiter glanced at Portia. "You're in good hands," he said, indicating that Colombine was a regular there. Portia agreed with him, then said to Colombine, "I like the service here almost as much as at the Salón Versalles."

"The two best restaurants in town happen to be located in downtown Medellín," Colombine said. "I can't allow a nasty drug war to get in the way of enjoying our delicious cuisine."

"Evidently, you're not the only one who feels that way." Portia swept an arm toward the crowded room. She leaned forward in her chair. "Are all the men at the bar bodyguards?"

"Probably . . . That's our way of life these days. Hopefully not forever. Someday life will return to normal. Our new mayor's committed to ending the drug war."

"So I hear. I certainly hope he succeeds. It must be difficult to live with the constant fear of danger."

"You'd be surprised what you get used to," Colombine said, then turned the conversation back to art. "I was pleased you liked Luis Caballero's latest drawings."

"I think they're dramatic and subtle at the same time."

She told Portia how pleased she was that she could see his work at her gallery and the Obregóns at the Alfonsos' villa. "They own his most important paintings."

"They blew me away. Again, it was thanks to you I could see them."

"It was all Maria's doing. She took an immediate liking to you, and then you saved her life. It was a huge compliment to dine at their home." She reminded Portia that Carlos could be quite possessive of his family. "He really doesn't like entertaining guests."

Portia's heart fluttered at the thought that she might have been prevented from gaining entry into the Alfonsos' villa. She took several more sips of wine.

"Their villa is beautiful, and their art collection is fantastic. What a lovely woman."

"She's my best client, and, as you know, we're old friends. One of the many qualities I admire in Maria is she doesn't flaunt her wealth. Didn't I tell you that you'd like her?"

"You did. I'm so impressed with her generosity." Then Portia leaned closer to Colombine. "You've told me that Don Pedro is ruthless," she whispered. "How is that possible when Maria is so gracious?"

"He behaves one way as a father and another as the cartel boss. As you know, my husband has always been fiercely critical of his drug activities, which has put a strain on my relationship with Maria."

"I can only imagine . . . Yet your friendship has lasted."

"Thanks to Lucia, Maria's mother." She told Portia that Lucia came from a cultured family and had been the major influence in her daughter's life. "Maria is a loyal friend, continually going out of her way for former school chums like me. When I had my appendix removed last spring, she came to visit me in the hospital every day. And she's devoted to her children and her charity work."

"Wow . . . she does it all," Portia said. "Is her husband involved with the cartel?"

"Carlos's managing the hotels has nothing to do with Don Pedro's cocaine operation."

"Glad to hear that," Portia said and took the last bite of her meal. It was as tasty as Colombine had described. She thought that Don Pedro and Carlos had done a good job of fooling the Colombians. Or perhaps Colombine was invested in protecting her best friend's husband.

"What did you think of him?" Colombine asked.

"He's sharp, witty, and passionate about art."

"He's sometimes so over the top, I wonder if art's more important to him than anything else." Colombine rummaged in her purse for a lipstick tube and a small, heart-shaped mirror before putting a fresh application on her lips.

"We got along very well," Portia said. "I also met their children. Toto's bright, terribly precocious, and Diana's adorable."

"They're dear. The entire family dotes on them."

The two women sat and planned the next few days: several visits to galleries, a lunch with Luisa Heilbrun, a day excursion to the Andes, and the highly anticipated museum tour.

Colombine insisted on paying the bill. "You're in my country," she said. Portia thanked her friend for the delicious dinner before heading to the bar and tapping Jaime on the shoulder. Then both women and their respective bodyguards walked out into the starry night.

Across the street, Portia noticed two unshaven men smoking under a streetlight. One passed a dark object to the other. Jaime put a protective arm around her as they hurried past them into the car. She could feel their eyes following her. Once inside, Portia felt angry with herself for taking this unnecessary risk as the car sped toward El Poblado. Roberto and Sean were right. She should have met with Colombine in a safer place. Although she couldn't help wondering if Colombine would have been as open with her in a more formal restaurant that was not of her choosing.

When Portia returned to the hotel, she called Sean, as promised. "I'm back. Colombine sends her best, and we have great plans for the next few days."

"Well done," a sleepy Sean replied. "Now get a good night's rest. You deserve it."

CHAPTER TWENTY-NINE

June 4, 1990

Colombian Culture at Its Best

On Monday afternoon, Portia and Sean had a wonderful time exploring the Museo de Antioquia. In her docent role, Colombine told them when each work of art had been executed and what had inspired the artist. Portia was surprised by how much more she liked Botero's paintings and sculptures now that she was seeing such a broad spectrum of his work. On the large plaza in front of the museum she was awed by a sculpture of an oversized masculine head that was impossible to miss. Inside, she was charmed by Botero's Latin American street scenes and his clever portrait of Cézanne as a Boteroesque figure holding an artist's palette as he stands in front of his canvas. She had dismissed Botero before as an artist whose whimsical portrayals of rotund people blurred the boundaries between reality and fiction, but as they walked from one gallery to another, Portia and Sean agreed that Botero deserved his outstanding international reputation. As she, Colombine, and Sean stood in one of the well-lit viewing rooms, she pointed at the

Botero painting of a large policeman holding a tiny whip as he sat on a small horse. "His sense of humor is infectious," she said and burst out laughing. She had almost forgotten how good it felt to laugh.

The Obregóns at the museum were dramatic, but none of them equaled the political ones she had seen at the Alfonsos' villa. "Maria and Carlos own the best," Portia said.

"They weren't afraid to experiment," Colombine said.

Sean had brought a small magnifying glass so that he could read the artist's signature on each painting. It made him look like an official art expert.

That evening, Portia and Sean had an early dinner at La Gran Conchita and agreed that Carlos was right about the hotel's food being exceptional. Gianfranco had cooked a superior sancocho, a traditional soup with large pieces of meat, tubers, and vegetables floating in a broth, topped off with a few sprigs of cilantro. The next course was a moist roasted hen served with rice and plantain. They went to bed feeling well-fed but also anxious about the upcoming raid scheduled for early Friday morning.

They were sound asleep in their rooms when shortly after 11:00 p.m. a siren woke them. The blaring noise sounded like an air-raid drill . . . only worse. As they raced down the stairs, along with the other guests, to the brightly lit reception area, all the lights, as well as some strobes that the police had brought with them, were on full blast. Portia felt terrified that their real purpose had been discovered.

"We've been found out," she whispered in his ear, but Sean shook his head no.

The mood at the normally peaceful hotel was chaotic as guests poured out of their rooms wearing white terry cloth bathrobes with the hotel insignia stitched onto the right breast pockets. A tall, willowy blonde and her short, red-haired, big-faced partner looked disheveled and disoriented. Portia couldn't help wondering who they were. They looked vaguely familiar. She couldn't place them until she suddenly remembered a scene in *The Public Enemy*, an old James Cagney film, where he had played a tough guy who pushed a grapefruit into his costar's face. The resemblance was uncanny.

After they arrived at the reception area, Sean and Portia overheard Carlos having a heated argument with two local policemen. The police were young and brash, waving their guns in his direction, as they demanded they must conduct a room-by-room search. Carlos said that the young Brazilian man they were looking for had checked out earlier that evening. The police informed the guests that the thief had been stealing small valuable objects from elegant jewelry and luggage shops in the upscale neighborhood sometime during the late morning. His booty included a Louis Vuitton briefcase, a Bulgari watch, Cartier earrings, and a large emerald ring.

"He had good taste," Portia whispered again to Sean. He put a finger to his lips.

The police acted as if they did not believe Carlos and said none of the guests were allowed to leave. They locked all the doors. There were fifteen guests milling around the reception area, some smoking, some drinking wine to calm their nerves, and some leafing through old magazines. The room, which normally smelled of the fresh roses that Maria ordered every day, reeked of cigarette smoke. Despite Sean's assurances, Portia was terrified that Carlos had engineered this so that the police could arrest them under some phony pretext. Although the hotel was air-conditioned, she was perspiring.

Finally, the police left and they were allowed to go back to their rooms. Carlos apologized to everyone. Portia had a sleepless night.

The following morning at breakfast, she overheard the news that the police had found the Brazilian thief at the airport. Both Sean and Portia looked exhausted yet relieved as they ate spicy huevos rancheros and drank brimming cups of Colombian coffee.

Over the next couple of days, Sean and Portia made the rounds of galleries with Colombine. They had a marvelous lunch with Luisa Heilbrun at their favorite outdoor restaurant in the InterContinental. At the last moment, Rupert was able to get away from the bank and join them. Sean found them both great company. "So intelligent and fun," he said. Portia felt grateful that they could have pleasant moments interspersed with the almost-constant tension.

Sean checked in with Roberto every day on the plans for the raid. He was assured that everything was under control, but with the passing of each day, Portia's nerves became increasingly frayed. Her yoga practice was of no help.

On June 6, the day before she was scheduled to leave, Portia ran into Maria at the hotel. They exchanged greetings, and Maria asked about her project of finding artwork. Portia told her about some of the gallery visits Colombine had arranged. She asked after Carlos, Toto, and Diana and promised to drop her a note when she was back in the States.

Portia went shopping that day to buy gifts. She found the perfect leather wallet for Stansky and a funny papier-mâché pig for Alexa. That night she called Stansky from the café phone booth across from the hotel. She forgot to ask Jaime to accompany her.

"Alexa is sick," he said. "She's running a temperature and wants her mother."

"Let me speak with her." Portia felt flooded with guilt.

"Okay."

"Sweetheart, I'll be home very soon," Portia said to her daughter.

"Don't worry, Mom. I'll get better."

"I miss you and can't wait to see you." She put her lips together and made a kissing sound before saying goodbye.

After she hung up, Portia's eyebrows knitted together in concern for her daughter. She ran back to her room at the hotel on the lookout for the shadowy man. She sighed in relief that he wasn't there.

She had entertained the possibility of showing up for the raid and surprising Roberto, but now she knew she absolutely had to get back to Alexa.

On Thursday morning, June 7, the gallant Rupert chauffeured her to the airport. As his Mercedes sedan sped toward Jose Maria Cordova International, she smiled at him. "I'm so pleased that I've found artwork for my New York client. I'll also be representing a few Colombian artists in Boston."

"That's great," he said. "I knew you'd be impressed."

Portia had been away for seventeen days in all and was longing to return to the familiarity and safety of her own home. She really needed to be there for Alexa and prayed she was feeling better.

Rupert turned to look at her when he stopped for a red light. "I'm glad your trip was fruitful. Thank goodness you didn't run into any serious difficulties."

"How could I, with you and Colombine shepherding me around?"

"More to the point, I was relieved that you and your friend, Sean Findlay—how is he by the way?—hired good bodyguards. I didn't tell you before, but I checked out Jaime's references when you gave me his name," he said.

"You're wonderful. Thank you, Rupert."

While they talked, Rupert kept his eyes on the road. "Now that you've been here, I'm sure you realize you can't be too careful. Did you hear about the car bomb that exploded this morning near the Museo El Castillo?"

"Sadly, I overheard a conversation about it at breakfast."

"Yes, a five-year-old girl and her mother were killed because they happened to be standing nearby," Rupert said as he gripped the steering wheel.

"What a horrible tragedy. It makes me very sad." Portia numbly gazed out the window at the passing landscape, while Rupert lamented the bad luck of innocent bystanders.

"You asked about Sean," Portia continued. "He's planning to return to New York in two days. He needs to tie up some business here. He sold most of his Old Master drawings through our wonderful Colombine, so of course he's very pleased with his trip."

"He's charming," Rupert said. "Although I thought the way he tipped his hat was a bit much."

Portia couldn't help laughing. "Don't you think his knowledge of art makes up for a little pretense?" she asked.

"If you say so," Rupert replied.

When she arrived at her gate, Portia was surprised to see Sean there.

"I had to make sure you got on the plane," he told her.

"Finding artwork in Medellín wouldn't have been as successful without you." Portia held out her hand for him to shake.

"You're the one who did all the groundwork," he said, after they shook hands.

"You made it happen."

"Bon voyage, Portia. I'll be in touch." He tipped his hat and waved goodbye as she was ready to board.

What a guy, Portia thought as she entered the plane. *He's a maverick* and *he's gallant.* Fortunately, she was not attracted to him, but she sure appreciated his good qualities.

On the plane, Portia ordered a glass of champagne and drank it in one long and delicious gulp. Then she took a short nap and awoke refreshed. She would have many stories to tell Stansky, Alexa, and Paul Travigne. Paul had encouraged her to become an art sleuth, and because of him, she had experienced the greatest adventure of her life. Her few conversations with him had been so supportive, unlike the ones with Stansky, who had let her know in his gruff voice just how irritated he was with her. "You missed a parent-teacher night," he had said when she called him the day before to remind him that she'd be home today.

She finally realized that Stansky's irritation was because he feared for her safety. And she was also aware that it was easier to have a pleasant conversation with a new friend than a worried, critical husband. Perhaps her painful divorce from Henry had made her more mature.

While she was in Medellín, the possibility of death had hovered around her. Now that she was safely on the plane, she took out her photos of Stansky and Alexa and almost cried as she touched them.

Portia sat next to an attractive woman in her late twenties named Gail. She had been dozing again when she heard a loud click that sounded like a gunshot. She opened her eyes in shock to see Gail bolting the brass locks on her leather briefcase after she'd taken out some papers.

"Please excuse me," Gail apologized. "I must finish some work before we land in Miami."

"No problem." Portia noted that her seatmate wore a sizable diamond ring on her left hand. An hour later, they began to chat about their work and their respective cities, and Portia complimented her on her beautiful ring.

Lunch arrived, and Gail talked nonstop. "I'm having problems with my Argentinian fiancé, Alejandro. He's a businessman, and I suspect he's already married."

"Why do you think that?"

"Sometimes he whispers into the phone when he thinks I'm sleeping. And he's never available on weekends."

"He sounds married to me. Why don't you confront him?"

"I don't know." Gail cleared her throat several times before taking more bites of her chicken salad sandwich.

Portia looked at her watch to check the time. She thought Julian must be with Castellano at his villa, going over the details of tomorrow's early morning raid.

Over their meal, she learned more than she wanted to know about Gail's love life. For a rash moment, in the spirit of sharing confidences, Portia was tempted to ask her seatmate if she'd ever run into the Alfonso family, but she knew that would be unwise. One could never be sure whom the stranger might know. Her small amount of FBI training had taught her to be cautious. She had almost slipped because her glass of bubbly made her light-headed. Now she understood why FBI employees weren't allowed to drink on the job.

When Gail finally got back to her work, Portia mused about Carlos and Maria. She liked him and was very fond of Maria. The morning before she met Colombine at the Museo de Antioquia, she'd overheard two maids chatting in the hallway about their boss being *un hombre simpatico*. As she passed their cleaning carts on her way to the elevator, they were still singing his praises with approving looks on their faces. She wondered what he had done for them, because they now liked him much more than when she first arrived. She knew the maids' now-positive opinions didn't change Carlos's being a sexual harasser and, despite Colombine's beliefs to the contrary, involved in the drug trade. Roberto's local contacts had verified those rumors. And no matter how gracious Maria was, Portia suspected that she knew about the theft and had been Carlos's accomplice to the crime, either before or after the fact. *Yet the forces of dark and light are not at work in Maria. Only in Carlos and in the art he probably stole*, she wrote in her notebook now that she was out of the country.

Portia had seen that Maria worked hard to give back to her community. Perhaps, she thought, as a way of compensating for her father's nefarious dealings. Regardless of her motivations, Portia had been impressed by Maria's support of local artists. She bought their work and helped them obtain museum and gallery shows. Her devotion to charity work at the local hospital and museums was well known in town and greatly appreciated by the appropriate beneficiaries. Portia had been touched by Maria's dedication. They had formed a real bond over the past two weeks.

Taking into account that Maria seemed to love Carlos and that most of his employees respected him, Portia imagined that he must have some humanitarian values. But he was also a selfish and conniving thief. Now that she knew more about both of them, she was certain that the paintings Carlos had chosen to steal from the Gardner were ones that embodied the clash between the light and dark forces he found within himself. The raging conflict between wanting to do good while being tempted by evil was undoubtedly the story of his life. What was once her hypothetical profile had become real.

As the plane continued to soar toward Miami, it was hard for Portia to contain her mixed emotions about what she had just been through. Another glass of champagne nudged her back to sleep.

CHAPTER THIRTY

June 7, 1990

Safe Return

As the plane prepared for landing, Portia's rapid heartbeat told her just how excited she was to see Alexa and Stansky again.

She remembered when she and Stansky had first met at the party he had held in his loftlike townhouse, and his eyes stayed focused on hers. It felt like minutes, but it must have been seconds. And then their first date at Nadia's, a local Lebanese restaurant, where they had talked nonstop until the owner asked them to leave when it was time to close.

Then they went to the Averof, a Greek restaurant in Cambridge, on a hot summer night. When Stansky picked her up, he was wearing a blue-and-white Greek fisherman's shirt for the occasion. "It does bring out the blue in your eyes," she teased.

"Very funny."

Stansky parked the car, and as they walked toward the restaurant, he told Portia he wanted to know all about her life. "Pretend I'm your shrink," he said.

"My former shrink told me I reminded him of Shirley Temple with clenched teeth," she said. "It must have been my dimples."

"You also have a photogenic face," Stansky said. "Do you tap-dance?"

"Now *you're* funny." Portia blushed a little while she fixed the barrette in her hair.

As they ate their egg lemon soup, Stansky asked, "What was it like to grow up Italian American?"

"Mostly wonderful. Although I suppose my Calabrian grandfather transmitted his fear to us because, all through my adolescence, I sometimes had nightmares about Mafia killings." She told him that prejudice against Italians was strong then, and that some of her high school friends used to ask if her father was in the Mafia. "Imagine . . . they thought every Italian kid had a Mafia connection."

"Unfortunately, the same prejudice existed in Pepper Pike. What did your dad say when you told him?"

"He got angry. He was a successful lawyer and was proud of his Italian heritage." She told him that Mario Cuomo, who was representing resident groups in Queens at the time, was her dad's hero. "I'd have to beg my father not to go to my school and talk with the principal about how I was being stereotyped."

"That's touching." Stansky put his hands behind his head and leaned back in his chair as comfortably as if he were in his own home.

Portia had fond memories of her courtship with Stansky. He had shown compassion toward her, and until the Gardner robbery had encouraged her to take risks. She needed to remember this.

As she found her way to baggage claim, she saw them waiting. She ran toward Alexa, who looked a little wan, and Stansky, who was wearing his blue-and-white shirt, her favorite. They surrounded her with bear hugs. Stansky pressed his lips to her neck. Then he sniffed the air and said, "Our lily of the valley is back."

Portia gave Alexa a big kiss, put a hand on her cool forehead, and was thankful she no longer had a temperature. As they walked toward the car, she showed her photographs of Toto and Diana and explained a little about each child. "They want to meet you someday."

"They look nice. You got the paintings back, right?"

"Yep, I hope so. I'll know more tomorrow."

Once they were inside their car heading home, Stansky drove with his left hand on the wheel. His right hand stayed on Portia's knee. "I really missed you, baby."

Alexa brought her up to date on school activities. "Can't wait to go bowling," she said.

When they arrived home and Portia entered her Vermeer kitchen, there was a vase filled with a dozen white roses on the table. She opened the card that lay next to it. "Welcome home, princess," it said, and the signature was Nick Moretti's.

"He beat me to it," Stansky said with a grin.

CHAPTER THIRTY-ONE

June 8, 1990

The Raid

The raid took place at 5:00 a.m. that Friday, the day after Portia flew back to Boston.

Julian stayed at Castellano's villa that morning, waiting to help crate the paintings once they had been removed from the van and placed on the front lawn.

At the last moment, Castellano decided that he shouldn't stay in the van. "I'd better be on the scene, in case the unexpected happens," he told Julian just before he left.

In the end, it was a good thing he was there.

The early morning assault did take the roadside guard by surprise, and the two policemen were able to handcuff him and give him a strong sedative. The guard at the front door had been sleeping, so subduing him was not difficult, either.

When they opened the door to Ludovico's room, he was asleep. Fortunately, the bodyguard didn't sleep with his gun. He put up a fight, and it took all their strength to contain his flailing body as he tried to break loose from their grip. Ludovico tried to injure his captors by kicking his legs at their private parts. They discovered just how strong and nasty the man was before they finally handcuffed him.

"You bastards," Ludovico shouted. "When Don Pedro hears about this, you'll pay with your lives." Castellano knew this was not an idle threat. He and his five police accomplices wore ski masks so they couldn't be identified.

Finally, at 5:45 a.m. Ludovico was brought downstairs and shoved into a waiting police car, which rushed him off to the local jail, where he would be questioned about Carlos. Three of the five policemen accompanied him. Once inside the car, of course, the driver removed his mask. Ludovico was blindfolded as he sat in the back with a police officer on either side of him.

Two of the policemen stayed on at the villa to help Pepé. He had a more difficult time than expected keeping the four servants calm during their confinement. The women sobbed as they tried opening the door before they were stopped. The men looked sullen. The bedroom was large enough for them to sit on the bed or on one of the two easy chairs. Light still came into the room through the half-shaded windows. All eyes were focused on the gun Pepé wore in a holster across his chest.

When one of the men stood up to look outside, Pepé yelled at him to sit down. He grimaced, and his hands shook. Then the steely-eyed Pepé, realizing they must still be scared and uncertain about what was going to happen, reassured them their lives were not in danger.

It wasn't until the two policemen brought in buttered toast and coffee from the kitchen that the remaining Alfonso staff settled down. After this early breakfast, the policemen made light conversation with the servants, asking them about their families. They answered in short staccato sentences. Finally, Pepé was able to keep them occupied for the time being by giving them a pile of the latest magazines to read— fashion and cooking for the women and sports for the men. Castellano had been very clever in anticipating that Pepé might need such props to divert the servants' attention away from their confinement.

The Interpol contractors went in search of the stolen paintings. When they arrived upstairs, they accidentally walked right instead of left. Once they made their way into the master suite, the out-of-plumb wall was difficult to find, at first because the vertical misalignment was subtle, and there was more than one Obregón painting on the bedroom walls. After Castellano joined them, he remembered Portia's slide of Maria standing in front of *The Dead Student.*

It took the master locksmith ten minutes longer than they had anticipated to spring the lock to the hidden room. The Interpol contractor who had accompanied him kept looking at his watch with each passing minute. Castellano was biting his nails. He urged the locksmith to hurry up. Castellano had been on the walkie-talkie with his assistant, who was waiting in a parked van at the front of the villa. When the locksmith finally succeeded, they rushed into the hidden room.

They turned on the lights and stood still, awed by the beauty of the paintings.

"That man, the one whose eyes keep following me around this room, looks real," the locksmith said as he pointed to Rembrandt's *Portrait of the Artist as a Young Man* and then removed the etching from the wall.

The other Interpol contractor pointed to the scene with Christ on the boat that was about to capsize. "That's powerful," he said. He crossed himself twice before he slid Rembrandt's painting off a brass picture hook.

"I prefer the elegant Vermeer," Castellano said, carefully removing it from the wall. He wanted to spend a few minutes studying it but fought off the temptation. "We better hurry this up," he said as much to himself as the others. One of the contractors had a list of the stolen paintings on a clipboard. He called out the name of each art object and then checked it off as it was taken down from the wall or removed from a shelf. Each object was carefully wrapped in a soft cloth before it was brought downstairs.

Once the paintings were outside the front door, Castellano personally brought each one to the waiting van. When all thirteen art objects were in the van, he gave his assistant instructions: "Drive quickly. We need to get these crated at my villa and then drive them to the airport in time for them to be boarded on the cargo plane that leaves at noon."

Julian kept looking at the clock in Castellano's kitchen while the raid was taking place. He ate whatever he could find in the refrigerator: some cheese, cold cuts, fruit. He wished he could drink a beer to calm his nerves. Out of respect for FBI rules he did not give in to this temptation. He hoped that Castellano was now on his way to the villa and would arrive soon.

The raid took slightly longer than the two hours they anticipated. Castellano got the cloth-wrapped paintings to his villa at 7:35 a.m. Julian spotted his van in the driveway from the kitchen window and rushed outside to meet him.

Portia stayed up late the night before talking with Stansky about her experiences in Medellín. She was bleary-eyed when the alarm went off in the morning. She had breakfast in her Vermeer kitchen with Stansky and Alexa before they left for Buckingham Browne & Nichols.

She received the call from Julian in her office. "We got them back," he told her. "All of them. Roberto just arrived, so we can crate them now."

"I'm thrilled," she told Julian. "Congratulate Roberto on pulling this off."

Julian promised to call her again when he arrived in Boston with the paintings. He hurried to get off the phone so he could help Roberto and his contractors.

Portia reveled in their success. She had a hard time concentrating on the mail in her office, so she wandered through the gallery, stopping to straighten a frame on one of the paintings. She could not have been happier until she thought about Carlos and Maria. She hated to think of the lovely Maria languishing in a jail cell, although she did want Carlos to be punished for the theft. She knew his darling children would have a hard time adjusting to life. At least Lucia, their grandmother, could take care of them.

She tried to work in the gallery that day, but she was too high-strung to engage with potential art buyers. She asked Brenda to take over. She called Stansky to tell him the good news. They would celebrate that evening. She left early and went for a quick walk in the Public Garden before she headed home.

Once he learned that Julian had successfully boarded the cargo plane with the crated paintings, Castellano informed the Interpol office in Caracas. They had tracked down Carlos's plane reservation to Medellín. He was known to prefer commercial flights because he had more faith in the pilots' skills, and he still liked to pretend he was an ordinary citizen in some ways. He and Maria were listed on the 4:00 p.m. Avianca flight leaving from the Simón Bolívar International Airport in Maiquetía, about seventeen miles north of Caracas.

Three muscular undercover policemen arrived at the boarding area and casually walked around, on the lookout for Carlos and Maria. Castellano had sent them recent photographs, taken by one of his men who had posed as a newspaper reporter when he told Carlos and Maria he was writing a story about La Gran Conchita for the local newspaper.

The boarding area held the usual group of people. Some milled about, some sat in chairs reading a book or newspaper or just staring into space. Parents with children were trying to keep them entertained so they wouldn't cry or annoy anyone. A small handful of people waited in line at the customer service desk. Others stood against the wall. The plan was for a policeman to put a tissue to his lips after he recognized the Alfonsos. When one of them gave this signal, the other two would walk as quickly as possible, without creating any commotion, to meet him. Once they recognized their quarry, they would have to act fast.

The largest of the three men, a man with hooded eyes that made him look more like a thug than a policeman, put a tissue to his lips as he stood next to Carlos, away from the crowd, to the right of the boarding desk. At the signal, two policemen came up behind Carlos and held him tight, while the other clamped handcuffs on his wrists. Carlos looked stunned.

"What's going on?" he demanded.

"You know what," the tall man said. "Now shut up."

There was a lot of noise in the boarding area as Carlos tried to kick his way out of the hold the men had on him. Some of the women started screaming, and children began to cry. The airline attendants looked frightened. One policeman patted Carlos's body and found the gun, holster, and small revolver in his boot before they dragged him from the waiting area. They brought Carlos out of the airport and put him in the back of a waiting police car. The car raced through traffic to the maximum-security prison in Caracas.

CHAPTER THIRTY-TWO

June 8, 1990

Where's Maria?

Maria was just coming out of the ladies' room near the boarding area when she heard the commotion and saw what was happening to Carlos. Instinctively, she hurried away toward the terminal's entrance, where she found a phone booth to call her father. Without thinking, she called him on his home number, instead of at his office.

"Papa, three men have handcuffed Carlos at the gate. What shall I do?"

"My darling! This can't be happening! Listen to me. Put on your sunglasses and a scarf."

"Yes, Papa."

"Go downstairs and get out of the building. Don't run or attract attention. Take a taxi to our special place. Call me from there on the secret number, and I'll tell you where to go."

She did as she was told. The taxi drove the distance to El Caserio, the designated restaurant, where she found the pay phone in the noisy bar and called her father on his secret line.

"What about Carlos? What will they do to him?"

"I don't know. I told you he shouldn't have stolen the paintings. I knew that was a big mistake."

"Oh no, Papa! Did they find out?"

"Yes. We called the villa right after you called, and there was no answer. I had Rodrigo drive over and he found your servants locked in a room. Please listen. Don't try to rescue Carlos. You're in danger. They'll be looking for you."

"All right, Papa. I'm scared. I'll do whatever you say. Where are Toto and Diana?"

"They're on their way home from Cartagena with your mother," Don Pedro said. He told Maria he'd need two days to have false passports made, put together lots of cash, and pack clothes for her and the children. He told her to go to the InterContinental Hotel in downtown Caracas and register under her false name. "Pay cash for the room. Stay there until I call you. Once everything is in order, I'll have Rodrigo travel with the children on a private plane to Caracas, so the three of you can be together."

"Will they be all right?"

"Yes, I promise you that," he said. "I'll have to send you to a safe place far away from here. Your mother and I will miss you and the children more than I can say."

Maria then called a taxi service and asked them to meet her outside El Caserio in five minutes. She asked the driver to take her downtown to the InterContinental Hotel. She was heartsick about her husband's arrest. *How could this be happening? Our life was so blessed,* she thought. Her handkerchief was soaked from tears, and she didn't have any tissues, so she wiped her cheeks with her jacket sleeve.

Maria almost went crazy waiting in her hotel room for two full days. Her father had forbidden her to call anyone but him. She couldn't even call her mother or sisters. She couldn't call Colombine. She was completely alone. Maria had a lot of time to think, and it came to her. Portia. Colombine's so-called friend. She must have been casing her villa when she came to see the Obregóns. What a fool she had been to trust her.

When Don Pedro finally called Maria on Sunday, she told him her suspicions. She wanted revenge. "My dear, I'm sorry, but I can't do anything. If something happened to Portia Malatesta, Interpol would arrest me. They've left me alone up until now, but Interpol must know she worked for the FBI. Better to forget her and concentrate on your safety." He told her to go to the private airfield the next morning and wait inside the small terminal for Rodrigo to find her.

Maria checked out of the hotel in the morning and did as her father told her. She knew she had to stop crying for the children's sake. She had misplaced her sunglasses and was sure that the other people in the waiting area were staring at her puffed-up face. She buried her head in a fashion magazine, until she felt a gentle tap on the shoulder. It was Rodrigo. She followed the portly man onto the tarmac. He guided her inside the waiting plane, and to her delight, the children rose to greet her. Maria was so happy to see Toto and Diana that she couldn't stop hugging and kissing them. Not wanting to worry them, she tried controlling her tears. Rodrigo gave her the false passports and several sealed envelopes with cash inside. Suitcases full of clothes were already on board.

They were to go to Madrid, Rodrigo told her. Don Pedro had a friend who had already arranged a place for them to live and found a school nearby for the children. Rodrigo would accompany them there.

The following day, they were settled in a luxurious three-bedroom apartment with a balcony, on a street off the seventeenth-century Plaza Mayor. In the early evening, Maria took the children for a walk under the Plaza's porticos to show them the elegant shops full of clothes and furnishings and the illuminated cafés that made this old neighborhood of Madrid so appealing. Having been brought up in the country, the children were shocked by the noise of the city traffic and the way people lived so close to one another.

Now they seemed to be out of danger, yet Maria could not relax. She continued to think about Carlos several times a day, wondering where he was and how he was doing. What made missing him even more painful was that she could not communicate with him. Toto and Diana kept asking her where their papa was.

"Doesn't he love us anymore?" Diana asked.

"Of course he does." Maria gave her daughter a hug and then held the child against her body for a few tender moments.

"Then why doesn't he come to see us?" Toto asked.

"He's away on a long business trip in Brazil."

Maria didn't have the courage to tell her children the truth about their father. One day soon she would have to let them know.

Over the next few days she tried her best to keep them entertained. They made two consecutive visits to the Zoo Aquarium. The first day the children particularly enjoyed the dolphin show. They had never seen anything like it before. As they were leaving, Maria noticed a tall man ahead of them who walked with his feet turned out like Carlos. She felt a sharp pain in her chest.

The following day they explored the zoo. The most impressive exhibit was the aviary, where ordinary and exotic birds flew free within its nets. Maria had bought them binoculars so the children could see some of the birds up close. She helped identify the various species for them. Toto made notes in a small spiral notebook.

On Sunday, she took them to the Buen Retiro Park, where they rented a rowboat on the lake. Afterward, they bought sandwiches at a food stand and had an impromptu picnic on the grass. They finished eating in time to watch a Punch-and-Judy puppet show at a nearby booth. The children were not used to spending so much time with their mother. "We love having you all to ourselves," Toto said. They often asked about their father and grandparents, and she lied, saying they would be coming to visit in a month or so.

She brought them for interviews at the nearby private school and enrolled them in classes for September. Toto told her that he liked the idea of being with boys his age. He hoped he could try out for the soccer team. Diana did not quite understand what school meant.

Over the next few weeks, Maria had difficulty sleeping. She broke out in a rash on her arms and legs. A doctor gave her some sedatives, which helped her sleep. Yet the pain from the loss of Carlos festered, wrapping around her like a scratchy sheath. She hired a maid for the family who could double as a babysitter. She was not as intelligent as Clare, but she was warm and caring.

Madrid was very hot in the summer, and she arranged for a driver to take her and the children to Calella de Palafrugell, a small seaside resort along the Costa Brava for the first week of August. The children found the water much colder than the seaside in Cartagena and complained to her. They also told her that the beach, with its umbrellas and lounge chairs everywhere, was much too crowded. She actually found it comforting to be lost in a crowd of people, but she couldn't explain to Toto and Diana why this was so.

Maria knew she would need to make friends if she was going to survive in Madrid. She hoped she could meet some of the other parents in the fall. She was going to have to make up a good story about the whereabouts of her husband.

On a cloudy day in late August, more than two months after they'd arrived in Madrid, Maria responded to a fortune-teller sign in their neighborhood. She found herself in a poorly lit room with peeling paint and a dirty rug on the floor. She sat down at a small table with a middle-aged gypsy, who wore a caftan and a scarf tied around her head. The gypsy took her right hand, turned it over and sighed. She told Maria that her husband "would be dead within a year." Maria couldn't stop crying. The gypsy gave her tissues. She patted her hand. "You'll have a long life ahead of you. You'll marry again, and your children will like their new father."

Maria tried putting the gypsy's prediction out of her mind. She felt all right during the day, but almost every night she woke up with nightmares about Carlos starving in prison. If only she could see him again and tell him how much she loved him. While her father was still angry with him for putting her life at risk, she had forgiven Carlos. Every morning she went to Mass at the Basilica de San Francisco el Grande, and as she knelt in a pew, her initial anger toward him dissipated a little more each time.

A month after being apprehended at the airport in Caracas, Carlos was extradited to the United States, where he was put on trial in Boston. He was found guilty of art theft and drug trafficking and was sent to the federal penitentiary in Lompoc, California, for twenty years. Daily life was hard, but he felt grateful that some of the prison guards spoke

Spanish. They accompanied him for exercise in the yard each day, and he was able to exchange a few words with them. They kept him up to date on world events and sometimes gave him extra food. He hoped to find a way to send a message to Maria through them. Since he had not heard otherwise, he figured that she had probably escaped. At least he hoped so.

Carlos looked gaunt. His eyes were sunken. His Adam's apple sharply protruded from his neck. The once-handsome man now resembled El Greco's portrait of the martyred Saint Sebastian; only the arrows in his chest were missing. He constantly berated himself. *What a fool I've been! Don Pedro was right. I've risked a wonderful life with my devoted family for mere possessions. How I wish I'd learned this lesson earlier. At least my dear mother, who must be in heaven, won't suffer for what I've done.*

Trying to drink the liquid that passed for coffee at the prison made Carlos long for the delicious Bahareque Premium blend he used to sip every morning from small glasses in his office. He closed his eyes and imagined himself sitting at his large mahogany desk as he reviewed the hotel's nightly register and accounts. Gloria, his efficient secretary, brought him fresh coffee whenever he caught her eye.

After he was settled at the office, Carlos used to telephone the general managers in Caracas, Mérida, Bogotá, and Cartagena to listen to their summaries of the previous week's operations. If there were any difficulties, he would strategize with the general manager in question until they found a solution.

One morning Carlos had a vivid dream.

He was lying in his large canopy bed at the villa, and the breeze outside swept sweet fragrances into the bedroom, especially the jasmine and gardenias planted beneath the windows. He looked around at the sleek built-ins and admired their design. Maria came into the room, kissed him on the check, and asked him to get dressed. "It's Sunday morning, and we want you to join us for breakfast."

When he entered the sunlit room, Toto was the first to jump up to greet him. "Papa," he said as his glasses fell down his nose. "Where are we going this summer?"

"Your mama and I will discuss this soon and let you know," Carlos said. "It will be someplace special, I promise you."

"Oh goody," Diana said. She threw her small arms around Carlos's neck. Her affection smelled so good. Carlos watched his daughter bend down to feed crumpet pieces to her little Scottie dog, Nina, who sat under the table at her feet.

Clare, their English nanny, was seated between his children, sipping her coffee. Carlos greeted Clare and offered to refill her cup. As the sun shone into the white breakfast room with its animal crockery display above the sideboard, he heard Maria laugh. Her laugh became louder. And louder.

Carlos woke up, surprised to find he was in a prison cell and that a guard was banging on the bars.

Why did I give up that sweet life? Carlos asked himself, forgetting for a moment that Don Pedro's using him in the drug trade had been troubling and unpleasant.

How long will I have to stay in this godforsaken place?

He understood why he had been tried for art theft but was shocked when his contact with the Boston Mafia resulted in another charge of drug trafficking.

CHAPTER THIRTY-THREE

June 9, 1990

The Paintings Are Reacquired

Back in Medellín, immediately following the raid, Roberto Castellano had chastised the Venezuelan police for arresting Carlos when Maria was not with him. "They didn't meet our standards," he complained to Julian Henderson on the phone. "Portia Malatesta was far more professional."

Julian had brought the paintings to New York because he had learned the day before that the cargo plane wouldn't fly directly to Boston. Making arrangements in Latin America was chaotic at best. Once he landed in New York, he was shocked by the difficult time he had getting them through customs. Prior to takeoff, Julian had alerted the FBI about his expected arrival time at Kennedy with the recovered art. Despite his request, no one was there to meet him. A supercilious customs official refused to believe Julian's story about returning the stolen paintings, and although Julian showed him his FBI badge, he didn't trust that it was real. "How can you work for the FBI when you have a British accent?"

"My mother's American." Julian called the man a jerk under his breath.

"You could be lying."

"I don't believe this is happening."

After placing a call to his superiors, who had been told by the FBI about the paintings but neglected to inform the people on the ground, the customs official agreed the paintings could reenter the country. Just as Julian was about to leave the international arrivals area, an FBI agent came rushing through the door.

"You're a little late." Julian gave him a hostile look. This was definitely not his morning to be nice. He had been under a great deal of stress going undercover in Colombia, and now these stupid bureaucrats were mucking things up.

"The traffic was worse than usual," the young man with a crew cut said, wiping sweat from his brow with a handkerchief.

"Well, you're here now, so help me wheel these crates to the truck."

At least North American Van Lines got things right, and the truck was waiting at its designated spot in the cargo area. After the precious cargo was loaded, a Port Authority squad car led the way out of the airport, followed by an NYPD squad car, the moving truck, and then a chauffeured car with Julian and the local FBI agent. Once they were out of the airport, the NYPD car took the lead so that they could get through traffic as smoothly as possible. At the Connecticut border, the Connecticut state troopers took over from NYPD until they reached the Massachusetts border. Then the Massachusetts state troopers escorted the moving van and Julian's chauffeur-driven car to the Gardner Museum in Boston.

Julian called Portia when he arrived in Boston, as promised. He told her what had happened at the airport.

"You must be a wreck." She had closed her office door at the gallery so that her staff could not hear.

"I hate petty officials who take themselves too seriously."

"Thank goodness you and the paintings are back. Is it all right if I meet you at the Gardner?"

"I'm afraid not. I don't want your name in the newspaper. I promise to let you know when the paintings are safely installed there. By the way, Maria has escaped."

"Thank God," Portia blurted out. "I probably shouldn't have said that to you, Julian. But you know how much I like her."

"I won't tell anyone you said that."

After Portia hung up, she paced up and down the gallery floor. Fortunately, it was a slow day, so she couldn't scare off any potential customers with her intensity. She was a jangle of nerves, terrified that something could still go wrong, although she knew it was unlikely.

When the truck drove up and the priceless cargo had been transported inside, Julian was greeted with great fanfare. All the members of the board of directors, the curators, and the staff were there, shouting and clapping as they waited to shake his hand. Julian had asked the staff beforehand not to inform the press, and they were happy to comply.

Afterward, he called Portia from his hotel room to let her know. "Our children are home."

"This is the best news. Great work, Julian."

"I wish you were here to celebrate with me, but we still need to be careful."

"I understand."

The following morning, when she was making lunch for Alexa to take to school, she felt like dancing around her kitchen. "Splish-splash, I was takin' a bath," Portia and Alexa sang to Bobby Darin's music as they twisted around the room. Stansky told them, "You're crazy," but their joy about the recovered paintings was infectious.

The next day, Nick Moretti stopped by the gallery and gave Portia a big hug.

"I knew you could do it, kid."

She thanked him for the roses. It felt good to be home.

A week later she would go by herself to pay silent homage to *The Concert*. Only then would she be able to celebrate her own part in the return of the paintings. Only then would she be able to speak with Antonio as she sat on their bench near his favorite painting.

After the paintings were returned to their former places in the Gardner Museum, the director organized a celebration for the public.

Portia went to the late-November gala with Stansky. She went as a docent, and no one suspected her role in the sting. The press was there, busily snapping photographs of the guests and asking Julian more questions about the operation. The Guarneri String Quartet played Bartók and Beethoven in the Gardner's concert room while more than four hundred guests milled about.

Portia was visited by Isabella at the party held in her museum. Lacing a delicate arm through hers, Isabella whispered, "Ms. Portia, I knew you could do it." Then she bent down, picked a blue bachelor button from the courtyard flowers, and pinned it to the lapel of Portia's black Armani suit. Portia could not have been happier, except for the fact that Julian kept his distance from her. She understood he was protecting her. Yet after their close relationship in Medellín, his standoffish behavior seemed weird.

Later that evening, when she was relaxing in their library, with her bare feet up on the Victorian sofa, she considered another special woman. Portia thought about Maria Alfonso and how happy she had felt when Julian told her that Maria had escaped. Despite her culpability, Portia would have hated to think about this simpatica woman in a lonely jail cell, far away from her beloved children. She knew it would be hard for Maria to live without her husband and hoped that someday she would be able to move forward.

Portia had to admit that she felt a little nervous about Carlos being in her country instead of Colombia. She didn't think he could hurt her or her family from prison, but his presence in the States did not please her. What if he were able to escape? Although she knew it was unrealistic, Portia hoped Carlos never figured out her role in the sting. Interpol and the FBI had kept her name out of the news, much to her own and Stansky's relief.

CHAPTER THIRTY-FOUR

December 3, 1990

The Aftermath

Diego, who had read about Carlos's trial and sentencing in the *Boston Globe* and also heard about his whereabouts in an emotional telephone call from Don Pedro, had been calling Lompoc to ask for permission to visit Carlos but was continually refused. The warden finally relented and gave him a ten-minute pass. He flew to California to see Carlos, despite the brief amount of time that they could talk.

He landed in Los Angeles and drove a rental car to Santa Barbara on the way to Lompoc. He couldn't believe how beautiful Santa Barbara County was. He found it strange that a medium-security federal prison was surrounded by such fertile farmland.

When Diego entered the run-down prison building, he was taken to a sparse room where a row of low seats stood against a half-solid wall. The top half of the wall was barred. Carlos came in from the opposite direction and sat down in front of Diego, who almost didn't recognize him.

The two men shook hands through the bars.

"How is Maria?" Carlos asked.

"Maria and the children are safe, but I don't know where they're living," Diego said.

"I'm relieved." Carlos slipped a note through the bars to Diego. "Please send this to Maria."

"I'll do my best to get it to her." Diego took the note because he didn't want to disappoint Carlos. He knew Don Pedro wouldn't risk having it delivered because Interpol and the Colombian police were watching their every move.

"I suspect that the Boston art dealer, Portia Malatesta, had something to do with my getting caught."

Diego nodded his head yes, but before he could respond, the guard told them that their time was up.

Diego called Don Pedro after he returned to his brother's Lexington home and conveyed Carlos's suspicion about the Boston art dealer.

"I know, I know," Don Pedro said. "But what can I do?"

Don Pedro lost his appetite. His beloved daughter was living in Spain with his grandchildren. He felt so depressed by his loss that he failed to pay close attention to his many businesses. He couldn't find anyone he trusted to manage the hotels. Don Miguel, the head of the Cali cartel and Don Pedro's rival, heard about the tragedy that had befallen Don Pedro's family and took advantage of the situation. He began making inroads into the Medellín cartel's territory. In the past this would have meant war, but now Don Pedro didn't have the heart to fight. His wife, Lucia, was also depressed. She told Don Pedro that she'd never forgive him for bringing Carlos into their home.

During the past year, Don Pedro had considered stepping down from the cartel leadership. Now that Carlos was in prison, he had no idea who could replace him as his successor. Maybe in a year or two, when news about the Gardner robbery died down, he and Lucia could visit Maria and the children in Madrid. He was afraid this might be wishful thinking.

Don Pedro considered a plan to further protect his precious daughter. He thought about asking his lawyer to subtly let Interpol know, via whatever contacts he deemed appropriate, that the American art dealer from Boston, who had led them to his daughter's villa, would be in danger if anyone tried to track down Maria and her family. At the last moment he decided against this ploy. Interpol could have the local police arrest him for this threat. Waiting for time to pass was the best strategy, but it was hard. Very hard.

"What do you want from me?" Carlos asked, pushing his face up against the bars as he looked at the FBI agent with a buzz cut and an earnest face. "You have the goddamn paintings." Carlos had aged considerably in the short time he had been in Lompoc. His hair had turned completely gray. He had difficulty sleeping, and his eyes were bloodshot.

A prison guard opened the door to allow the FBI agent inside Carlos's cell. The agent loosened his tie and took his jacket off. He offered Carlos a cigarette, which he refused.

"We want you to tell us who helped you steal the art."

"I'll only talk after you find a way for me to communicate with my wife."

"I'll see if we can make a deal." The FBI agent held his hand out for Carlos to shake. He warned him that organizing this would be difficult.

Carlos guessed that Don Pedro would never admit to knowing Maria's whereabouts.

"I'll ask Diego Augustin to mail or carry your letter to your wife via Don Pedro if necessary," the FBI agent said.

"I hope that Don Pedro will find a way to get my letter to Maria, and that the same process could be repeated the other way around— then I'll talk."

After the FBI agent left, Carlos sat on the thin mattress with his head in his hands. He wore a harsh cotton uniform with black stripes. The sheets on his cot were wrinkled and coarse. The food was tasteless. There was no window in his cell. The rough-textured walls with their peeling paint reminded him of his mother's home in Santo Domingo Savio. He wished he had never heard of the Gardner Museum.

CHAPTER THIRTY-FIVE

June 10, 1991

Back to Normal

Summer finally arrived in Boston, and when Portia opened the windows of Alexa's bedroom to let in some fresh air, she could smell the roses blooming in her garden below. Aside from the happy twittering of birds, the street was quiet. She felt sure that she'd hear a refrain from a Beethoven sonata when she walked past the Brevard house on the way to her gallery that morning.

Now that it was all over, Portia had returned to being a wife, mother, and gallery owner. Her new Stockwell show of Vermont barns had been a great success, and she was pleased about that. Life didn't have to be complicated. She was beginning to appreciate the joys of simplicity. That had not precluded her from inviting Paul Travigne to dinner. He had met her family after she returned, and they'd become friends. Stansky found Paul great company, and Alexa enjoyed the way he teased her. Whenever Paul came to dinner, Portia told him, "Without your help, the Gardner paintings might still be in Medellín."

She enjoyed seeing his gap-toothed smile. And Stansky seemed to be all right with Paul getting the credit. "You're a good guy," he said as he poured more Sancerre into Paul's glass.

She took Alexa bowling on Sunday at Kings Dining & Entertainment on Dalton Street. She made sure that Alexa won most of their games. When Alexa hit all the duckpins, Portia jumped up and down and hugged her. They shared a whole pizza together before they left for home.

A few months later, when Julian Henderson called her with the possibility of another international assignment, Portia didn't hesitate to agree. Domesticity was great, but recapturing stolen art had become her métier.

AFTERWORD

A Discerning Eye is a work of fiction. Names, characters, places, and incidents are either the product of the author's imagination or have been fictionalized. The events following the Gardner robbery are completely imaginary.

Some stolen paintings do turn up in private collections, although "eighty percent of what is stolen is never found again," according to Robert E. Spiel, a private security consultant to the fine arts community based near Chicago. "We never know where it really is."

The following are a few examples of art stolen for or from private collections:

> 1) "Italian police have recovered a Renoir painting that was stolen from a private collection thirty-three years ago. Following a tip from the flamboyant art critic Vittorio Sgarbi, who was enlisted to evaluate the work by a gallery owner in the city of Riccone, the police arrested the gallery owner and two other suspects. The oil painting of a nude woman, valued at $883,000, was stolen from a family in Milan in 1975. The owner's daughter vouched for the authenticity of the painting by identifying a mark made by a ball that she hit it with in the early 1970s."
>
> —ABC News (Australia), September 27, 2008

2) "Five 17th-century paintings stolen in 2002 from the Frans Hals Museum in Haarlem, the Netherlands, have been recovered by the police. The paintings were insured for a total value of $4.3M. Three people have been arrested in connection with the case. Louis Pirenne, a museum spokesman, said three of the works had been damaged, and a lawyer was one of the defendants. They were found in a house in 's-Hertogenbosch, the Netherlands."

—"Dutch Art Recovered," *New York Times*, September 16, 2009

3) "On Sunday, February 11, 2008, three men wearing ski masks walked into the Emile Bührle Foundation, a private museum in Zurich, in daylight, barely a half hour before the 5:00 p.m. closing time. They grabbed four 19th-century masterpieces, tossed them into a van and sped off. They took a Cézanne, a Degas, a Van Gogh and a Monet, together worth an estimated $163 million, but not the most valuable works in the collection. The four paintings just happened to be hanging in the same room. The mix of value and quality added to the impression that the robbery was as haphazard as it was brazen. One of the thieves pulled a handgun and ordered terrified staff members and visitors to lie down on the floor, as the other two men pulled the paintings off the wall. The police said the paintings appeared to be sticking out of the back of the white van the men used to make their getaway. Two of the four paintings (the Van Gogh and the Monet) were later recovered in a nearby parked car."

—Uta Harnischfeger and Nicolas Kulish, "At Zurich Museum, a Theft of 4 Masterworks," *New York Times*, February 12, 2008

4) "Stéphane Breitwieser, a thirtysomething French waiter, admitted to stealing 238 artworks and other

exhibits from museums traveling around Europe; his motive was to build a vast personal collection. 'I enjoy art. I love such works of art. I collected them and kept them at home.' He began stealing art in March of 1995 and was arrested in November of 2001 on the grounds of the Richard Wagner Museum in Lucerne, Switzerland. Keeping the stolen loot, worth about $1 billion, he stored the paintings in his mother's flat in Eschentzwiller, France. Breitwieser specialized in Old Master paintings from the 16th to 18th century. In January 2005, Breitwieser was given a twenty-six-month prison sentence. Unfortunately, over sixty paintings, including masterpieces by Brueghel, Watteau, Francois Boucher, and Corneille de Lyon were chopped up by Breitwieser's mother, Mireille Stengel, in what police believe was an effort to remove incriminating evidence against her son."
                                    —BBC News, January 7, 2005

5) "*The Scream* and *The Madonna* by Edvard Munch were stolen in Norway in August of 2004. They were recovered by a police operation in 2006. 'The thieves had difficulty finding someone to take them,' the police chief, Iver Stensrud, said. 'They were obliged to multiply their contacts and proposals, and that increased the chances for the police to find them.'"
                                    —BBC News, August 31, 2006

6) "The curious case of William Milliken Vanderbilt Kingsland, a threadbare eccentric and an amateur genealogist, began in the summer of 2006, when a few months after he died, it was discovered that his birth name was Melvyn Kohn . . . He left more than 300 pieces found in his apartment—including stolen works by Picasso, Copley, Fairfield Porter, and Odilon Redon. 'Many of the Kingsland artworks,' FBI agent James Wynne said, 'appeared to have last belonged to

galleries in New York, but it was difficult to track down
when they were last seen.'"

—Eric Konigsberg, "Two Years Later, the FBI
Still Seeks the Owners of a Trove of Artworks,"
New York Times, August 11, 2008

The abbreviated version of Portia Malatesta's list of thirteen artworks
stolen from the Gardner Museum on March 18, 1990:

Johannes Vermeer, *The Concert*, 1658–60. Oil on canvas, 28.5 x 25.5 inches. (Dutch Room, in a gilt frame
attached to a stand on a table by the window facing the
doorway.) Bought at Hôtel Drouot auction in Paris in
1892 from the estate of Théophile Thoré, a prominent
art critic instrumental in reviving Vermeer's reputation. One of only thirty-six known Vermeer paintings.
Realistic composition of three musicians playing music
together. Light pours into the room from an unseen
window and falls on the tiles of the black-and-white
floor as well as on the harpsichordist's skirt.

Rembrandt, *A Lady and Gentleman in Black*, 1633.
Oil on canvas, 51.6 x 42.9 inches. Inscribed at the bottom. (Dutch Room, in a large frame on the south wall
of the gallery, at left.) A formal portrait of a standing
husband and a seated wife facing an empty chair. The
couple's white ruffled collars and pale faces stand out
against their heavy black clothes.

Rembrandt, *Christ in the Storm on the Sea of Galilee*,
1633. Oil on canvas, 63.7 x 51.1 inches. Inscribed on
the rudder. (Dutch Room in a large frame on the south
wall of the gallery, at right.) Rembrandt's only seascape,
it was purchased through Bernard Berenson. Based on
the Gospel of Luke, light coming from a break in the
sky pours onto the calm face of Christ while the disciple sailors anxiously try to right the sail in a dark,

angry sea. Rembrandt's face appears on a disciple who is staring out at the viewers. He is holding on to his cap in one hand and the rope in the other.

Rembrandt, *Portrait of the Artist as a Young Man*, ca. 1634. Etching, 1.75 x 2 inches. Self-portrait of the artist at age twenty-eight. (Dutch Room, on the side of a cabinet beneath Rembrandt's *Self-Portrait* of the artist at age twenty-three, oil on wood, 35.3 x 28.9 inches.) This self-portrait shows a contemplative Rembrandt with intense dark eyes, a mustache, and an unkempt beard. The left half of his face is in shadow. The much larger self-portrait had been taken off the wall but was left behind. Presumably it was too cumbersome to carry because it was painted on wood.

Édouard Manet, *Chez Tortoni*, 1878–80. Oil on canvas, 10.2 x 13.4 inches. (Blue Room, beneath the oil-on-canvas portrait of Manet's mother, which was out for cleaning on the day of the robbery.) In *Chez Tortoni*, a dapper mustachioed gentleman dressed in a black top hat and coat is seated at an outdoor café table with light pouring into the space. The gentleman's face is half in shadow.

Govaert Flinck, *Landscape with an Obelisk*, 1638. Oil on oak panel, 21.5 x 28 inches. (Dutch Room, in similar frame to Vermeer, the painting stood against the same customized stand that was attached to a table by the window, but it faced the opposite direction of the Vermeer.) Formerly attributed to his master, Rembrandt. It was purchased through Bernard Berenson as a Rembrandt at a time when Isabella Gardner was losing interest in his paintings. Foreboding landscape on the right, with an ethereal light shining on a magical obelisk on the left.

Edgar Degas, *Three Mounted Jockeys*, 1885–88. Black ink, white, flesh, and rose washes, probably oil pigments, applied with a brush on medium brown paper, 12 x 9.4 inches. (Short Gallery, on a cabinet.) One seated jockey leaning back on a horse. Two jockeys below are drawn upside down. Jockeys intrigued Degas, and he frequently painted them.

Edgar Degas, *La Sortie de Pesage*, nineteenth century, exact date unknown. Pencil and watercolor on paper, 3.9 x 6.3 inches. (Short Gallery, on a cabinet.) A subtle rendering of a mounted jockey entering a race. The jockey has his back to the viewer. Dressed in orange and white, he sits on a tall, dark horse. Another mounted jockey stands about five paces ahead. Several attendees line up at a window to the left.

Edgar Degas, *Cortège sur une Route aux Environs de Florence*, 1857–60. Black pencil and white wash on paper, 6.3 x 8.3 inches. (Short Gallery, on a cabinet; originally in a single frame with *La Sortie de Pesage*.) Elaborate funeral procession in the Italian countryside appears in the middle diagonal of the composition. The church and town appear from a distance in the top third. Underbrush is painted below the procession in the bottom third.

Edgar Degas, *Program for an Artistic Soirée*, 1884. Charcoal on buff paper, 8.2 x 11.8 inches. (Short Gallery, on a cabinet.) Sketches of ballet dancers and musical instruments.

Edgar Degas, *Program for an Artistic Soirée*, 1884. Charcoal on white paper, 9.5 x 12.2 inches. (Short Gallery, on a cabinet. Combined in a frame with drawing above.) This sketch is less detailed than the one above. Otherwise, it is exactly the same.

Chinese bronze beaker, or *Gu*, representative of the Shang dynasty, 1200–1100 BC. Height 10½ inches, diameter 6 1/8 inches, weight 2 lbs. 7 oz. (Dutch Room, on a table to the right of Rembrandt's *Christ in the Storm on the Sea of Galilee*, and under Francisco Zurbarán's *A Doctor at Law*.) The thieves had to cut through layers of fabric on the table and then pry the beaker off its metal base.

Finial in the form of an eagle, 1813–14. French. Gilt metal (bronze). Height approx. 10 inches. (Short Gallery—above a Napoleonic flag.) Its widespread wings measure close to two inches in each direction. The finial originally sat on top of the pole support of a silk Napoleonic flag, which remains.

ACKNOWLEDGMENTS

The theft of thirteen art objects at the Isabella Stewart Gardner Museum in Boston took place on March 18, 1990. Since then we art lovers have been deprived of viewing a precious Vermeer, three Rembrandt masterpieces, and a mysterious Manet. My dearest wish is that this novel helps publicize the art that has been missing for thirty years, and that you, the reader, will recognize a stolen piece that's been hidden somewhere. All it takes is one.

I have read two source books for this novel: Louise Hall Tharp's engaging and well-documented biography *Mrs. Jack* and *Eye of the Beholder: Masterpieces from the Isabella Stewart Gardner Museum*, edited by Alan Chong, Richard Linger, and Carl Zahn. These two books have given me insights into Isabella Gardner's extraordinary character. Many years ago I visited Bernard Berenson's villa, I Tatti, in Settignano.

Thank you to my editor, Faith Black Ross, for her insightful manuscript review, to Katie Meyers for her marketing expertise, to Devon Fredericksen, for overseeing the book production, and to my talented web designer, Mina Manchester.

My wonderful writing group at the New York Society Library has been particularly helpful with their comments over six years of ongoing chapter submissions and revisions. Jack Buchanan, our group leader and author of several books on the Revolutionary War, Shelley

Rogers, Jennifer Jestin, Andrew Ross, and Henrik Petersen—you are the best.

Nancy Cohen helped me with the initial book outline about ten years ago and also asked me tough questions about character and plot along the way. Nancy and I were in my first New York writing group along with Henny Durst and author Sue Ribner. Doriana Molla later joined our small group. She inspired Sue and me to travel to Albania, where we met Doriana's lovely family, who lived in Tirana. Sadly, Henny and Sue are no longer on this earth. Doriana's family has since moved from Albania to join her in Brooklyn.

I was also in a New York writing group with authors Cassie Farrelly, Maria Granovsky, and Jan Schmidt. Thank you for your comments during the early stages of this novel. Cassie recommended me to Girl Friday Productions, who produced her beautifully written novel *The Shepherd's Calculus* for Cavan Bridge Press.

I appreciate the insights and comments from the following readers: author and TV creator Marilyn Horowitz, author Marcy Dermansky, author Nicole Bokat, Jane Cavolina, Lois Safian, Patricia Booth, Marilyn Yanowitch, author Gabe Habash, Pam Liflander, and Jane Rosenman.

My former West Canton Street neighbor, the author Jean Gibran, also gave me useful feedback on an early version of the first few chapters. I was fortunate to receive a helpful editorial letter from Christine Kopprash several years ago.

I have attended some illuminating writers' workshops, especially Squaw Valley's Community of Writers, the Writer's Hotel, the Muse and the Marketplace, Kauai Writers Workshop, and Catalyst. Shanna McNair and Scott Wolven, the Writer's Hotel directors, read my entire manuscript before their conference in June 2019. I am grateful for their helpful feedback.

The author and teacher Susan Shapiro has taught me about the craft of writing. When I first moved to New York in 2001, I attended Susan's nonfiction writing seminar at the New School. Since then I have participated in many writing seminars with Susan over the eighteen years I have lived in New York. Her book, *Byline Bible*, is a must-read for anyone who wants to write for online publications, newspapers, or magazines.

A big thank you to Molly Stern, Paul Berman, Alexandra Nordlinger, Marlene Stone, Amanda McGowan and Loren Comstock for their ongoing support.

READING GROUP QUESTIONS AND TOPICS FOR DISCUSSION

1. When we first meet Portia, she is driving to meet her younger brother, Antonio, at the Isabella Stewart Gardner Museum. What kind of first impression does Portia make on the reader?

2. It's understandable that Portia Malatesta is devastated by Antonio's suicide. Can suicide be prevented? Is Portia's grief more protracted because Antonio took his own life?

3. What are the many ways that Portia deals with her grief? Which of those ways might work for the reader if he/she experienced a loss?

4. Portia Malatesta hates the Mafia. Yet she wants to meet with two Mafia art collectors. Are her values compromised?

5. How does Portia develop her discerning eye? Who else in the story has a discerning eye?

6. How is the Isabella Stewart Gardner Museum in Boston different from the Frick Museum in New York, the Barnes Foundation in Philadelphia, and the Norton Simon Museum in Pasadena, California?

7. Did you know that Bernard Berenson was considered the foremost authority on Italian Renaissance art in his day? Have you ever been to Villa I Tatti, his estate in Settignano, outside Florence? It's now the Harvard University Center for Italian Renaissance Studies and

houses his art collection as well as his personal library of books on art history and humanism.

8. What motivates some wealthy people to become art collectors? Why do some collectors donate their art collections to established museums, such as the Metropolitan Museum of Art, while others establish their own museums?

9. What motivates art thieves? Why do they steal art instead of robbing a bank or a jewelry store?

10. How is Stansky a supportive husband? How is he not?

11. In many ways *A Discerning Eye* follows the rules of the mystery genre, but it also subverts them. How does the novel differ from other mysteries you've read? How would you classify it—mystery or family drama? Why?

12. What makes Carlos Alfonso a complex character? We first meet him at his Colombian villa, where he fires the night guard for falling asleep on the job, but then he runs after him to offer another job, in the kitchen. Carlos seems to have it all: a beautiful, loving wife, two darling children, and a great job managing La Gran Conchita hotels. What drives Carlos?

13. Is it possible for Diego Augustin to be indirectly involved in the drug trade and not be tainted by it?

14. Roberto Castellano plays a crucial role in the sting operation. Was he right to insist that Portia Malatesta return home before the raid takes place?

ABOUT THE AUTHOR

© Kirk Donnan

Carol Orange has worked in the art world for more than twenty years. She began as a research editor on art books in London and later became an art dealer in Boston. She lived in Paris for two years, where she researched George Sand's life and writing. Her short story "Delicious Dates" was included in Warren Adler's 2010 short story anthology. Another story, "Close Call," appeared in the *Atherton Review* volume 102. She currently lives in Chicago near her daughter and her family. Readers can find her on Instagram (@carolorange2), on Facebook, on Twitter (@COrangeAntiques), and at www.carolorange.com. *A Discerning Eye* is her first book.

Made in the USA
Middletown, DE
14 October 2020

21965254R00168